Airship Memoirs

"The Reluctant Pirate"

Airship Memoires is a production of Phantom Script Publishing,
a subsidiary of **Twelfth Pillar Solutions**

ISBN: 9798758380789

ANSI (ebook):

Airship Memoirs

"The Reluctant Pirate"

With a love for the writing styles of Murray Leinster (William Fitzgerald Jenkins), Jules Verne, Sir Arthur Conan Doyle, Alexandre Dumas and Phillip K. Dick I've made an attempt to expound on visions past to create a world of action, mystery, adventure and more. I give many thanks to all of the authors before me who have helped to shape this world and all of its unique characters. May the worlds and characters created give you just as much joy reading as they gave me to create.

I can only hope to honor those who came before me with my attempts to expand on a genre that I enjoy.

Like all of my writings, I dedicate this to my daughter, Laurel, who has given me the inspiration to follow my dreams. Every time I look in her face, I never see who I am, but rather who I am to her.

Luv Ya Baby Girl!

~~***~~

Table of Contents

Prologue

This isn't where our story starts, but it is where it begins. For not everything starts at the beginning, nor is an ending always the end.

March 13, 1759; a Tuesday that started off as any other Tuesday; the only thing newsworthy of the day was that the clockmaker, John Harrison, had created a new marine chronometer that allowed for new, more accurate, measurement of time on land, sea or air that, in turn, could and would lead to later advances in astrogation…

More importantly, it is also the day that *they* came and the day that Edmond Halley's name would become a swear word in the annals of history. It wasn't for Halley himself, by no means or afflictions of his own, for he was a gentle man who never met ill with anyone. No, it was his blasted comet that caused so much disgruntled angst with those who spoke of the subject.

It was dusk as the sun was setting behind the mountains; Halley's comet with its magnanimously long tail shot across the sky. For its third day now, it could be seen before the North Star had even appeared. People would gaze up every night like clockwork to see how much it had moved across the sky. By now, it was coming near its last night to be seen… at least until *they* arrived.

A large hole appeared in the dusky outer orbit of our aether. Firstly, it started as a mild disturbance in the air, but then quickly grew to a large turbulence that began to quake the ground and churn the seas. The hole, as was seen by those who were not running for shelter, was, in fact a door. Some sort of gateway, if you will, opening to allow an armada of very unfamiliar and unfriendly looking flying vessels of every shape and size to take space just outside of our aether.

The vessels all seemed to be connected by a greenish light that resembled that of a spider's web; connecting sinews between the ships with a singular thread focusing from the lead vessel down to the mountains. This making one to assume that the armada was being pulled in unison down toward the mountain's tip. If this entire armada were to have landed, it would have taken up the entire lower section of the new world.

As the history books describe the event, with the first line of vessels making their way close enough to the ground that the seams of their aether bladders and boltings could be seen. With a blast from an unknown source, the singular thread of green light connecting this invading armada gave way of its connections with the solitary beam from the lead ship changing direction to point upwards in the direction that Halley's comet was now passing. As with the disturbances on the ground, this beam had a similar effect as it struck the comet.

Those who watched the events unfold had not taken into account the effects that this had on the comet at the time. In reality, the concern was all on the visitors. There were rumors and rumors of rumors as to the origins, but the most prolific was centered on the unrest that was taking place in Austria. It was believed that this Armada was a secret weapon compiled by Prussian technologies and used during King George's war. Many believed it was something he would have used, but none knew how anyone of modern means could create such an ominous spectacle without raising suspicion of creation. The massive collection gave belief that it would take years to amass such an armada.

With the comet being independent and unattached to any larger surface, unlike the mountains previously used as an anchor for the lead ship to tether itself, the beam now forced the comet to change in direction and was now heading toward us with the same level of speed that originally pulled it toward the horizon.

Though green light was only spun in the direction of Halley's comet for, what seemed to be seconds before shutting down, it was enough to change the comet's trajectory from one of beauty and wonder to that of a Nostradomian cataclysm of apocalyptic proportions.

Three days passed; the armada blanketed the sky overhead. There was scuttlebutt about the armada engaging in conversation with our leaders, but for those not privy to such information, it appeared that the vessels were waging war against us.

"Beware the ides of March" a man named Shakespeare once said. No one would have guessed that this simple statement from a playwright would be an edict for the world, as we knew it then anyway.

The comet quickly stormed across the sky, leaving long trails of snow, ice and debris in its wake. No one could fathom the length of its tail, as it seemed to go on for miles. It blasted through the armada, taking out a third of its vessels before crashing into the sea.

This event was not the worst, no, not by any stretch of the imagination. The impact of the large mass caused instant waves hundreds of feet in the air, which destroyed coastlines and submerged large landmasses almost instantly. What were once vast continents now appeared to be scattered islands floating in one large sea.

The hope of the waters receding was short lived as it was apparent that the warm waters of the sea, with the vigorous force that the aether placed on the comet as it came to rest, would create permanent water rise along with contaminations in the seas.

Earthquakes and volcanoes, erupting from the impact, further added to the sinking and rising of landmasses, creating even more randomly placed islands.

It is years past from that eventful history, and as I write this, those who survived the cataclysm have since rebuilt, each to their own preference. Some, wanting to avert another situation on the surface, created flying islands that stayed in the mid aether, while others had the mind that one day the waters would recede, so they built floating islands that were not transfixed to any one particular location, but could navigate the sea to avert any future situation. This all while allowing them to have an established set of communities as the water recanted back to the depths and the floating island could rest aground. Then there were those with no technologies or skills that merely stayed on the land surfaces, accepting any fate dealt them from future events.

Again, this isn't where our story starts, but it is where it begins. For, not everything starts at the beginning...

Chapter 1

It was not by impulse or a last-minute whim that Vash Rayburn was on his way to the floating sky city of Nemo Vesta by sneaking aboard the very ship that had come to his homeland of Gibbit Cove for the sole purpose of insuring every last one of his relatives hang from the highest tree.

No, quite the contrary, he had been planning his escape at length and now was the time to put his carefully worked out scheme into action. He obviously wasn't expecting, nor looking forward to the hanging of his relatives, however he knew that they'd be able to get out of it in some way or another as they have so often done in the past. He rather frequently thought that if they weren't professional sky pirates, that they would make most formidable politicians. But while the family was working on their escape plans, Vash, setting his escape into motion, stowed away on the would-be executioners' vessel.

Though presently in a state of destitution, hiding from his family's captors in the very ship that brought the would-be executioners here, his ambition was to reach Nemo Vesta where his plans of a new life could be played out, so he set about getting there even if it meant placing himself in danger to do so; he is from a family of sky pirates you know.

Making it safely to the sky port of Tomar Bay, Vash was able to slip off of the vessel while the crew was pre-occupied with cargo exchange. Being from the pirate background that he was, he knew a thing or two about the operation, mechanics and general maintenance involved in caring for dirigibles of just about every make, thanks to his grandfather's teachings, so he merely passed himself off as port maintenance by jumping in and disconnecting the charging hoses from the helium bladder and walked off with the real port maintenance when they were finished with recharging the ship's helium. Now one thing of note, the crew of this vessel did just come from trying to kill his family for piracy and, though his family members were all able to get away, Vash still had a score to settle for the dishonor of his blood, so he did not properly seal the bladder's cap, thus creating a slow leak that would render the large leviathan grounded after only a few hours of flight.

From there, he made two more stow away maneuvers before making it onboard a vessel heading toward Nemo Vesta. He fell asleep in the cargo hold rather content with himself as he envisioned the looks on the faces of the aristocrats of Nemo Vesta when he showed them his engineering abilities. Yes, he was on his way to greatness; Step one would be complete.

I guess some explanation is in order; Vash Rayburn's plan wasn't to just leave his homeland of Gibbit Cove, but it was much more extensive than that. You see, On Nemo Vesta, Vash intended, in this order, to (1) achieve greatness as an engineer and inventor, (2) grow satisfactorily wealthy, (3) marry a delightful girl of proper upbringing, and (4) end his life as a well-respected member of a community that honored him for his accomplishments instead of hunting him because of his pirate past.

Once on Nemo Vesta, he found himself a steady job where he was able to set his plans into motion.

Six months later…

One night before the police broke down the door to his one-room domicile, Vash went to bed and slept soundly. He was calmly assured that his ambitions were about to be realized. At practically any instant the magistrate would discover his brilliant intellect and he'd be honored with lavish accolades of appreciation, his friend Derk would have more admiration for him than previously, and even Jessica would probably decide to marry him on the spot, not giving care to what her father thought. She was the delightful girl of part three in his plan. Such prospects, with the sound of rain dancing on the roof, made for a very good sleep.

Nemo Vesta was a fine city to be sleeping on. Outside the capital city its sky port received shipments of luxuries and raw materials from all around the world. Its landing grid reared skyward with large grappling arms by which to hoist ships into loading bays to insure safe and expedient landing and departure, something that most sky ports (and ground ports for that matter) lacked. There was commerce, high end manufacturing as well as many examples of wealth and culture, and Vash modestly admitted that its standard of living was the highest in the entire regatta of sky cities, with the capital floating island being the wealthiest of all the floating suburbs connected by cable bridges as they maintained balance in the aether. Its citizens had no reason to worry about anything but a supply of tranquilizers to enable them to stand the doldrums of their unexciting existences between social events.

Even Vash became lulled into a state of satisfied bliss and doldrums, as of the moment. On Gibbit Cove there wasn't even a landing grid. The few, battered, cobbled ships the inhabitants owned had to take off precariously by the use of older steam pressure booster systems and to land in port was at the discretion and skill of the vessel's captain. They came back blackened and sometimes more battered than when they left, and sometimes they would not even land at port, but rather on the water and sail in as if they were water ships instead of sky ships. The people of Gibbit Cove gave always-affected innocent indignation when an embattled sky ship of strangers came and furiously demanded that they be towed in.

Yes, Nemo Vesta seemed a very fine place in comparison. So, as it was every night, Vash went confidently to bed, realizing that his prior actions would set all of his plans in motion and he soundly fell asleep, well until five hours after sunset. That's when the police breaking in his door awakened him from his dreams of success.

The constable, with four brutish lackeys made a tremendous crash as they turned the threshold of, what was, the doorframe, into a splintered mess on the floor. It was apparent that they were in great haste to achieve some goal. The noise woke Vash from a strange nightmare of a situation that took place back home when he was young as he blinked his eyes open. Before he was even fully awake, two of the four uniformed men grabbed him and dragged him out of bed. They searched him frantically for any weapons. They then stood him against the west wall of his apartment, all the while pointing two stun-pistols at him, and all of this happening as the constable and the other two lackeys began to tear his room apart, the countenance on their faces telling in inaudible screams that they were looking for something of great importance. Vash, finally getting a grip on what was happening, noticed his friend Derk walk hesitantly into, what was previously, Vash's doorway and looked at him with a somewhat remorseful look about him as he wrung his hands and paced nervously against the wall.

"I had to do it, Vash," he said with a nervous breaking in his voice. *"I just had to do it!"*

Vash looked at him with a sudden realization that he was just sold out, but for what and why by his friend? He was now becoming more irritated than concerned. He came from a family, heck! An entire cove of professional pirates of which, not one would have sold him out without fair warning of doing so. Now it began to look as if the police had gone from a simple search to deliberate vandalism as one of the officers slit open his pillow and began to poor its contents onto the floor. Another cop was ripping the seams of his mattress to look inside. Somebody else was going carefully through a little pile of notes that Jessica had written to him, squinting at them as if he were afraid of seeing something that he'd wish he hadn't. This violation of privacy became too much *"What's happened?"* asked Vash incredulously to Derk, knowing that the officers wouldn't answer him. *"What's the meaning of this?"*

Derk said miserably: *"You killed someone, Vash. An innocent man! You didn't mean to, but you did, and ..."*

"Me kill somebody? That's ridiculous!" protested Vash as he looked again to the officers who had now destroyed anything in his room that could have been used as a container for whatever they were looking for.

"The body was found outside the powerhouse," said Derk, anxious wanting to get out of there. *"Outside the steam converter relay station that you—"* Derk looked at the constable hoping that he would stop him from speaking and tell him he could go home.

"The steam converter relay station? Oh!" Vash seemed to let out a sigh of relief. It was amazing how relaxed he became, almost as if he suddenly became lost to the reality that he was just accused of murder. The relief came because, up to this point, it had mulled over in his mind that somebody might have found out he'd been born and raised on Gibbit Cove—which would have ruined everything. It was almost impossible to imagine that this brought relief, but still it was a great relief, nonetheless, to find out he was *only* suspected of a murder he knew he had not committed. And

the only reason that he was suspected was because his first great achievement as an electronic engineer on Nemo Vesta had been discovered. *"They found the thing at the relay station, eh? I can assure you that I didn't kill anybody and, other than a cut lock, there's no harm done. My invention has been running for almost a week now and I had planned on going to the Power Board with it in a couple of days anyway."* He addressed the constable. *"So now that I know what's up,"* he said. *"Be so kind as to hand me the pair of pants on the chair that you didn't tear apart."*

One of the lackeys quickly waved a stun-pistol in his face, brushing the barrel along Vash's jaw line. *"One more sarcastic word, and—pfft!"*

"Don't talk, Vash!" said Derk in panic. *"Just keep your mouth shut! It's bad enough as it is! Don't make it worse on yourself!"*

The constable handed Vash his pants, but not before deliberately slicing a hole down the left leg. With a look of defiance, Vash took the pants and put them on. He became aware that the cop seemed overly agitated; in fact, it seemed as if everyone in the room was overly agitated about something that wasn't being spoken, information that hadn't been revealed yet. Everybody in the room was in a state of acute fear except himself, as if they were all expecting him to try something heinous. He, again, started to wonder if they had found out where he came from. Vash found himself incredulous at this point. People acted this way in Gibbit Cove, but higher classed, sky city civilians just didn't act this way in a civilized, upper crust society such as Nemo Vesta.

"Who'd I kill?" he demanded. *"And why would I have killed this person?"*

"You wouldn't know him, Vash," said Derk soulfully. *"You didn't mean to kill him, but it's by luck and grace that he was the only one that you killed, instead of everybody in that sector!"*

"Everybody—?" Vash stared confused.

"No more talk!" snapped the nearest cop. His teeth were grinding as he brought the stun pistol closer. *"Keep quiet Rayburn or else!"*

While the constable and his lackey squad completed the examination of his room. Vash still had no idea of what they might be looking for. When they began to rip up the flooring and pull down the wall coverings, a new set of lackeys showed up and led him outside.

To his amazement, there was a fleet of steam trolleys in the shaded street outdoors. They quickly piled him in one, and four cops climbed in after him, keeping stun-pistols trained on Vash during the entire maneuver. Out of the corner of his eye he noticed Derk climbing into an adjacent steam trolley. The entire fleet sped away together. The police had taken the whole affair with enormous seriousness as if Vash were some sort of a terrorist, or dare I say it…a sky pirate.

They rolled off the expressway and down a cleared avenue. Vash recognized the looming, sanitized walls of the Detention Building as its huge hydraulic system churned the heavy gears causing the gate to swing wide while making a sound of grinding that sent chills to anyone entering who were uncertain of their situation. The steam trolley that held Vash rode in as the others trailed off. The gate closed. Vash took note of the grim, sterile wall on the west courtyard which had a surprising number of guards at the ready to sweep the open space with gunfire should anybody be so inclined to make a suspicious gesture.

He shook his head in disbelief as to the lengths and severity that they had went to in order to get him here. In his mind, all they needed to do was ask him to come down and he would have gladly done so, that is what a respectable gentleman would have done. As of yet, no one had mentioned Gibbit Cove, so this simply didn't make sense. From day one on Nemo Vesta his conscience was whole-heartedly clear and he had been truthful about everything minus the part about where he was raised. This was insanity! He was not escorted to a cell, but rather curiously directly into the hearing room. His guards, then surrendered him to courtroom guards and went away with almost hysterical haste. It was as if no one wanted to be near him.

Vash stared about; the courtroom was highly informal. The chief justice sat at an ordinary desk with minimal ornamentation. The chairs were bearable. The air was clean and not stuffy as most buildings of this caliber, which Vash had seen many of. The atmosphere was that of a conference room in which reasonable men could discuss differences of opinion in calm leisure. *"Finally,"* he thought, "*a respectable amount of normality. Maybe now I can find out what's going on."* Only on a place such as Nemo Vesta would a prisoner be brought in by police under the previous pains to be dealt with in such meager, unassuming surroundings.

Derk came in by another door. He was with a man Vash recognized as the attorney who had represented Jessica's father in certain past legal interviews. There had been no mention of Jessica or the plan to marry her, so it couldn't have anything to do with that. It had been strictly business with her father. Jessica's father was Chairman of the Power Board, a director of the Polynational Association of Sky City Manufacturers, a committeeman of the Banker's League, and other important goings on. Vash had been thrown out of her father's offices several times. He now scowled ungraciously at the lawyer who had been the one to give that order on many of the occasions. He saw Derk wringing his hands in agitation once again.

Another man in court attire came to his side. *"Apparently this is my counsel,"* thought Vash, *"He is just as scared of me as the others, some counsel this is."*

"I'm the Citizen's Representative," he said uneasily. *"I'm to look after your interests. Do you wish to acquire a personal attorney?"*

"Why?" asked Vash, still feeling confident that there was simply some misunderstanding.

"For the charges— Do you wish a psychiatric examination—so as to make the claim of no responsibility to the act?" asked the Representative somewhat nervously. *"It might ... it might really be best under the circumstances."*

"Psychiatric Examination! I'm not crazy," said Vash, *"though I am beginning to wonder about everyone else here."*

The Citizen's Representative spoke to the justice.

"Sir, the accused waives his right to psychiatric examination, without prejudice or malice to a later claim of no responsibility should he wish to change his mind."

The attorney of Jessica's father watched with bland eyes to the entire affair which was taking place.

Vash said impatiently, *"May we just get on with it so that some since will come from all of this? I know what I've done and more importantly, what I haven't. What monstrous crime am I charged with?"*

"The charges against you," said the chief justice politely, *"are that on the night of March 12th at half past eight, you, Vash Rayburn, entered the fenced-in grounds surrounding the Nemo Vesta South Steam Converter Relay Station, which supplies power to the south quadrant propellers of the city. It is charged that you passed, not one, but two no-admittance signs before coming to a door marked 'Authorized Personnel Only.' You broke the lock of thus said door. While inside, you smashed the power receptor diverting steam pressure from the air chambers. This power receptor converts pressure to power for the industrial blades by which the entire south side propeller system operates. You smashed the receptor, minimizing the thrust capabilities of the entire south side."* The justice paused. *"Do you wish to challenge any of these charges as contrary to fact?"*

The Citizen's Representative said hurriedly: *"You have the right to deny any of them, of course."*

"Deny them? Why should I?" asked Vash. *"I did do everything that his honor said! But what I will deny is killing someone, what is this about me killing somebody? Why'd they say that I...?"*

"Don't mention that!" pleaded the Citizen's Representative. *"Please don't bring that up! You will be much, much better off if that doesn't get mentioned!"*

"But I didn't kill anybody!" insisted Vash, *"and what does that have to do with me diverting power from the relay station?"*

"Nobody's said a word to me about any of this," said the Citizen's Representative, jittering. *"Please, let's not have it in the record! The record has to be published."* He turned to the justice. *"Sir, the facts are conceded by the witness as stated."*

"Then Mr. Rayburn," said the chief justice to Vash, *"do you choose to answer all of these charges at this time?"*

"Why not?" asked Vash incredulously. *"Of course! Let's sort all of this out right now."*

"Then, if there are no objections, proceed," said the chief justice.

Vash drew a deep breath as he tried to understand why a man's death, charged to him, was not even mentioned and, in fact, was almost stricken from public record all together. He didn't like the nervous and agitated way everyone seemed to be looking at him. But—

"About diverting the pressure," he said confidently. *"What did I do in the power station before I diverted the pressure?"*

The justice looked at the attorney who now, was obviously there as representation for Jessica's father and his power company.

"Why," said that gentleman quite sternly, *"speaking in behalf of the Power Board as the chief complainant, before you diverted the pressure and smashed the standard receptor you connected a device of your own design across the power-leads just past the turbine converter. It was some sort of electric receptor unit of an apparently original pattern. It appears to have been a very interesting device as stated by the company engineers who examined it."*

"I had offered up the plans and prototype to the Power Board," said Vash, with a slight hint of arrogance, *"and I was thrown out...You! You specifically had me thrown out! What did it do? Tell the people in this courtroom what your engineers saw."*

"It substituted for the turbines that you had diverted the power from," said the attorney.

"Go on," said Vash, feeling as if he was about to be vindicated for his efforts.

"It continued to supply more than ample amount of power to the stabilization propellers" added the attorney, *"with overflow diverting back into the South side's power grid. In fact, your crime was only discovered because the original turbines had to be maintained every six hours or they would dry out and stick—naturally—there was concern when the readings never warned us of seizing. Plus, there was a drop in the average carbon burn that generally took place. Your device adjusted to the load and did not burn carbon. So, when the attendants went to see how the turbine was not seizing, they discovered what you had done."*

"It saved carbon, then," said Vash triumphantly beaming with delight. *"That means it saved money. I saved the Power Board plenty while my invention was connected. They wouldn't believe me when I explained it to them...you wouldn't believe me. Now they know. I did know what I was talking about!"*

The chief justice then broke in:

"Completely irrelevant. You have heard the charges. In legal terms, you are charged with burglary, trespass, unlawful entry, malicious mischief, breach of the peace, sabotage, and endangering the lives of everyone on Nemo Vesta, should your contraption not have worked and the south side propellers stopped functioning. Discuss the charges, please!"

"I'm telling you!" protested Vash. *"I offered the thing to the Power Board. They said they were satisfied with what they had and wouldn't listen. So, I proved that it worked! That receptor saved them ten thousand credits worth of carbon in just the first few hours that it was running. It'll save more than a million credits a year if placed in every power station on Nemo Vesta! If I know the Power Board, they never unhooked it and are still using it as we speak!"*

The courtroom, in its entirety, visibly shivered as they murmured amongst each other.

"Well? Are they?" demanded Vash belligerently to the attorney, "*tell me I am wrong!"*

"They are not," interrupted the attorney, tight-lipped. *"It has been smashed and even been melted down."*

"Then look at my patents!" insisted Vash. *"This whole thing is stupid."*

"The patent records," said the attorney with unnecessary vehemence, *"have been destroyed. Your possessions have been searched for copies. Nobody will ever look at your drawings again—not if they are wise!"*

"Wha-a-at?" demanded Vash incredulously. *"They were wha-a-at?"*

"I will amend the record of this hearing before it is published," said the chief justice rather uneasily. *"I should not have made that*

comment. I ask permission of the Citizen's Representative to amend."

"Request granted," said the Representative before he had even finished with his words.

The justice said quickly:

"The-charges have been admitted by the defendant. Since the complainant does not wish punitive action taken against him—"

"He'd be a blasted fool if he did," grunted Vash under his breath.

"And merely wishes security against future repetition of the offense," the chief justice continued, *"I rule that the defendant may be released upon posting his bond on the promise of good behavior in the future. That is, he will be required to post bond which will be forfeited if he should at any time, again, enter a relay station enclosure, passes any no-trespassing signs, ignores any no-admittance signs and/or smashes any apparatus belonging to the complainant."*

"All right," said Vash indignantly. *"I won't try to help any more. If they're too stupid to save money, that's not on me— How much is the bond?"*

"The court will take it under advisement and will notify the defendant within the customary two hours," said the chief justice at top speed. He swallowed. *"The defendant-will be kept in close confinement until the bond is posted. This hearing is concluded."* As his gavel slammed the wooden sound block on his table.

He did not look at Vash. Courtroom guards put stun-pistols against Vash's body and ushered him out in the same quick fashion in which he had been ushered in.

Presently his friend Derk came to see him in the cold dank cell in which he had been placed. Derk looked white as if the smell of the place, or maybe that he just played a role in getting his friend arrested, made him sick.

"I'm in trouble because I'm your friend, Vash," he said miserably, *"but I asked permission to explain things to you. After all, I caused your arrest. I urged you not to connect up that infernal contraption without permission!"*

"I know," growled Vash, *"but there are some people out there that are just so stupid you have to show them everything. I didn't realize that there are people so stupid you can't show them anything."*

"You ... showed something you didn't intend to," said Derk in a low melancholy voice. *"Vash, I ... I have to tell you. When they went to charge the carbon bins at the Relay station, they ... they found a dead man, Vash!"*

Vash sat up in anticipation that he was going to finally find out what all of this had to do with a dead man.

"What's that about a dead man?"

"Your machine—killed him. He was outside the building at the foot of a tree. Your receptor killed him through a stone wall! It broke his bones and killed him.... Vash—" Derk never seemed to stop wringing his hands. *"At some stage of power-drain as your receptor was transferring energy, it seems that you inadvertently created some sort of death ray device!"*

Vash had had a good many shocks today. When Derk arrived, he'd been incredulously comparing the treatment he'd received and the panic about him, with the charges made against him in court. They didn't add up. This new, previously undisclosed item left him speechless. He goggled at Derk, who wept as if he had been the one to kill the poor chap.

"Don't you see?" asked Derk pleadingly. *"That's why I had to tell the police it was you. We can't have someone in Nemo Vesta creating death rays! The police can't let anybody go free who knows how to create a weapon like that! This is a wonderful place to live, but there are lots of evil people out there; what if this were to fall into the hands of, say, someone from Gibbit Cove?"* Vash almost snickered at the fact Derk had no clue that the machine was built by someone from Gibbit Cove. *"They'll do anything! The police dare not let it even be suspected that death rays can be made! That's why you weren't charged with murder. People all over the planet would start doing research, hoping to satisfy all their grudges by committing murders from a distance with no trace of the culprit! For the sake of civilization your secret has to be suppressed—and you with it. It's terrible for you, Vash, but there's nothing else to do!"*

Vash said almost dazed:

"But the chief justice said all I needed to do was pay my bond to get out."

"The ... the justice," said Derk tearfully, *"he didn't name it in court, because it would have to be published in public record, but he's set your bond at fifty million credits! There's nobody who could raise that for you in any reasonable amount of time, and with the reason behind the bond, there is no way that an appeal will ever get it reduced."*

"But anybody who looks at the plans of the receptor will know it can't make death rays!" protested Vash blankly.

"Nobody will look," said Derk morosely. *"According to multinational law, anyone who knows how to make it will have to be locked up. They checked the patent examiners. They've forgotten. Nobody dared examine the device you had working. They'd be jailed if they understood it! Nobody will ever risk learning how to make death rays—not on a sky city as civilized as this. Civility is only as good as the person who can get away with murder. You have to be locked up forever, Vash. You just have to!"*

Vash, succumbing to the reality of Derk's words, simply replied with an almost inaudible: *"Oh...I see."*

"I beg your forgiveness for having you arrested," said Derk in a sorrowful wail, *"but I couldn't do anything but tell—"*

Vash just stared at his cell wall. Derk went away weeping. He was an admirable, honorable, however, not-too-bright young man who had been Vash's only friend outside of Jessica.

Vash stared blankly at nothing. As an event, the entire thing was preposterous, and yet it was sorely believable in presentation. When in the course of human endeavors someone does something that puts someone else to the trouble of adjusting the numb routine of his or her life, the one being forced into adjustment is oftentimes resentful. The richer he or she is at the time and the more satisfactory their life, the more resentful he or she is at any change, however minor. And should, out of all of the changes that offend them, the changes that require them to think back on past mistakes, is most disliked.

The high brass in the Power Board considered that everything was moving smoothly. There was no need to consider new devices. Vash's drawings and plans had simply never been bothered with, because there was no recognized need for them. And when he forced acknowledgment that his receptor worked better than the antiquated steam operated turbines, the unwelcome demonstration was highly offensive in and of itself. It was natural; it was inevitable that it should have been infallibly certain that any possible excuse for not thinking about the receptor would be seized upon. And a single dead man found near the operating demonstrator.... If one assumed that the demonstrator had killed him, —why one could react emotionally, feel vast indignation, frantically command that the device and its inventor be suppressed together, and go on living happily without doing any thinking or making any other change in anything at all.

Vash was appalled. Now that it had happened, he could see that it had to. The geo political world of sky cities, more specifically, that of Nemo Vesta was at the very peak of human culture. It had arrived at so splendid a plane of civilization that nobody could imagine any improvement—unless, of course, the afore mentioned better tranquilizer that could actually be designed to make life more endurable.

Nobody ever really wants anything he didn't think of for himself. No one can want anything he doesn't know exists—or that he can't imagine existing. On Nemo Vesta no one wanted anything, unless it was relief from the tedium of ultra-civilized life. Vash's new power device did not fill a human need; only a mechanical one. It had, therefore, no value that would make anybody hospitable towards it.

And Vash would now spend his life in jail for failing to recognize that one small detail.

He revolted, immediately. He wanted something, he wanted out. And because he was the son of a pirate, the grandson of a pirate, the nephew of a pirate with piracy in his veins, he could not be content with spending any portion of his life as a captive so he began to put his mind to work devising *alternatives* to his captivity, he set about designing his escape in immense detail. With his newly enforced change in perspective, he took the view that he must seem, at least, to give his captors and jailers and—as he saw it—his persecutors what they wanted.

They would be pleased to have him dead, provided their consciences were clear. This brought back a vivid memory of how his father once escaped the captivity of a sky marshal's vessel once when he was captured for looting a supplies barge. Vash built on that as a foundation for his plan.

Shortly before nightfall he performed, what would seem to some as, cryptic actions. He unraveled threads from his shirt and laid them aside for the time being. There would be a vision-lens in the ceiling of his cell; the blasted things are all over the place here on Nemo Vesta, and somebody would certainly notice what he did. He made a light. He put the threads in his mouth, set fire to his mattress, and laid down calmly upon it. The mattress was of excellent quality. It would smell very badly as it smoldered.

And it did. Lying flat, he kicked convulsively for a few seconds. He looked like someone who had possibly ingested poison. Then he waited.

It seemed like a very long time before he could hear his jailer come down the cell corridor, dragging a fire hose. Vash had been correct in assuming that he had been watched through the vision-lens. His actions had been those of a man who'd anticipated a possible need to commit suicide, and who had hidden poison in a part of his shirt for such a time, should the situation warrant it. The jailer did not hurry, because if the inventor of a death ray actually committed suicide, everyone would feel a little less anxious. They allowed Vash a reasonable time in which to die. *"It would be the gentleman's thing to do,"* he thought.

He seemed impressively dead by the time his jailer actually opened the old, rusting cell door and dragged him out. The Jailer then removed the un-scorched furniture in order to preserve it, and then proceeded to set up the fire hose on its widest spray in which to put out the fire as quickly as possible. He went back to the corridor to wait for the fire to be extinguished.

Thinking Vash dead and leaving him to his own devices, the jailer was caught unaware as Vash crowned him with a stool, with Vash feeling an unexpected satisfaction in the act as the jailer collapsed in a heap on the floor. *"Thank you pop,"* Vash said out loud as he gloated inside for the memory of his father's escape.

One minor setback did occur, however. The Jailer did not carry keys. The system was set up for him to be let out of this corridor by a second guard posted outside the door. Vash growled as he picked up the fire hose. He turned its nozzle back to make a stream instead of a mist. Water came out at about four hundred pounds of pressure. He knocked on the door and as the second guard began to open it, Vash used the newly acquired water cannon to blast the door open the rest of the way, rendering the second guard unconscious. He took this guard's uniform, stun-pistol, and keys then casually open another door leading to the courtyard. He marched out, waved at two guards who sighted him, and walked right out of the prison into the very steam trolley that had brought him here. He climbed into the driver's seat as a partially naked guard came into the courtyard yelling at the guards to lock down the gates. Seeing that his cover had been blown, he cranked the trolley's gauge to maximum pressure and burst through the gate as it was grinding shut, whirling into the street outside.

Vash was now free, but only temporarily. Around him lay the city capital of Nemo Vesta—the highest civilization in all of the sky cities. Trees lined its ways. Towers rose splendidly toward the skies, with thousands of less ambitious structures scattered in between. There were open squares and parkways and malls, and it did not smell like a city at all, nor would you suspect this perfected city to be poised miles above the earth. Before he had the time to get overly sentimental, he was loosed on the streets not more than three or four minutes before the communicator in the trolley squawked the all-police alarm for him.

It was to be expected, of course. The entire city would shortly be one enormous man hunt, set on the united purpose of catching one Vash Rayburn. There was only one place on this floating mantrap for him to go, somewhere he could be safe—and he wouldn't be safe anywhere on Nemo Vesta if he had actually been officially charged with murder. But since the police had tactfully failed to mention murder in his charges, he could get at least breathing-time by taking refuge in the Inter-colonial Embassy.

He headed for it, bowling along splendidly. The police trolley hummed on its way for half a mile. The Inter-Colonial Diplomatic

Service represented humanity at large upon each individual continent, sky city, deluge city, and Stratos city on the planet. The lead ambassador was the only person Vash could even imagine as listening to him, and that was because the ambassador was not from Nemo Vesta, but came from the deluged city of Kanerdale, not too far from the coastal lines of Gibbit Cove. But he mainly counted upon a breathing space in the Embassy, during which to make more plans as yet unformed as his main objective was to get out of sight. Pondering how a memory of his past just saved him from a life locked away, he began to see some virtues in the simple, lawless, piratical world in which he had spent his childhood despising.

Another steam Trolley rushed frantically toward him down a side street. Stun-pistols made little pinging noises against the body of his vehicle. He put on more speed, but the other trolley overtook him. It ranged alongside, its occupants waving stern commands to halt. And then, just before it swerved to force him off the highway, Vash swung instead at them and drove their trolley into a tree. It crashed thunderously. One of Vash's own wheels collapsed from the impact. He drove on with the crumpled wheel producing an up-and-down motion that threatened to make the seasoned member of a pirate community sea-sick. Then he heard yelling behind him. The cops had piled out of the trolley and were in pursuit on foot.

The tall, rough-stone wall of the Embassy was visible, now, beyond the monument to the First Settlers of Nemo Vesta. He leaped to the ground and ran. Stun-pistol bolts, though a little beyond their effective range, still bit the skin with a sting like fire. They spurred him on.

"NO! NO! NO!" Vash exclaimed as he shook the gates. The gates of the Embassy were closed. He bolted around the corner and, using his years of experience climbing ship masts to work on vessel sails, he darted up the conveniently rugged stones of the South wall. He was well aloft before the cops spotted him. They fired at him from, what seemed to be every angle and the charges popped and crackled all around him.

But he found himself at the top and had both arms over the parapet before a charge hit his legs and stunned them—paralyzing him from the waist down. He hung fast, ready to curse fate for letting him get that far only to be caught at that moment.

Then hands grasped his wrists. A white-haired man appeared from within the walls just on the other side of the parapet. The man took a good, solid grip, and heaved. He drew Vash over the breast-high top of the wall and let him down to the walkway inside it.

"A near thing, that was!" said the white-haired man pleasantly. *"I was taking a walk in the garden when I happened upon the excitement. It seems that I arrived just in time."* He paused, then added, *"I do hope you're not just a common murderer with the police after him! We can't offer asylum to such—only a breathing space and a chance to start running again. But if you're a political offender—"*

Vash began trying to work sensation and usefulness back into his legs. Feeling finally came back, and the sudden awakening of the nerves was not pleasant to say the least. *"I never envy a man shot by a stun pistol,"* said the white-haired man.

"I'm the Inter-Colonial Ambassador," said the white-haired man politely. *"Let me help get you inside while you regain your land legs."*

"My name," said Vash bitterly, *"is Vash Rayburn and I've been framed for trying to save the Power Boards millions of credits a year!"* Then he said more bitterly: *"If you wish to know my business, I ran away from Gibbit Cove trying to leave claim to my past and be a civilized man, to live a civilized life. It was a mistake! I'm to be permanently jailed for using my brains!"*

The ambassador cocked his head thoughtfully to one side.

"Gibbit Cove, you say?" he said with a ponderous curiosity. *"The name Rayburn fits to that somehow. Oh, yes! Sky-piracy! People say the people of Gibbit Cove capture and loot a dozen or so ships a year, only there's no way to prove it was them. And there's a man named Rayburn who was reported as to head a particular ruffian group that call themselves the Equalizers."*

"That would be my grandfather," said Vash with an almost slight hint of pride in his voice at the prospect that his legend had made it this far around the world. *"So, what are you going to do about it? I'm outlawed! I've defied the sky city government! I'm disreputable by descent, and worst of all I've tried to use my brains!"*

"Deplorable!" said the ambassador mildly. *"I don't mean outlawry is deplorable, you understand, or defiance of the government, or being disreputable. But trying to use one's brains is bad business! A serious offense in these parts! Are your legs all right now?"* Vash nods his head yes as he continues to rub life into his stiffened knees. *"Then come on down with me and I'll have you given some dinner and some fresh clothing and so on."*

"Offhand," the white-haired man added, *"it would seem that using one's brains would be classed as a political offense rather than a criminal one on Nemo Vesta. We'll see I guess; we'll see."*

Vash gaped up at him shocked at the words he just heard. He had figured that the man would immediately turn him over to the authorities.

"You mean there's a possibility that—"

"Of course!" said the ambassador to the amazement of Vash. *"You haven't phrased it in so many words, but you're actually a rebel. A revolutionist. You defy authority and tradition and governments and such things. Naturally, by the founding principles, the Inter-Colonial Diplomatic Service is inclined to be on your side. What do you think it's for?"*

Chapter 2

About two hours had now passed. Vash was ushered into the ambassador's office. He'd been refreshed, his torn clothing replaced by more respectable garments, and the places where stun-pistols had stung him was now soothed by ointments. More importantly though, he'd worked out and firmly adopted a new point of view as it pertained to his current situation.

He'd been a misfit at home on Gibbit Cove because he was never content with the humdrum and monotonous life as a member of a sky pirate community. Piracy was a matter of dangerous take-offs in cranky airships, to be followed by weeks or even months of tedious and uncomfortable boredom in high altitudes thinly veiled with oxygen so as to have to wear a re-breather mask for most of the time on board. No voyage ever contained more than 10 to 15 seconds of satisfactory action. Regardless of the result of the actions, one had to get away fast when it was over, lest overwhelming forces swarm up from nearby air marshal stations. It was intolerably devoid of anything an ambitious young man would want.

Even when one had made a good haul—with the lifeboats darting frantically for ground—and after one actually made it back to Gibbit Cove with a captured ship, even then there was little satisfaction in a piratical career. Though Gibbit Cove had never had a large population, piracy could not support a large number of people. Gibbit Cove couldn't attempt to defend itself against even single heavily-armed ships that sometimes came in passionate resolve to avenge the disappearance of a rich freighter or a fast new liner. So as for the people of Gibbit Cove, in order to avoid hanging, they had to frequently play innocent as well as use other distinct means of presenting themselves as convincingly simple, harmless folk who cultivated their fields and led quiet, blameless lives. They might loot, but they had to hide their booty where investigators would not find it; they couldn't really benefit by it. They had to build their own houses and make their own garments and grow their own food. So, one could say that life on Gibbit

Cove was dull to say the least. Piracy was not profitable in the sense that one could live well by it with the exception of a select few. It simply wasn't a trade for a man like Vash.

So Vash decided at a young age that he would abandon it. He would study mechanics and inventing and whatever else he found in books taken from looted passenger-ship libraries. Within months of arrival on a law-abiding sky city, he would be able to earn a living using mechanical engineering as an honest trade.

Unsatisfactory was the life, at least not as satisfying as Vash had dreamed. Law-abiding communities were no more thrilling or rewarding than piratical ones. A payday now and then didn't make up for the tedium of labor. Even when one had money there wasn't much to do with it. On Nemo Vesta, to be sure, the level of civilization was so high that many people needed psychiatric treatment to stand it, and neurotics vastly outnumbered more normal folk. Within the floating confines of Nemo Vesta, engineering was yet another trade like piracy, and nothing more.

He should have known it would be this way. His grandfather had often discussed this frustration with him saying, *"We common creations of the Almighty who made us,"* it was his grandfather's habit to say, *"don't make much sense! There are some of us that work so hard we're too tired to enjoy life. There's some that work so hard at enjoying it that they don't get any fun out of it. And the rest of us spend our lives complainin' that there just ain't any fun in life no matter what. The man that, over all others, has the best time of any is one that picks out something he hasn't got a chance to do, and spends his life rebelling because he's continually stopped from doing it. When"*—and here Vash's grandfather tended to be a bit more emphatic and almost theatrical—*"he wouldn't think much of it if he could!"*

What Vash actually craved, of course, was a sense of achievement, of doing things worth doing, and doing them well. Technically there were opportunities all around him. He'd developed one, and it would save millions of credits a year if it were adopted. But nobody wanted it. He'd tried to force its use, he was in trouble for doing so, and now he could complain justly enough, but despite his grandfather's words, he was not the happiest man he knew no matter which position he had taken.

The ambassador received him with a cordial wave of the hand.

"Things move fast," he said cheerfully. *"You weren't here half an hour before there was a police captain at the gate. He explained that an excessively dangerous criminal had escaped jail and been seen to climb the Embassy wall. He offered very generously to bring some men in and capture you and take you away—with my permission, of course. He was shocked when I declined."*

"I can understand that," said Vash.

"By the way," said the ambassador. *"A young man like yourself—am I right to assume there is a girl involved in this?"*

Vash considered. *"A girl's father,"* he acknowledged, *"is the real complainant against me."*

"Does he complain," asked the ambassador, *"because you want to marry her, or because you don't?"*

"Neither actually," Vash told him. *"She hasn't quite decided that I'm worth defying her rich father for."*

"That's good!" said the ambassador. *"Less of a mess that way, you can't blame a woman for being practical."* Changing subjects to veer away from Vash's personal life, the ambassador sharply spoke, *"I've checked your story. Allowing for differences of viewpoints of course, it agrees with the official version. I've ruled that you are a political refugee, and so entitled to sanctuary in the Embassy. And that's that."*

"Thank you, sir," said Vash.

"There's no question about the crime," observed the ambassador, *"or that it is primarily political. You proposed to improve a technical process in a society, which considers itself beyond improvement. If you'd succeeded, the idea of change would have spread, people now poor could see potential to get rich, while people now currently rich would have gotten poor from the loss in revenue, and you'd have done what all governments are established to prevent...individual liberty. You proposed to change an entire economic structure that would take the power away from the government and the power barons, so you'll never be able to walk the streets of this city again in safety. You've honestly scared people. People, most anyway, are like sheep and as such, they*

prefer the confinement of a penned in yard with rations that they know over the freedom of an open, unexplored field where they can have their fill."

"Yes, sir," said Vash. *"It's been an unpleasant surprise to them, but I truly wasn't expecting the backlash that I had received."*

The ambassador, both elbows planted firmly on his desk, put the tips of his fingers together on his lips as if heavily contemplating on the next words to come from those lips.

"Do you realize, Mr. Rayburn," he asked, *"that the whole purpose of civilization is to take the surprises out of life, so one can be absolutely bored out of one's mind...that a culture in which nothing unexpected ever happens is called its Golden Age? An age when nobody can even imagine anything happening unexpectedly, that they later fondly refer to as the Good Old Days is the lump sum of one's view of a prosperous society?"*

"I hadn't quite ever thought of it in just those words, sir—". Vash said somewhat hesitant.

"Believe it or not, it is one of the most avoided facts of life," said the ambassador. *"Government, whether local, state-to-state or in a world sense of the word, is an organization for the suppression of adventure. Taxes are, in part, the insurance premiums one pays for protection against the unpredictable. And you have offended against everything that is the foundation of a stable, orderly and tedious way of life—against civilization, itself."*

Vash frowned with a perplexed look on his brow. *"Yet you've granted me asylum—"*

"Naturally!" said the ambassador. *"The Diplomatic Service works for the welfare of humanity. That doesn't mean stuffiness. A Golden Age in any civilization is always followed by collapse. In ancient days savages came and camped outside the walls of super-civilized towns. They were unwashed, unmannerly, and unsanitary. The super-civilized people, refusing to even think about them, soon found themselves at the present mercies (or lack thereof) of those very savages as they stormed the city walls and then, yet another civilization went up in flames."* Shaking his head, the ambassador added, *"It doesn't matter if you are on a land-based city such as Gibbit Cove or a sky city such as Nemo Vesta, civilizations which*

rest on their laurels and stay content only to concern themselves with what is on their side of the wall, often gets destroyed by that which is on the other side."

"But now," objected Vash, *"there are no savages."*

"Ahh, my dear Mr. Rayburn, but there are. They have just reinvented themselves," the ambassador told him. *"My point is that the Diplomatic Service cherishes individuals and causes which battle this stuffiness and complacency and get people out of this Golden Ages mentality to see the potential monstrous things that could be on the other side of the wall. Not common criminals, of course, they are merely bothersome creatures like body lice, but rebels and revolutionaries who prevent hardening of the arteries of commerce and furnish wholesome exercise to the political class—they're worth cherishing!"*

"*I ...I think I see, sir,"* said Vash.

"I honestly hope you do," said the ambassador. *"My actions on your behalf are pure diplomatic policy. To encourage the dissatisfied is to insure against universal law and a one-world hypocrisy—which can be bland to the individual. Nemo Vesta is in a bad way. You are the most encouraging thing that has happened here in quite a long time. And you're not a native, which adds to the delight of seeing the old codgers faces."*

"No, I am not a native," agreed Vash. *"I come from Gibbit Cove, a civilization of sky pirates and ruffian buccaneers and never thought I would be one to cause so much grief to an entire city."*

"Never mind any of that now." The ambassador pulled out a dusty atlas and opened up on the desk. *"Consider yourself a good symptom, and valued as such, a counterweight to the current leanings of a society close to tipping, or maybe a virus to a body that has not had its immune system tested. If you could spread that virus and start a contagion, you'd force your fellow citizens to rise up and take back the keys to the paddock that they have for so long been locked in."* with a smirk, the ambassador glanced over at Vash, *"savages can always reinvent themselves, even those from Gibbit Cove. But enough ramblings from an old man disgruntled with political life. Let us set about your affairs."* He looked down at the atlas. *"Where would you like to go, since you obviously must leave Nemo Vesta?"*

"Not too far, sir, — if I can help it " said Vash as he leaned over to look at the atlas.

"The girl, eh?" The ambassador did not smile. He ran his finger down a page. *"There are a few close proximity cities and ports as well as one land-based civilization that didn't get destroyed in the water rises, what are you looking for? Something more secluded or something screaming more of lively commercial activity, where one with mechanical engineering skills should easily find employment? Ah Ha!"* exclaimed the ambassador, *"I have it, Port Barogate. It is said to be progressive and there is much organized research— Now it is a floating port docked next to the east side of Her Majesty's Isle, so the piracy tidbit might need to stay hidden."*

"I wouldn't want to be kept in the position of an engineer, sir," said Vash apologetically. *"I'd rather ... well ... putter on my own."*

"Impractical, but a recluse inventor type might be sensible. It would afford you seclusion and anonymity without question," commented the ambassador. He turned to another page in the atlas. *"There's Toffpoint. Its social system is practically feudal, a little under-developed for my taste, but... There's a landing grid for dirigibles. Its main exports are skins and metal ingots and practically nothing else. There are no power relays for you to modify,"* the ambassador said jokingly. *"Strangers find the local customs difficult. Though it is scattered with quite a few communities, you won't find any larger than eight thousand people, and most don't even approach that size. If I had to describe it, I would say that it is like a scattered mess of small baronies surrounding a feudalistic society of aristocrats, and roads are usually in such disrepair that you will not see a vehicle such as a steam trolley anywhere, just not practical you see."*

The ambassador leaned back and said in a slightly detached voice:

"I received a letter from there a couple of months ago. It was rather arrogant and rude to say the least. The writer was one Emory Demetrius Fairbeard, and he explained that his dignity would not let him make a commercial offer, but an electronics tinker who put himself under his protection would not be the loser for it. He signed himself prince of this, lord of that, baron of the other thing and claimant to the dukedom of something else. Are

you interested? There are no kings on Toffpoint, just feudal chiefs."

Vash thought it over.

"I think that I'll go to Toffpoint," he decided. "It's bound to be better than Gibbit Cove if they are looking for Tinkers, and it can't be worse than Nemo Vesta."

The ambassador looked impassive. An Embassy servant came in and offered an indoor communicator. The ambassador put it to his ear. After a moment he said:

"Show him in." He turned to Vash. *"My dear boy, you did kick up a heck of a storm! The Minister of State, no less, is here to demand your surrender. I'll counter with a formal request for an exit-permit. I'll talk to you again after he leaves."*

The ambassador walked out with an almost elated tone in his voice and a barely audible statement, *"Yes, my boy, you definitely scared them."*

Vash went out. He paced up and down the other room into which he was shown. Toffpoint would definitely not be in a Golden Age! He was wiser now than he'd been that morning. He recognized that he'd made mistakes in trying to go from a sky pirate to a noble pillar of society on one of the most lavish sky cities on the planet. Now he could see rather ruefully how completely improbable it was that anybody could put across a technical device merely by proving its value, without the market wanting it. He shook his head regretfully at the blunder, swearing that mistake would not be made again.

An hour or so had past and the ambassador sent for him.

"I've had a pleasant time," he told Vash genially. *"There was a beautiful row of accompanying officials with the Minister of State. You've really scared people, Mr. Rayburn! You deserve well of the republic! Every government and every person need to be thoroughly terrified occasionally. It limbers up the brain."*

"I agree, sir," said Vash. *"I've—"*

"The residing counsel for the United Sky City Justice Department," interrupted the ambassador relishing an official letter recently handed to him, *"insists that you be turned over to authorities*

immediately to be locked up with no chance of parole because you know how to make death rays. I, of course, said it was nonsense, and you were a political refugee in sanctuary and requesting asylum. The Minister of State said the Cabinet would consider removing you forcibly from the Embassy if you weren't surrendered. I said that if the Embassy was violated no ship would clear for Nemo Vesta from any other civilized port. They wouldn't like losing their global trade! Then he said that the government would not give you an exit-permit, and that he would hold me personally responsible if you killed everybody on Nemo Vesta with your death ray, including him and me. I said he insulted me by suggesting that I'd permit such shenanigans. He told me that the government would take an extremely grave view of my attitude, and I said they would be silly if they did. Then he went off with great dignity—but shaking with panic—leaving me with the letter of demand I have in my hand."

"Evidently," said Vash in relief, *"you believe me when I say that my gadget doesn't make death rays."*

The ambassador looked slightly embarrassed.

"To be honest," he admitted, *"I've no doubt that you invented it independently, but they've been using a device, similar to the one you described, for half a century in the Strato-Cetus Mining sector to run their soil grinders. They've had no trouble with people being destroyed by death rays."*

Vash winced, slightly upset at the knowledge his invention wasn't completely original. *"Did you tell the Minister that?"*

"Hardly," said the ambassador. *"It wouldn't have done you any good. You're in open revolt and have performed overt acts of violence against the police and the city at this point. Also, it was impolite enough for me to suggest that the local government was stupid. It would have been proportionately more undiplomatic of me to prove it."*

Vash then had an immediate uneasy feeling.

"I'm thinking that the cops—quite unofficially of course—might try to kidnap me from the Embassy. They'll deny that they tried, especially if they manage it. But I think they'll try none the less."

"Very likely," said the ambassador. *"We'll take precautions."*

"I'd like to make something—not destructive—but just in case," said Vash. *"If you would trust me not to make death rays,"* Vash smirked. *"I'd like to make a generator of directed low-impulse microwaves. What happens is they ionize the air wherever they strike. That's all. They make the air in the affected region a high-resistance conductor. Nothing more than that."*

The ambassador said: *"There was an old-fashioned way to make ozone...."* When Vash nodded, a little surprised that the ambassador knew the device he was referencing. The ambassador said, *"By all means go ahead. You should be able to get parts from your room's vision-receiver. I'll have some tools given you."* Then he added: *"Diplomacy has to understand the things which control events. Once it was social position; for a time, it was weapons. Then it was commerce. Now it's technology. But I wonder how you'll use the ionization of air to protect yourself from kidnappers!* Placing his hand in the air to halt Vash from saying anything, *"Don't tell me! Don't even hint, I'd rather have fun trying to guess."*

He waved his hand in cordial dismissal and an Embassy servant showed Vash to his quarters. Ten minutes later another staff man brought him tools such as would be needed for work on a vision set. He was then left to his own devices.

He delicately disassembled the set in his room and began to put some of the parts together in a uniquely novel yet wholly rational fashion. The science of electronics, like the science of mathematics, had progressed way beyond the point where all of it had practical applications. One could spend a lifetime learning things that research had discovered in the past, and industry had never found a use for. On Gibbit Cove, industriously reading pirated books; Vash didn't learn where utility stopped. He'd kept on learning long after a practical man would have stopped studying to get a paying job, but the boredom of Gibbit Cove afforded much time for his hobby of exploratory learning.

Any electronic engineer could have made the device he now assembled. It only needed to be wanted—and apparently, he was the first person to want it. In this respect it was like the receptor that had gotten him into trouble in the first place. However, as he put the small parts together, he felt certain hollowness of heart. A man Vash's age needs to have some girl admire him from time to time to make him feel reason for his accomplishments. If Jessica had been sitting cross-legged before him, listening intently while he rambled on about his creations, Vash would probably have been perfectly happy. But she wasn't. It wasn't likely she ever would be as Vash scowled to himself remorsefully.

Inside of an hour he'd made a hand-sized, 3.5-watt, wave-guide projector pistol using waves of eccentric form. Within the beam of the projector pistol, air became ionized. Air would become a high-resistance conductor comparable to nichrome wire, wherever the projector sent its microwaves.

He was wrapping tape about the crudely fashioned pistol grip when a servant brought him a scribbled note. A woman who fled after leaving it had handed it in at the Embassy gate then disappeared in the night. It looked like it could be Jessica's handwriting. It read like Jessica's phrasing. It appeared to have been written by somebody in a highly emotional state. Yet something about it wasn't quite—not absolutely—convincing.

He went to find the ambassador. He handed over the note. The ambassador read it and raised his eyebrows.

"Well?"

"It could be authentic," admitted Vash.

"In other words," said the ambassador, *"you are not sure that it is a booby trap—an invitation to a date with the authorities?"*

"I'm not sure," said Vash. *"I think I need to check it out none-the-less. If I have any illusions left after this morning, I'd better find it out. I thought Jessica was of the same heart that beats within me, so I must investigate."*

"I make no comment or judgment," observed the ambassador. *"I was young once too. Can I help you in any way?"*

"I have to leave the Embassy," said Vash, *"and there's possibly a solid gauntlet of police outside the walls in wait. Could I borrow some old clothes, a few pillows, and a length of rope?"*

The ambassador just nodded with a sideways smile at the prospect of another puzzle that he would get to ponder on; another game of 'what's he making now?'

Half an hour later a rope began to uncoil itself at the uttermost outside corner of the Embassy wall. It dangled down just feet off the ground. This was at the rear of the Embassy enclosure. The night was bright with stars, and the city's towers glittered with many lights. But here there was almost complete blackness and that silence of a sleeping city only interrupted by the dull roar of the flight blades from underneath, keeping the city stationed.

The rope remained dangling from the wall with no signs of life. No light reached the ground where it hung. The tiny crescent of the moon cast an insufficient glow. Nothing could be seen by it, but incandescent shadows stretching here and there.

The rope suddenly went up, as if it had been lowered merely to make sure that it was long enough for its purpose. After pulling completely up, it descended once again. This time a midsized humanoid shadowy figure dangled at its end. It came down, swaying a little. It reached the blackest part of the shadow at the wall's base. It stayed there for what seemed to be an eternity.

Nothing happened. The figure rose swiftly, hauled up by a rapid pulling of the rope. Then the line came down again and once again a figure descended, but, unlike the previous attachment, this figure moved. The rope swayed and oscillated back and forth as if the figure was having trouble with footing. The figure came down a good halfway to the ground. It paused, and then descended with much movement to two-thirds of the way from the top.

After the momentary pause, something seemed to alarm it. It began to rise with violent writhing and tugs of the rope. It ascended quickly.

There was a crackling noise; that of a stun-pistol! The figure seemed to climb more frantically. More crackling sounds broke the silence. Half a dozen or so sharp, snapping noises came up from the ground below. They were stun-pistol charges alright and there were tiny sparks where they hit. The dangling figure seemed to convulse a few times then went limp, but it did not fall. More charges poured into it. It hung motionless halfway up the wall of the Embassy just dangling as if dead.

Roused movements began in the darkness below. Men appeared, talking in low tones and straining their eyes toward the now motionless figure. They gathered underneath it. One went off at a run, carrying a message. Someone of authority arrived, panting. There was more low-toned argument. More and still more men appeared. All at once, there were now forty to fifty figures at the base of the wall with stun pistols at the ready should the figure begin to move once again.

One of those figures began to climb the rope hand over hand. He reached the motionless object. He exclaimed in a shocked and incoherent voice. He was shushed from below. He let the figure drop. It made next to no sound when it landed.

Then there was a rushing, as the guards about the Embassy went furiously back to their proper posts to keep anybody from slipping out. Only two men remained ranting bitterly over a dummy made of old clothes and pillows. But their ranting was in vain and fell on deaf ears.

Vash, by the time of the discovery, was now a number of blocks away. He now suffered painful doubts about the note that allegedly came from Jessica. The guards about the Embassy would have tried to catch him in any case, but it did seem very plausible that the note had been sent in order to get him to leave the Embassy. On the other hand, a false descent of a palpably human-like dummy had been plausible, too. He was able to draw all the guards to one spot by his seeming doubt and by testing out their vigilance with a dummy. The only thing improbable in his behavior had been that after testing their vigilance with a dummy, he'd made use of it. Not one of the shadows below suspected that Vash would use his dummy to create a diversion.

A fair distance away, he turned sedately into a narrow lane between two buildings. This paralleled another lane serving the home of Jessica and her father. The note had named the garden behind her home as a perfect rendezvous point. But Vash was not going to be at that garden. He wanted to be sure whether the cops had forged the note or not.

He judged his position carefully. *"If I climbed this tree, —hm-m-m...."* Vash thought as he hung his full weight from a low branch. He thought it generous of the city-planners of Nemo Vesta to use trees so lavishly on a sky city—if he climbed this tree he could look into the garden where Jessica, in theory, waited in tears. He climbed it. He sat astride a thick limb in magnolia-scented darkness and watched. He brought out his 3.5-watt projector pistol, which he had fashioned earlier. There was reason for suspicion and Vash was going to take every precaution.

Neither in Jessica's house, nor in any of the houses between, was there a single lighted window. This was peculiar and increased Vash's uneasiness.

Vash adjusted the wave-guide and pressed the stud trigger of his instrument as he pointed it carefully into the nearer garden.

From the darkness of the grove, a figureless male voice grunted in a startled and surprised tone. There was a stirring. Vash changed the direction of his projector pistol and yet another man's voice rang out with a startled exclamation. The words seemed inappropriate to a citizen merely breathing the evening air.

Vash frowned. The note from Jessica had, at present, seemed to have been a forgery. To make sure, he readjusted the wave-guide to project a thin but fan-shaped beam. He aimed again. Painstakingly, he traversed the area in which men would have been posted to jump him, in the event that the note was forged. If Jessica were there, she would feel no effect. If police lay in wait, they would notice. And notice they did.

A man howled. Two men yelled together in harmony like two alley cats. Somebody bellowed. Somebody squealed. Someone, in charge of the flares made ready to give light for the police, was so startled by a strange sensation that he jerked the cord. An immense, cold-white brilliance appeared. The garden where Jessica definitely was not present became bathed in incandescence. Light spilled over the wall of one garden into the next and disclosed a squirming mass of police in the nearer garden also. Some of them leaped wildly and ungracefully while clawing behind them. Some stood still and struggled desperately to accomplish something that pertained to their hind quarters, while others gazed blankly at them until Vash swung his instrument their way, also.

A man tore off his pants and swung over the wall to get away from something intolerable. Others imitated him, save in the direction of their own flight. Some removed their trousers before they fled, while others tried to get them off while fleeing. Those last did not fare too well. Mostly they stumbled and other men fell over them, when both fallen and fallen-upon uttered hoarse and profane lamentations—A comedy of errors was afoot to say the least.

Vash let the confusion mount past any unscrambling, and then slid down the tree and joined in the rush. With the glare in the air behind him, he only feigned to stumble over one figure after another. Once or twice he even grunted as he appeared to have scorched his own fingers. But the daring move brought him out of harm's way into the adjacent lane with a dozen stun-pistols, gifts from the officers. Mostly uncomfortably warm from the microwaves, but sufficient trophies from the would-be ambush.

As they cooled off, he stowed them away in his belt and pockets, strolling away down the tree-lined street. Behind him, cops becoming aware of their trouser-less condition that was quickly brought to their attention by the sudden nip in the air and were now appealing to householders to notify headquarters of their state.

Vash did not feel particularly disillusioned by the success of the getaway and his new acquisitions. It occurred to him that even though this particular event would likely help him get off of Nemo Vesta, if he were to leave against the cops' will, he needed to have them at less than top efficiency. And it would stand to reason those men who have had their pants scorched off them are not apt to think too clearly and may take extreme measures to get their man and reclaim their pride. The more Vash thought about it, the more he felt a certain confidence increase in his mind.

He began to feel that he had worked things out very nicely, so Vash began to gloat to himself as he pondered over the effectiveness of his latest invention as if giving a training lecture at a university. If ionization made air a high-resistance conductor, then an ionizing beam would make a high-resistance short between the power terminals of a stun-pistol. With the power a stun-pistol carried, that short would get hot. So would the pistol. It would get hot enough, in fact, to scorch clothing and skin that came in contact with it. Which had happened as his theory predicted.

If the effect had been produced in the soles of the policemen's feet, Vash would have given every cop a hotfoot. But since they carried their stun-pistols in their hip pockets—well the comedy that ensued was worth the loss of a perfectly good vision receiver.

The thought of Jessica diminished his satisfaction, however. The note could be pure forgery, or the police could have learned about it through the treachery of the servant she sent to the Embassy to present it. It would be worthwhile to know. He turned around and headed back toward the home of her father. If she were loyal to him—why it would complicate things considerably. But he felt it necessary to find out.

He neared the spot where Jessica lived. This was an especially desirable residential area of Nemo Vesta that only the high in power lived. The houses were large and gracefully designed with their high Victorian style columns and lavish gardens. Vash could hear music ahead—live music. He went on. He came to a place where strolling citizens had paused under the trees of the street to listen to the melody and the sound of voices that accompanied it. The music and the festivity were coming from the house in which Jessica dwelt. She was having a party, on the very night in which he'd been framed for life imprisonment.

It was a shock to the system as one might guess. Vash had very little time to dwell on it, however as there was a sudden rush of vehicles and police trolleys descending on the front lawn. They formed a wall of blue coats about the house, while some knocked and were admitted in haste. Then Vash nodded disenchanted to himself as he watched the spectacle of reality unfold.

His escape from the Embassy was now known as well as the failure of the trap Jessica's note had baited. The police were now turning the whole city into a trap for one Vash Rayburn, and they were looking first at the most probable places, then they'd search the possible places for him to be, and by the time that had been accomplished they'd have cops from other surrounding ports and cities pouring into Nemo Vesta and they'd search every square inch of it for him. And most certainly and assuredly they would take the most urgent and infallible precautions to make sure he didn't get back into the sanctuary of the Embassy.

It was a situation that would have appalled Vash only that morning. Now, though, he only shook his head sadly. He moved on. Vash had gotten into trouble by trying to make an industrial civilization accept something it didn't want—a technical improvement in a standard device. He'd gotten partly out of trouble by giving his jailers what they definitely desired—the sight of him apparently a suicide in the cell in the Detention Building. He'd come out of the Embassy, again, by giving the watchers outside a view they urgently desired—a figure secretly descending the Embassy wall. He'd indulged himself at the ambuscade, but now the way to get back into the Embassy...

It was not far from Jessica's house to a public-safety kiosk, decoratively placed on a street corner. He entered it. It was unattended, of course. It was simply an out-of-door installation where cops could be summoned or fires reported or emergencies described by citizens independent of the regular home communicators. It had occurred to Vash that the global authorities would be greatly pleased to hear of a situation, in a place, that would seem to hint at his presence. There were all sorts of public services that would be delighted to operate impressively in their own lines. There were bureaus, which would rejoice in a chance to show off their efficiency.

He used his microwave projection pistol upon the apparatus in the kiosk; which remember, at short enough range would short-circuit just about anything. It was perfectly simple, if one knew how. He worked with a sort of tender thoroughness, shorting this item, shorting that, giving this frantic emergency call, a fib here, an exaggeration there. When he went out of the kiosk, he walked briskly toward an appointment he had made.

And presently the murmur of the city at night had new sounds added to it. They began as a faint, confused clamor at the edges of the city. The uproar seemed to moved central and grew louder as it came by. There were clanging bells and sirens and beeper-horns warning all nonofficial vehicles to keep out of the way. On the raised-up expressway snorting metal monsters rushed with squealing excitement. On the fragrant lesser streets, small vehicles rushed with proportionately louder howling. Police trucks poured out of their cubbyholes and plunged valiantly through the dark. Broadcast-units signaled emergency and cut off the air to make the placid radio waves available to authority.

Not soon after, the outer parts of the city regained their former quiet festiveness as the tumultuous noises of the authorities soon left their scattered positions to congregate in one central location, save that there was less music. The broadcasts were off. But the sound of racing vehicles clamoring for right-of-way grew louder and louder, and more and more peremptory as it concentrated toward the large open square on which the Embassy faced. From every street and avenue fire-fighting equipment poured into that square. In between and behind, hooting loudly for precedence, police trolleys, with blaring sirens and billowing clouds of steam from overworked boilers, accompanied and fore-ran them. Emergency vehicles of all the civic bureaus appeared, all of them with a grandiose pompous conviction of their importance over the other.

That space that lay before the Embassy was large and well open. From its edge, the monument to the First Settlers of Nemo Vesta placed in its center looked small. But even that vast plaza filled up with steam trolleys of every imaginable variety, from the hose towers which could throw streams of water four hundred feet straight up, to the miniature trouble-wagons of Electricity Supply. Staff trolleys of fire and police and sanitary services crowded each other and bumped fenders with tree-surgeon carriages prepared to move fallen trees, and with public-address ground vessels ready to lend stentorian tones to any voice of authority who may choose to speak up without just cause.

But the irony was, there was no situation, well except for the fact that there was no situation. There was no fire. There was no riot. There was not even a stray dog for the pound wagons to pursue, nor broken water mains for the water department technicians to shut off and repair. There was nothing for anybody to do but ask everybody else what the heck they were doing there, and presently to yell at each other for cluttering up the way.

The din and clamor of arriving horns and sirens had stopped, and was eventually replaced by mutterings of irreverence and maledictions were developing, when a last vehicle arrived. It was an ambulant mobile and it came purposefully out of a side avenue and swung toward a particular place as if it knew exactly what it was about. When its way was blocked, it hooted impatiently for passage. Its red tinted gaslights swaying violently demanding clearance. A giant fire-fighting unit pulled aside. The ambulant mobile ran past and hooted at a cluster of police trolleys. They quickly made way for it, hoping that somehow, they would be able to shine light on this impromptu gathering of city forces. It blared at a gathering of dismounted, irritated city personnel, weaving side to side as it made its way through them. It moved in a straight line for the gate of the Embassy.

Approximately a hundred yards from the gate, its horn blatted irritably at the aether-ran flying carriage of the acting head of municipal air marshals who was on his way home when noticing the conglomeration of city forces and descended to investigate. That car obediently made way by taking loft again, making another landing attempt by the founding fathers' statue.

The ambulance rolled briskly up to the very gate of the Embassy. There it stopped. A figure got down from the driver's seat and walked purposefully in the gate.

Thereafter nothing happened at all until a second figure rolled and toppled itself out on the ground from the passenger side. That figure kicked and writhed on the ground. A policeman went to find out what was the matter.

It was the real ambulance driver. Not the one who'd driven the ambulance to the Embassy gate, but the one who should have been driving. He was bound hand and foot and not too tightly gagged. When released he, through horse panting, exclaimed that he had been captured and bound by someone who said he was Vash Rayburn and was in a hurry to get back to the Embassy and needed a ride.

There was no uproar. Those to whom Vash's name had meaning were struck speechless with rage. The fury of the police was even too deep for tears as many of them slightly rubbed their backsides in remembrance of a recent encounter which only fueled their fury.

But Vash Rayburn, now safely back in the quarters assigned him in the Embassy, unloaded a dozen cooled-off stun-pistols from his pockets and sent word to the ambassador that he was back, and that the note ostensibly from Jessica had actually been a police trap as the ambassador had suspected.

Getting ready to retire for the night, he reviewed his situation. In some respects, it was not too bad. All but Jessica's share in trying to trap him, and having a party the same night.... He stared morosely at the wall. Then he saw a clearer perspective that, very simply, she might not have known even of his arrest. She had lived a highly sheltered life after all. Her father could have had her kept completely in ignorance....

He cheered immediately at this revelation. This would be his last night on Nemo Vesta, if he were lucky, but vague plans already revolved in his mind. Yes.... He would achieve splendid things, he'd grow richer than Jessica’s father, he'd come back and marry that delightful girl, and end as a great man. Already, today, he'd done a number of things worth doing, and on the whole, he'd done them well.

Chapter 3

When dawn broke over the capital city of Nemo Vesta, the sight was appropriately glamorous, despite the torn-up courtyard in front of the Embassy. There were shining towers and curving tree-bordered ways, above which innumerable small birds flew tumultuously avoiding upper air disturbances caused by turbine draft. The dawn, in fact, was heralded by high-pitched chirpings everywhere. During the darkness of the earliest point of dawn, there had been only a deep-toned humming sound, a dull, yet audible sound all over the city. That was the landing grid in operation out at the sky port, letting down a twenty-thousand-ton liner from the Cetus Horn exchanging goods and supplies needed by the city. Shortly it would take off for Nemo Krim, Port Barogate, and then Toffpoint, and if Vash were lucky he would be on it. But at the earliest part of the day there was only tranquility over the city and the square, giving the Embassy the feel of an unvisited mausoleum with no direct means to get to the vessel as of yet.

At the gate of the Embassy enclosure, staff members piled up boxes and bales and parcels for transport to the sky port and thence to destinations whose names were practically songs. There were dispatches to Delil bay, where the Inter-colonial Diplomatic Service had a sector headquarters, and there were packets of Embassy-stamped invoices for Lohala Colony, the floating city of Tralee and sky city of Nemo Famagusta. There were boxes for New England Proper and the Isle of Maja Minor, and metal-bound cases for Kent proper, which is the remaining landmass which was formally known as South America. The early explorers of this part of the world reclaimed from the waters had set up small villages and territories that were, as yet, still not fully self-sustainable—which less than one human being in ten thousand had seen since the waters receded oh so long ago.

The sound of the stacking of freight parcels was crisp and distinct in the morning hush. The dew deposited during darkness had not yet dried from the pavement of the square or the deep gouged tracks made from the commotion the night before. Damp, unhappy figures loafed nearby. They were obviously secret police, as yet unrelieved after a night's vigil about the Embassy's rugged wall. They were sleepy and their clothing stuck wet to them, and not one of them had had anything warm in his stomach for many hours. They also had not expected as much from their superiors.

Vash was again in sanctuary inside the Embassy they'd guarded so ineptly through the dark. He had made it out without their leave, and made a number of their fellows unwilling to sit down for a while and then made all of the municipal authorities of the city look ridiculous by the manner of his return. The police guards about the Embassy were very positively not in a cheery mood. But one of them saw an Embassy servant he knew. He had stood the man drinks, in times past, in order to establish a contact that might be useful at some point. He summoned a smile and beckoned to that man.

The Embassy servant came briskly to him, rubbing his hands after having put a moderately heavy case of documents on top of the waiting pile.

"That Rayburn character," said the plainclothesman, attempting hearty ruefulness, *"he certainly put it over on us last night!"*

The servant nodded hesitantly.

"Look," said the plainclothesman, *"there could be something in it for you if you ... hm-m-m ... wanted to make a little extra money."*

The servant looked down and then up slightly, as if pondering the idea.

"No chance," he said, *"He's leaving today."*

The plainclothesman jumped.

"Today?"

"*For Toffpoint*," said the Embassy servant. *"The ambassador is shipping him off on the liner that is currently docked at the grid."*

The plainclothesman dithered as he became more inquisitive to the servant's free information.

"So, how's he going to get to the liner?"

"I wouldn't know exactly," said the servant. *"They've figured out some way. I could use a little extra money... if you wish me to find that out for you."*

He lingered for a moment thinking if he should pay the servant or not, but the plainclothesman was staring at the innocent parcels about to leave the Embassy for distant parts. He took visual note of sizes and descriptions. "*No. Not yet.*" But if Vash were leaving he had to leave the Embassy. *"If he left the Embassy...."* he thought.

The plainclothesman bolted. He made a breathless report by the portable communicator that had been set up for just such use. He told what the Embassy servant had said, and the inference to be drawn from it, the suspicions to be entertained—and there he stopped short. Orders came back to him. Orders were given in all directions. Somebody was going to distinguish himself by catching Vash Rayburn, and undercover politics worked to decide who it should be. Even the job of guard outside the Embassy became desirable. So fresh, alert plainclothesmen arrived. They were bright-eyed and bushy-tailed, and they took over. Weary, hungry men yielded up their posts. They went home. The man who'd gotten the infallibly certain clue went home too, disgruntled because he wasn't allowed a share in the credit for Vash's capture. But he would find himself glad of it later.

Inside the Embassy, Vash finished his breakfast with the ambassador.

"I'm giving you," said the ambassador, *"that letter to the character on Toffpoint. I told you about him. He's some sort of nobleman and has need of an electronic engineer. On Toffpoint they're rare to nonexistent. But his letter wasn't too specific."*

"I remember," agreed Vash. *"I'll look him up. Thank you for everything, sir."*

"Somehow," said the ambassador, *"I cherish unreasonable hopes of you, Mr. Rayburn. A psychologist would say, if he were to read you, that your group identification is low and your cyclothymia practically a minus quantity, while your ergic tension is pleasingly high. What he would mean by all of that is with reasonably good fortune you would create more havoc than most. I wish you would and that good fortune follow. And Vash..."*

"Yes?" feeling a sense of honor that the ambassador referred to him by his first name.

"I don't urge you to be vengeful," explained the ambassador, *"but I do hope you won't be too forgiving either. Not of these characters who tried to have you jailed for life because you attempted to make their lives better. You've scared them badly. It's very good for them. Anything more that you can do along those lines will be really a kindness, and as such will positively not be appreciated, but it'll be well worth doing.... I say this because I like the way you plan things. And any time I can be of service—"*

"Thanks," said Vash, *"but I'd better get going for the liner."* He'd already planned to write Jessica from Toffpoint. *"I'll get set for it."*

He rose. The ambassador followed suit.

"I like the way you plan things," he repeated appreciatively. *"We'll check over that box together."*

They left the Embassy dining room together.

It was well after sunrise when Vash finished his breakfast, and the bright and watchful new plainclothesmen were very much on the alert outside. By this time the sun had lost its early ruddy-red tint, and the trees about the city were vividly green, and the sky had become appropriately blue—as the skies always are on high altitude sky cities. There was the beginning of traffic on the streets. Some were routine movements of goods and vehicles. But some were special.

For example, the dual stack steam trolley, which came to carry the Embassy shipment to the sky port. They were perfectly ordinary trolleys, hired in a perfectly ordinary way by the ambassador's assistant. They came trundling across the square and into the Embassy gate as they did once every two months. The ostentatiously loafing plainclothesmen could look in and see the waiting parcels loaded on them. The first load was quite unsuspicious. There was no package in the lot, which could have held a man in even the most impossibly cramped of positions.

But the police took no chances. Ten blocks from the Embassy the authorities stopped it and verified the licenses and identities of the driver and his helper. This was a moderately lengthy business. While it went on, plainclothesmen worked over the packages in the truck's body and put stethoscopes to any of more than one cubic foot capacity.

They waved the trolley on. Meanwhile the second trolley was back at the Embassy being loaded. And the watching, ostensible loafers saw that the second to the last item to be put aboard was a large box which hadn't been visible before. It was carried with some care, and it was marked fragile, and it was put into place and wedged fast with other parcels.

The plainclothesmen looked at each other with anticipatory glee. One of them reported the last large box with almost lyric enthusiasm. When the second trolley steamed off and left the Embassy with the last of the parcels and the curious large box, a police trolley came innocently out of nowhere and just happened to be going the same way. Ten blocks away, again the trolley load of Embassy parcels was flagged down and its driver's license and identity were verified. A plainclothesman put a stethoscope on the questionable case. He beamed as he made a suitable signal to the other officers.

The trolley went on its way while zealous, almost Machiavellian, plans were afoot.

Five blocks from the port, an unmarked steam trolley came hurtling down a side street where it sideswiped the trolley loaded with the parcels from the Embassy, and went careening away down the street without stopping. The trailing police trolley made no attempt at pursuit but, instead, stopped 'helpfully' by the damaged trolley which had been hit. A wheel was hopelessly mangled beyond service. So uniformed police, with conspicuously happy expressions, cleared a space around the stalled vehicle and stood guard over the parcels under diplomatic seal. With eager helpfulness, they sent for other transportation to take the Embassy's shipment to its destination on the liner.

A sneeze was heard from within the mass of guarded freight, and the policemen shook hands with each other. When substitute steam trolleys came—there were two of them—they loaded one high with Embassy parcels and sent it off to the port with their blessing. There remained just one, single, large-sized box to be put on the second vehicle. They bumped it on the ground, and a startled grunt came from within.

There was an atmosphere of innocent enjoyment all about as the police tenderly loaded this large box on the second truck they'd sent for, and festooned themselves about it as it trundled away. Strangely, it did not head directly for the sky port. The police carefully explained this to each other in loud voices. Then some of them were afraid the box hadn't heard, so they knocked on it. The box coughed, and it seemed hilariously amusing to the policemen that the contents of a freight parcel should cough. They expressed deep concern and—addressing the box—explained that they were taking it to the Detention Building, where they would give it some cough medicine.

The box then spoke ill demands at them, despairingly. They howled with childish laughter, and assured the box that after they had opened it and given it cough medicine, they would close it again very carefully—leaving the diplomatic seal unbroken—and deliver it to the sky port so it could go on its way.

The box spoke again, luridly. The trolley, which carried it now hastened as fast as it could without causing harm to its passengers. The box teetered and bumped and jounced with the swift motion of the vehicle. Bitter, enraged, and highly ungentlemanly language came from within.

The police were charmed. Even so early in the morning they seemed inclined to burst into song. When the Detention Building gate opened for it, and closed again behind it, there was a welcoming committee in the courtyard. It included a jailer with a bandaged head and a look of vengeful satisfaction on his face, and no less than three guards who had been given baths by a high-pressure hose upon Vash Rayburn's untimely departure from his cell. They wore unnamable expressions.

And then, while the box yelled very bitterly, somebody tenderly loosened a plank—being careful not to disturb the diplomatic seal—and pulled it away with a triumphant gesture. Then all the police could look into the box.

And they did.

Then there was dead silence, except for the voice that came from a two-way communicator strategically mounted in one corner of the box.

"And now," said the voice from the box—and only now did anybody notice what the muffling effect of the boards had hidden,

that it was a speaker-unit which had spoken and coughed and sneezed—*"we take our leave of the infernal sky city of Nemo Vesta and its happy police force, who wave to us as our liner lifts toward the skies. The next sound you hear will be that of their lamentations at our departure."*

But the next sound was not that of lamentation, but rather a howl of fury. The police were very much disappointed to learn that Vash hadn't been in the box, but instead only one-half of a two-way communication pair, and that Vash had coughed and sneezed and yelled at them from the other instrument somewhere else as he had now officially signed off.

The sky liner was not lifting off just yet. It was still solidly aground in the center of the landing grid. Vash had bid farewell to his audience from the floor of the ambassador's aether fueled ground-car, which at that moment was safely within the extra-territorial circle about the entry port next to the north-loading end of the vessel. He turned off the set, calmly got up and brushed himself off then got out of the car. The ambassador followed him and shook his hand.

"You have quite a touch," said the ambassador sedately. *" At times, you seem very inspired, Vash! You have a natural gift for infuriating constituted authority. You should plot as your business. You would go far!"*

He shook hands again and watched as Vash calmly shuffled up the ramp leading into the lift, which should and did raise him to the level of the loading dock entrance port of the liner.

Twenty minutes later the hydraulic arms of the giant landing grid lifted the liner smoothly upwards into the upper stratosphere and released. The twenty-thousand-ton vessel continued up for another fifty yards before engaging the turbines to its forward thrust propellers. There the ship jockeyed for line, and then there was that curious, momentary disturbance of all of one's muscles having sensations of being pulled, which was the effect of the turbines building up forward momentum. Then everything was normal again.

Time passed. The only sounds were that of the turbines coming on and off and the bladders losing helium in order to keep at a steady altitude. The liner, bearing Vash, now sped through the open sky with the cares of Nemo Vesta dissipating with every mile as Vash drifted to sleep in the cargo hold.

In time, Vash woke as the goliath dirigible made landfall on the eastern shores of Port Barogate. He went aground and observed the floating city. He found it odd that he had a fear of floating cities that they might, someday, sink into the depths of the ocean, yet at the same time, had no such compunctions toward sky cities that, if they lost power, would fall to the very same oceans from a much greater height only to sink to the depths of the ocean in the exact same manner. This port was new and bustling with tall buildings and traffic jams and a feverish conviction that the purpose of living was to earn more money this year than last. Its landing ports were chaotic and busy. Vash had time for swift sightseeing of one street market only and an estimate of what items of such a place would tickle his fancy. He saw slums and gracious public buildings, and went back to the landing port and rose up on the landing grid to re-board to his makeshift quarters Then there was again a jockeying for line, and the liner winked out of sight and was again journeying toward its next destination, Vash's new home.

Presently the liner that seemed so massive as it left Nemo Vesta appeared in optical finders of Toffpoint as the tiniest of shimmering pearly specks against the blue. To the north and east and west of the port, rugged mountains rose steeply. Patches of snow showed here and there, and naked rock reared boldly in spurs and precipices. But there were trees on all the lower slopes, yet there was not really a timberline to be seen.

The sky liner increased in size, descending toward the landing grid. The grid itself was a monstrous lattice of archaic steel, half a mile high and enclosing a circle not less in diameter. It filled most of the level valley floor, and horned out into the water.

The ship that previously seemed the size of a pea was presently the size of an apple. Then it was the size of a basketball, and then it swelled enormously and put out spidery metal legs with large splay metal feet on them and alighted and settled gently to the ground. The humming stopped. *"For the size and weight,"* Vash thought *"this vessel lands on its own quite well."*

As the loading bay began to open, there were shoutings. Whips cracked. Straining, horn-tossing bison heaved and dragged something, very deliberately, out from between warehouses under the arches of the grid. There were two-dozen of the bison, and despite the shouts and whip-cracking they moved with a stubborn slowness. It took a long time for the object with the wide-tired wheels to reach a spot below the liner. Then it took even longer for brakes to be set on each wheel, and then for the draught animals to be arranged to pull as two teams against each other. The entire sight was a spectacle of amazement and curiosity to Vash.

More shoutings and whip-cracking took place. A long, slanting, ladder-like arm arose. It teetered, and a man with a lurid purple cloak rose with it at its very end. The ship's air lock opened and a crewman threw a rope. The purple-cloaked man caught it and made it fast. From somewhere inside the vessel the line was hauled in. The end of the landing ramp touched the sill of the air lock. Somebody made other things fast and the purple-cloaked man triumphantly entered the liner.

There was a pause. Men loaded carts with cargo to be sent to remote and unimagined regions of the planet. In the air lock, Vash stepped to the unloading ramp and descended to the ground. He was the only passenger. He had barely reached a firm footing when objects and parcels being unloaded began following him down. His own ship bag—a gift from the ambassador—and then parcels, bales, boxes, and such nondescript items of freight as needed special designation, all came off as if in a parade for everyone to view. There were rolls of wire, long strings of brass objects all strung like beads on shipping cords as they made their way off of the liner. Plex skins of fluid, which might be anything from wine to fuel in less than bulk-cargo quantities, were handed off one at a time. For a mere fifteen minutes the flow of freight continued and then the liner was almost ready, once again, to depart; that is once it took on the shipments that it did need to take. Toffpoint was not an important center of trade, so there was no real need for the liner to stick around once its business had been met.

Vash stared incredulously at the town that lay to the east of the grid. It was barely a town at all and could almost be considered a village, at that. Its houses had steep, gabled roofs, of which some seemed to be tile and others thatch. Its buildings leaned over the narrow streets, which were unpaved. They looked like mud. And there was not a power-driven ground vehicle anywhere in sight, nor anything man made in the air for that matter.

The loading process ended. The man with the purple cloak, who had ridden the teetering belt-beam up, reappeared and came striding grandly down to ground. *"Somebody cast off, above,"* yelled the man in purple. Ropes writhed, fell and dangled; the ship's air lock door then closed.

There was a vast humming sound of turbines once again. The ship lifted sedately. It seemed to hover momentarily over the group of horses, bison and humans in the center of the grid's enclosure. But it was not hovering. It shrank as it was rising in an absolutely vertical line while its protruding legs folded back in as a dragon fly taking off from a reed. It dwindled to the size of a basketball and then an apple and then to the size of a pea. And then that pea diminished until the vessel had become the size of a dust mite in the wind and then could not be seen at all. It was at this point Vash realized that he was at his new home and there was no turning back now.

Vash shrugged and began to trudge toward the warehouses. The bison-drawn landing ramp began to roll slowly in the same direction. Carts and wagons loaded the items discharged from the ship. Creaking, plodding, with the curved horns of the bison rising and falling, the wagons overtook Vash and passed him. He saw his ship bag on one of the carts. It was a gift from the ambassador on Nemo Vesta. He'd assured Vash that there was a fund for the assistance of political refugees, and that the bag and its contents was normal. But in addition to the gift clothing, Vash had a number of stun-pistols, gifts that were formerly equipment of the police department of Nemo Vesta.

He followed his bag to a warehouse. Upon arrival there, he found the bag surrounded by a group of whiskered Toffpointian characters wearing felt pants and large sheath knives. They had opened the bag and were in the act of ferocious dispute about who should get what of its contents. Incidentally they argued over the stun-pistols, which looked like weapons but weren't because nothing happened when one pulled the trigger. Vash grimaced. They'd been in store on the liner during the voyage. Normally they picked up a trickle charge from kinetic broadcast power emitted from the turbines, on Nemo Vesta, but there was no kinetic broadcast power on the liner, and definitely not any on Toffpoint. They'd leaked their charges and were quite useless. *"The one in my pocket is about useless, too."* He thought as he grazed over the barrel with his palm.

Vash grimaced once again and swerved to the building where the landing grid controls must be. He opened the door and went in. The interior was smoky and ill smelling, but the equipment was wholly familiar. Two unshaven men—in violently colored shirts—languidly played cards. Only one, a redhead, paid attention to the controls of the landing grid; he watched dials. He turned and saw Vash.

"Who are you and what do you want?" he demanded sharply.

"A few kilowatts," said Vash. The redhead's manner was not amiable, truly a man with no admiration for wit.

"Get outta here!" he barked hoarsely.

The transformers and snaky cables leading to relays outside—all were clear as print on a paper to Vash. He moved confidently toward an especially understandable panel, pulling out his stun-pistol and briskly breaking back the butt for charging. He shoved the pistol butt to contact with two terminals devised for another purpose, and the pistol slipped for an instant and a blue spark flared giving the appearance of an oddly shaped Tesla Coil in action.

"Hey, quit that!" roared the redheaded man. The rest of the men pushed back from their card game. One of them stood up, smiling unpleasantly.

The stun-pistol clicked, the indication that the charge cells were at full capacity once again. Vash withdrew it from making the charge contact, flipped the butt shut, and turned toward the three men. Two of them bolted toward him suddenly—the redhead and the unpleasant smiler.

The stun-pistol hummed. The redhead howled. He'd been hit in the hand. His unshaven companion buckled in the middle and fell to the floor. The third man backed away in panic, automatically raising his arms in surrender.

Vash saw no need for further action. He nodded graciously with a tip of his hat and went out of the control building, twirling the recharged stun pistol on his index finger as if he had just won an old west style shoot out. In the warehouse, argument still raged over his possessions. He went in, briskly. Nobody looked at him. The casual appropriation of unguarded property was apparently a social norm, here. The man in the purple cloak was insisting furiously that he was a Toffpointian gentleman and he'd have his share or else—

"Those things," said Vash, *"are mine and I would much appreciate it if you would kindly put them back in the bag."*

The whiskered Faces turned to him, expressing shocked surprise. A man in dirty yellow pants stood up with a suit of Vash's underwear and a pair of shoes. He moved with great dignity to depart.

The stun-pistol buzzed once again. The old-timer leaped and howled then fled as he dropped Vash's possessions. Vash had aimed accurately enough, but prudence suggested that if he appeared to kill anybody, the matter might become serious. So, he'd fired to sting the man with a stun-pistol bolt at about the same spot where, on Nemo Vesta, he'd scorched members of a certain party of police who had laid in ambush for him. It was nice shooting. But this happened to be a time and place where prudence did not pay.

There was a concerted gasp of outrage. Men leaped to their feet. Large knives came out of elaborate holsters. Men wearing configurations in every style and color of the rainbow—all badly soiled—roared with indignation as they charged at Vash. They waved knives as they came.

He held down the stun-pistol trigger and traversed the rushing men. The whining buzz of the weapon was inaudible, at first, but before he released the trigger it was plainly to be heard. Then there was silence. His attackers formed a very untidy heap on the floor. They breathed torturously and labored on the floor. Vash began to retrieve his possessions. He had to roll over a few men for the purpose of gaining all of them.

A pair of very blue, apprehensive eyes stared at him. The man in purple had stumbled over one man and gazed at Vash utterly speechless at the ease in which he vanquished the would-be looters.

"Hand me that, please," said Vash. He pointed toward a pair of trousers at the feet of the man in purple.

The man obeyed, shaking. Vash completed the recovery of all his belongings. He turned. The man in the purple cloak winced and closed his eyes with a feeling of fear and dread.

"Hm-m-m," said Vash. He needed information. He wasn't likely to get it from the men in the grid's control room. He would hardly be popular with any of them, either, but he did need directions. He said: *"I have a letter of introduction to one Emory Demetrius Fairbeard, prince of something-or-other, lord of this, baron of that, and claimant to the dukedom of the other thing. Would you have any idea how I could reach him?"*

The man in the purple cloak gaped at Vash.

"He is ... my chieftain, sir," he said, aghast. *"I ... am Bazil, Bazil Trigg, his most trusted retainer."* Then he practically wailed, *"You must be the man I was sent to meet! He sent me to learn if you came on the ship! I should have fought by your side! This is disgrace!"*

"It is disgraceful," agreed Vash grimly. But he, who had been born and raised in a sky pirate community, should not be too critical of others. *"But being the gentleman that I am, I shall let it go. How do I find him?"*

"I should take you!" complained Bazil bitterly. *"But you have killed all these men. Their friends and chieftains are honor bound to cut your throat! And you shot Merrik, but he ran away, and he will be summoning his friends to come and kill you now! This is shame! This is—"* Then he said hopefully: *"Your strange weapon! How many men can you fight? If fifty, we may live to ride away and if more, we may even reach Emory Fairbeard's castle. How many?"*

"We'll see what we see," said Vash dourly. *"But I'd better charge these other pistols. You can come with me, or wait. I haven't killed these men. They're only stunned. They should come around presently."*

He went out of the warehouse, carrying the bag, which was again loaded with uncharged stun-pistols. He went back to the grid's control room. He pushed it open and entered for the second time. The redheaded man was still slightly dazed as he rubbed at his hand. The man who'd smiled unpleasantly still lay in a heap on the floor. The second unshaven man jittered visibly at first sight of Vash as he re-entered.

"I'm back," said Vash politely, *"for more kilowatts."*

He put his bag conveniently close to the terminals at which his pistols could be recharged. He snapped open a pistol butt and presented it to the electric contacts.

"Quaint customs you have here," he said conversationally. *"Robbing a newcomer, resenting his need for a few watts of power that comes free to you because of the water wheels that naturally crank the turbines with no deliberate actions on your part..."* The stun-pistol clicked. He snapped the butt shut and opened another, which he placed in contact for charging. *"Making him act,"* he said acidly, *"with manners as bad as one of the locals, going at him with knives so he has to be violent in turn."* The second stun-pistol clicked. He closed it and began to charge a third. He said severely: *"Innocent tourists—relatively innocent ones, anyhow—are not likely to be favorably impressed with Toffpoint!"* He had the charging process going swiftly now. He began to charge a fourth weapon. *"It's particularly bad manners if you ask me,"* he added sternly, *"to stand there grinding your teeth at me while your friend behind the desk crawls after an old-fashioned chemical gun to shoot me with."*

He snapped the fourth pistol shut and went after the man who'd dropped down behind a desk. He came upon that man, hopelessly panicked, just as his hands closed on a clumsy gun that was supposed to set off a chemical explosive to propel a metal bullet.

"Don't!" said Vash calm yet severely toned. *"Just don't. If I have to shoot you at this range, it'll leave blisters and scorched hair. You won't like it and, frankly, I don't like the smell."*

He took the weapon out of the man's hand. He went back and finished charging the rest of the pistols.

He returned most of them to his bag, though he stuck others in his belt and pockets to the point where he looked like the fiction-tape pictures that portrayed characters of pirates, which he found funny as he glanced at his reflection in the glass; not the real sky pirates, as Vash was one, but the almost comical versions that he had never once actually seen represented in life. He moved to the door. As a last thought, he picked up the bullet-firing weapon.

"There's only one service ship here a month," he observed politely, *"so I'll be around. If you want to get in touch with me, ask Emory Demetrius Fairbeard. I'm going to visit him while I look over professional opportunities on Toffpoint."*

He went out once more. Somehow, he felt more cheerful than a half-hour hence, when he'd landed as the only passenger from the sky liner. Then he had felt ignored and lonely and friendless on a strange and primitive colony. He still had no friends, but he had already acquired some enemies and therefore material for more or less worthwhile achievement. As he walked away from the panel, he surveyed the sunlit scene about him from the control-room door.

Bazil, the man in purple, had brought two shaggy-haired animals around to the door of the warehouse. Vash had sea legs, land legs and sky legs, but wasn't entirely sure of his footing on a horse. Bazil was frenziedly in the act of mounting one of them. As he climbed up, small bright metal disks cascaded from a pocket. He tried to stop the flow of money as he got feverishly into the saddle.

From the gable-roofed small town a mob of some thirty mounted men plunged toward the landing grid. They wore garments of yellow and blue and magenta. They waved long-bladed bayonet style knives and made bloodthirsty noises. Bazil saw them and bolted, riding one horse and towing the other by a lead rope. It happened that his line of retreat passed right by where Vash stood.

Vash held up his hand. Bazil then reined in.

"Mount!" he cried hoarsely. *"Mount and ride!"*

Vash passed up the chemical—powder—gun. Bazil seized it frantically.

"Hurry!" he panted. *"Emory Fairbeard would have my throat cut if I deserted you! Mount and ride!"*

Vash painstakingly fastened his bag to the saddle of the lead horse. He unfastened the lead rope. Not being too familiar with the steering of these animals, he'd noticed that Bazil pulled in the leather reins to stop the horse. He'd seen that he kicked it furiously to urge it on. He deduced that one steered the animal by pulling on one strap or the other. He climbed clumsily to a seat ready to take a riding position and learn as he went.

There was a howl from the racing, mounted men. They waved their knives and yelled in zestful anticipation of murder.

Vash pulled on a rein. His horse turned obediently. He kicked it. The animal broke into a run toward the rushing mob. The jolting motion amazed Vash. One could not shoot straight while being shaken up like this! He dragged back on the reins. The horse stopped.

"Come on!" yelled Bazil despairingly. *"This way! Quick!"*

Vash got out a stun-pistol. Sitting erect, frowning a little in his concentration, he began to take pot-shots at the charging horde.

Three of them got close enough to be blistered when stun-pistol bolts hit them. Others toppled from their saddles at distances ranging from twenty yards up to seventy-five yards. A good dozen, however, saw what was happening in time to swerve their mounts and hightail it away. But there were eighteen luridly-tinted heaps of garments on the ground inside the landing grid. Two or three of them squirmed and moaned in agony. Vash had partly missed on them. He heard the chemical weapon booming thunderously. Now that victory was won, Bazil was shooting valorously. Vash held up his hand for a cease fire. Bazil rode up beside him, not quite believing what he'd seen.

"Wonderful!" he said shakily. *"Wonderful! Emory Fairbeard will be pleased! He will give me gifts for my help to you! This is a great fight! We will be great men, after this!"*

"Then let's go and brag," said Vash with a smirk.

Bazil was shocked.

"You need me," he said commiserating over his own actions. *"It is fortunate that Emory Fairbeard chose me to fight beside you!"*

He sent his horse trotting toward the mostly unconscious men on the ground. He alighted from his saddle. Vash saw him happily and publicly pick the pockets of the stun-gun's victims. He came back, beaming and now swaggering in his saddle.

"We will be famous!" he said zestfully. *"Two against thirty, and some ran away!"* He gloated. *"And it was a good haul! We share, of course, because we are companions."*

"Is it the custom of Toffpoint," asked Vash mildly, *"to loot defenseless men?"*

"But of course!" said Bazil. *"How else can a gentleman live, if he has no chieftain to give him presents? You defeated them, so of course you take their possessions!"*

"Ah, I see," said Vash. *"To be sure!"*

He rode on. The road was a mere horse track. Presently it was less than that. He saw a frowning, battlemented stronghold away off to the left. Bazil openly hoped that somebody would come from that castle and try to charge them toll for riding over their lord's land. After Vash had knocked them over with the stun-pistol, Bazil would add to the heavy weight of coins already in his possession.

It did not look promising, in any way. But just before sunset, Vash saw three tiny bright lights flash across the sky from west to east. They moved in formation and at identical speeds. Vash knew a sky marshal scout troop when he saw them. He bristled, and muttered under his breath.

"What's that?" asked Bazil. *"What did you say?"*

"I said," Vash repeated dourly, *"that I've got to do something about Nemo Vesta. When they get an idea in their heads...."*

Chapter 4

According to the vision tapes, the colonized civilizations of the world vary wildly from each other. In cold and unromantic fact, it isn't so. Travel is too cheap and colonies too numerous to count, having popped up in the last century and a half since the flooding, that settlement and re-settlement is easy. There's no point in trying to live where one has to put on with policies or frivolities that one does not wish to engage in. There's no reason to settle on a colony, terrestrial or man-made, where one can't live with the familiarities of one's ancestors or re-invent themselves to opposite ends of how he was raised. It simply doesn't make sense!

Vash Rayburn encountered no remarkable features in the landscape of Toffpoint as he rode through the deepening night. There was grass, which was not luxuriant. There were bushes, which were not unduly lush. There were trees, and birds, and various other commonplace living things whose forbearers had been dumped on Toffpoint in its early settlement some century or so before. The ecological system had worked itself out strictly by hit-or-miss, but the result was not unfamiliar. Save for the star-pattern overhead, Vash could have believed himself on some parts of Gibbit Cove, or some parts of Nemo Vesta, or very probably anywhere, because, no matter the distance, there will always be familiarity, he thought.

There was, though, the star-pattern. Vash tried to organize it in his mind. He knew where the sun had set, which would be west. He asked the latitude of the Toffpointian sky port. Bazil did not know it. He asked about major geographical features—which direction was the seas and continents and so on. Bazil had no ideas on the subject.

Vash fumed. He hadn't worried about such things on Nemo Vesta. Of course, there he'd had one friend, Derk, and believed, as well, that he had a sweetheart, Jessica. There he was lonely and schemed to acquire the admiration of others. He ignored the sky. Here on Toffpoint he had no friends, but there were a number of local citizens now doubtless recovered from stun-pistol bolts and yearning to carve him up with large knives. He did not feel lonely, but the instinct to know where he was, was again in operation.

The ground was rocky and far from level. After two hours of riding on a small and wiry horse with no built-in springs, Vash hurt in a great many places he'd never known he owned. He and Bazil rode in an indeterminate direction with an irregular scarp of low mountains silhouetted against the unfamiliar stars. A vagrant night wind blew. Bazil had said it was a three-hour ride to Emory Fairbeard's castle. After something over two of those hours had past, Bazil said meditatively:

"I think that if you wish to give me a present, I will take it and not make a gift in return. You could give me," he added helpfully, *"your share of the plunder from our victims."*

"Why would I do that?" demanded Vash. *"Why should I give you a present?"*

"Because if I were to accept it," explained Bazil, *"and made no gift of equal or higher worth in return, I would become your retainer. Then it would be my obligation as a Toffpointian gentleman to ride beside you, be your counsel, fight in your defense, and generally uphold your dignity and honor."*

Vash currently suspected himself of having blisters in places that had no dignity about them at all. He said suspiciously:

"And what of Emory Fairbeard? Are you not his retainer?"

"Between the two of us," said Bazil, *"he's stingy. His presents are not as lavish as they could be. I can make him a return-present of part of the money we won in combat. That frees me of duty to him. Then I could accept the balance of the money from you, and become a retainer of yours."*

"Oh," said Vash.

"I feel that you need a retainer much more than the good Emory Fairbeard," said Bazil. *"You do not know the customs here. For example, there is enmity between his lordship, Emory Fairbeard and the young Lord Seymour. If the young Lord Seymour is as enterprising as he should be, some of his retainers should be lying in wait to cut our throats as we approach Emory Fairbeard's stronghold."*

"Hm-m-m," said Vash rather grimly at this new enlightenment. But Bazil seemed undisturbed. *"This system of gifts and presents sounds complicated. Why doesn't the good Emory Fairbeard simply give you so much a year, or week, or whatnot?"*

Bazil gasped aloud in shock at the mere proposal of the idea.

"That would be pay! A Toffpointian gentleman does not serve for pay! To offer it would be insult!" Then he said, *"Listen to me!"*

He reined in his horse to a slow trot. Vash quickly, yet rather clumsily followed his example. After a moment or two of scouting the terrain ahead, Bazil clucked to his horse and started off in a gallop once again.

"It was nothing," he said almost regretfully. *"I had rather hoped we were riding into an ambush."*

Vash grunted. It could be that he was being told a tall tale. But back at the sky port, the men who came after him waving large knives had seemed sincere enough.

"Why should we be ambushed?" he asked. *"And why in the world would you hope for it?"*

"Because your wonderfully amazing weapons would destroy our enemies," said Bazil placidly, *"and the pickings would be good."* He added: *"It would seem likely that we should be ambushed due to the fact that the good Lady Adeline refused to marry Lord Seymour. She is Emory Demetrius Fairbeard's youngest daughter, and to refuse to marry a man is naturally a deadly insult. So, he should ravage the Fairbeard's lands at every opportunity until he gets a chance to carry off the Lady Adeline and marry her by force. That is the only way the insult can be wiped out."*

"I see," said Vash ironically.

The two horses topped a rise at the edge or a precipice, and far in the distance there was a yellow light, with a mist above it as of illuminated smoke.

"That is Lord Emory Demetrius Fairbeard's stronghold," said Bazil. He sighed. *"It looks as if we may not be ambushed after all."*

They weren't. It was very dark where the horses forged ahead through brushwood. As they moved onward, the single light became two. They were great bonfires burning in iron cages some forty feet up in the air. Those cages projected from the battlements of a massive, cut-stone wall. There was no light anywhere else underneath the stars.

Bazil rode almost underneath the cressets and shouted upward. A voice answered. Presently a gate clanked open and a black, cave like opening appeared behind it. Bazil rode grandly in, and Vash followed. Now that the ride seemed over, he let his mind begin to wander to where he ached from the unaccustomed exercise. Everywhere. He also guessed at the area of his skin first rubbed to blisters and then to the discomfort of raw flesh underneath.

The gate clanked shut behind them as torches waved overhead. Vash found that he and Bazil had ridden into a very tiny courtyard. Twenty feet above them, an inner battlemented wall which offered excellent opportunities for the inhabitants of the castle to throw things down at visitors who after admission turned out to be undesired; arrow slits and meurtrière style murder holes.

Bazil shouted further identifications, including a boastful and entirely untruthful declaration that he and Vash, together, had slaughtered twenty men in one place and thirty in another, and left them lying in their own visceral gore.

The voices that replied sounded derisive. Somebody came down a rope and fastened the gate from the inside. With an extreme amount of creaking, an inner gate swung wide. Men came out of it to take the horses. Vash dismounted, and it seemed to him that he creaked as loudly as the gate. Bazil swaggered, displaying coins he had picked from the pockets of the men the stun-pistols had disabled. He said splendidly to Vash:

"I shall go now to announce your coming to his majesty, Emory Demetrius Fairbeard. These are his retainers. They will see to it that you have eat and drink." He added amiably, *"If you were given food, it would be disgraceful for my lord to cut your throat."*

He disappeared. Vash carried his ship bag and followed a man in a dirty pink shirt to a stone-walled room containing a table and a chair. He sat down, relieved to have a rest for his back. The man in the pink shirt brought him a pint of local vintage. He disappeared again.

Vash drank the sour wine and brooded. He was very hungry and very tired, and it seemed to him that he had been disillusioned in a new dimension. Morbidly, he remembered a frequently given lecture from his grandfather on Gibbit Cove.

"It's no use!" it was the custom of his grandfather to say. *"There's not a bit o' use in having brains! All they do is get you into trouble! A lucky idiot' is ten times better off than a brainy man with a jinx on him! A smart man starts thinkin', and he thinks himself into a jail cell if his luck is bad, and good luck is wasted on him because it ain't reasonable and he don't believe in it when it happens! It's taken me a lifetime to keep my brains from ruinin' me! No, sir! I hope none o' my descendants inherit my brains! I pity 'em if they do!"*

Vash had been on Toffpoint not more than four hours. In that time, he'd found himself robbed, had resented it, had been the object of two spirited attempts at assassination, had ridden an excruciating number of miles on an unfamiliar animal, and now found himself in a stone dungeon and deprived of food lest feeding him obligate his host not to cut his throat. And he'd gotten into this all by himself! He'd chosen it! He'd practically asked for it!

He began strongly to share his grandfather's disillusioned view of brains.

After a long time, the door of the cell opened. Bazil was back, chastened.

"The good lord, Emory Fairbeard wants to talk to you," he said in a subdued voice. *"He's not pleased."*

Vash then quickly gulped down the remainder of the sour ale, then picked up his ship bag and limped to the door. He decided painfully that he was limping on the wrong leg. He tried the other. No improvement. He really needed to limp on both. Vash thought to himself *"Should he decide to slit my throat, it would be much improvement on how I am feeling at this moment."*

He followed Bazil through a long stone corridor and up well-worn cobble stone steps until they came to a monstrous hall lit only by torches in large, gothic style holders on the side walls. It was barbarically hung with banners, and not exactly a cheery place for one visiting for the first time. At the far end of the hall, logs burned in a grand fireplace large enough to consume the body of a large man if the notion were to arise.

His lordship, Emory Fairbeard sat in a huge, what seemed to be mahogany, intricately carved throne beside the fire; wizened and white-bearded beyond his years, in a fur-trimmed black velvet robe, with a slight peevish, almost annoyed expression on his well weathered face.

"My chieftain," said Bazil somewhat subtly, *"here is the engineer that you had asked for from Nemo Vesta"*

Vash scowled back at Fairbeard, as if to mimic his peevishness. He did regard Vash with a flicker of interest, however. A stranger who, unfeigned in demeanor, would scowl at a feudal lord with no superior and many inferiors is a rare novelty in these parts.

"Bazil tells me", said Fairbeard fretfully, *"that you and he, together, slaughtered some dozens of the retainers of my neighbors today. I consider it unfortunate. They may ask me to have the two of you hanged, and it would be impolite for me to refuse."*

Vash retorted scathingly:

"Well, I should consider it impolite for your neighbors' retainers to march toward me at high rates of speed waving large knives and announcing what they intended to do to my innards with those knives!"

"Yes," agreed Fairbeard impatiently. *"I concede that point. It is natural enough to act hastily at such times. But still, knowing the ability that my retainer has for the dramatic and over fanciful— How many did you actually kill?"*

"None," said Vash curtly. *"I shot them with stun-pistols that I had just charged prior in the control room of the landing grid."*

Fairbeard sat up erect in his throne.

"Stun-pistols?" he demanded sharply. *"You used stun-pistols on Toffpoint?"*

"Of course, on Toffpoint," said Vash with tart sarcasm in his voice. *"This is where I was! But no one was killed. One or two may be nursing slightly blistered skin by now, but all of them had their pockets picked by Bazil. I understand that is a local custom. There's nothing to worry about."*

But Fairbeard stared at him, aghast with distain over the fact that stun pistols were used.

"But you do not understand how deplorable this is!" he protested. *"Stun-pistols used here? It is the one thing I would have given strict orders to avoid! My neighbors will talk about it! You could have used any other weapon, but of all things why did you have to use stun-pistols?"*

"Because that was the means of defense that I had on me," said Vash briefly.

"Horrible, just horrible!" said Fairbeard as his facial wrinkles began to increase. *"The worst thing you could possibly have done! I have to disown you. Unmistakably! You'll have to disappear at once. We'll blame it on Seymour's retainers."*

Vash asked somewhat shocked at the way the words were expressed:

"Disappear? Me?"

"You must vanish, you were never here." said Fairbeard. *"I suppose there's no real necessity to cut your throat, but you plainly have to disappear, though it would have been much more discreet if you had simply gotten killed."*

"Are you saying that I was indiscreet by not defending myself and surviving their attack?" demanded Vash, now more than visibly irritated at the direction of the conversation.

"Extremely so!" Fairbeard snapped back with equal irritation. *"Here I had you come all the way from Nemo Vesta to help arrange a delicate matter, and before you'd traveled even the few miles it took to get to my castle—within minutes of landing on Toffpoint, I might add! —You spoiled everything! I am a reasonable man, but these are the facts! You used stun-pistols, so you have to disappear. I think it generous for me to say only until people on Toffpoint forget that such things exist. But the two of you must vanish ... oh, for a year or so ... there are some fairly cozy dungeons in the lower corridors of the castle—"*

Vash, now seethed at the sudden possibility that he had done so much to escape a prison only to be hidden away in a dungeon. He'd tried to do something brilliant on Nemo Vesta, and had been framed for a murder he did not commit with a weapon that he did not create. He'd defended his life and property on Toffpoint, and nearly the same thing popped up as a prospect. Vash angrily suspected that both fate and chance had plotted plain conspiracy against him.

But there was an interruption. A clanking of arms sounded somewhere nearby. Men with long, gruesome, glittering spears came through a doorway. They stood aside. A girl entered the great hall. More spearmen followed her. They stopped by the door. The girl came across the hall.

Vash couldn't help but notice that she was a very pretty girl, yet it took on very little importance with so many other things currently going on, he had no time for girls, even one that looked as angelic as her.

Bazil, behind him, said in a quivering voice:

"My Lady Adeline, I beg you to plead with your father for his mercies on his most faithful retainer!"

The girl looked surprised at him for addressing her so direct. Her eyes fell on Vash, giving a look of hopeful interest. Vash, at that moment, was very nearly as disgusted and as indignant as a man could be in that moment. Needless to say, he did not return the same interest to her—which to the Lady Adeline, daughter of the Lord Emory Demetrius Fairbeard, who was prince of this and baron of that and so on, was news. In fact, he did not look at her at all. He ground his teeth, seething as he glared at Fairbeard.

"Don't try to use those doe eyes of yours to wheedle me, Adeline!" snapped her father. *"I am a reasonable man, but I indulge you too much since the death of your mother—even by allowing you to refuse that young imbecile Seymour, with no end of inconvenience as a result. But I will not have you question my decision about Bazil and this Rayburn Character!"*

The girl said pleasantly:

"Of course not, Father. But what have they done?"

"The two of them," snapped Fairbeard again, *"fought twenty men today defeating all of them! Bazil plundered them. Then thirty other men, mounted, tried to avenge the first twenty and they*

defeated them also! Bazil plundered eighteen. And all this was permissible, though highly irregular and unlikely. But they did it with stun-pistols! Everybody within news range will talk of it! They'll know that this Mr. Rayburn came to Toffpoint in order to see me! They'll suspect that I imported new weapons for political purposes! They will howl over every scheme I've had these twenty years!"

The girl stood still. A spearman leaned his weapon against the wall, raced across the hall, shifted a chair to a convenient position for the Lady Adeline to sit, and raced back to his fellows. She then gracefully sat down.

"But did they really defeat so many?" she asked, marveling at the prospect. *"That's wonderful! And Bazil was undoubtedly fighting in defense of someone you'd told him to protect, as a loyal retainer should do. Wasn't he?"*

"I wish," fumed her father, *"that you would not throw in irrelevances! I sent him to bring this Rayburn character here this afternoon, not to massacre my neighbors' retainers—or rather, not to not massacre them. A little blood-letting would have done no harm, but stun-pistols—"*

"He was protecting somebody he was told to protect," said Adeline. *"And this other man, this—"*

"Rayburn. Vash Rayburn," said her father irritably. *"Yes. He was protecting himself! Doubtless he thought he did me a service in doing that! But if he'd only let himself get killed quietly the whole affair would be simplified!"*

The Lady Adeline said with quiet dignity:

"By the same reasoning, Father, it would simplify things greatly if I let the Lord Seymour kidnap me, yes?"

"It's not the same thing at all" Fairbeard said with surprise that his daughter would turn his own words against him.

"At least," said Adeline, *"I wouldn't have a pack of spearmen following me about like puppies everywhere I go!"*

"It's just not the same." Her father repeated.

The Lady Adeline continued, *"The men of Lord Seymour's castle leering at me from all corners, their breaths smelling of wine and cheap pipe tobacco, and they breathe very noisily as they try to whisper to me how they could remove me from my situation if only I would provide a service to them"*

"It's not—", her father once again tried to interject before getting cut off once again by his daughter.

"So, father, doesn't it seem especially unreasonable," said the Lady Adeline with even greater dignity as she leaned back in her chair, knowing that she was about to win her case, *"when you could put Bazil and Mr. Rayburn, who can fend off twenty and thirty men at once all by themselves on duty to guard me. But instead, you would have them in the dungeon and me at the potential mercies of Lord Seymour, it doesn't seem to me that you think much of my safety; instead of using them to keep your daughter safe from that particularly horrible Seymour, they are locked away!"*

Fairbeard conceded to his daughter's argument as he spoke with cracked voice.

"To end the argument, I will think it over until tomorrow. Now go away! All of you."

Adeline, beaming, rose and kissed him on the forehead. He squirmed and coughed at the possibilities of onlookers seeing him as a father figure and not a ruler. She turned to leave, and beckoned casually for Bazil and Vash to follow her.

"My chieftain," said Bazil tremulously, *"do we depart, too?"*

"Yes! I said all of you, didn't I?" rasped Fairbeard. *"Get out of my sight!"*

Bazil moved with agility in the wake of the Lady Adeline's flared train that followed behind her. Vash picked up his bag and followed. This, he considered darkly, was in the nature of a reprieve only. And if those three airships overhead did come from Nemo Vesta…why were there three?

Vash followed the Lady Adeline up, what seemed to be an endless flight of painfully uneven cobblestone stairs. He thought to himself that this agony would never end, but suddenly stars appeared. The spearmen who guarded the lady stepped out on a flagstone level area that overlooked the coastal line below. When Vash finally made it to the opening, he saw that they had arrived at the battlements of one of the highest points of the castle wall. A glowing moon showed a rambling wall of circumvallation, with peaked roofs inside it. He could look down into a courtyard where a fire burned and several men busily did things beside it. But there were no other lights. Beyond the castle wall the ground stretched away toward a nearby range of rugged low mountains. It was vaguely splotched with different degrees of darkness, where fields and pastures and woodland corpses lay in the almost bone chilling void of blacks and grays.

"Here's a bench," said Adeline cheerfully, *"and you can sit down beside me and explain things. What's your name, again, and where did you come from?"*

"My name is Vash Rayburn," Though the lady did just save him from imprisonment, he found himself scowling with his words. *"I come from the coastal colony port of Gibbit Cove, where if you are not a sky pirate, you are a scoundrel hiding from the marshals for some other ostensibly nefarious reasons. My grandfather heads the most notorious of the pirate gangs."*

"Absolutely and most dreadfully wonderful!" said Adeline, admiringly. *"I knew you were no ordinary person to be able to fight as my father said you did today!"*

Bazil cleared his throat.

"Lady Adeline—"

"Hush!" said Adeline. *"You're a nice old fuddy-duddy that father sent to the sky port because he figured you'd be too timid to get into trouble. So, hush!"* Turning her attention back to Vash she said interestedly excited, *"Now, tell me all about the fighting. It must have been absolutely most wickedly terrible!"*

She watched him expectantly as if readying herself for an embellished story of adventure and excitement.

"The fighting I did today," said Vash angrily, *"was exactly as dangerous and as difficult as shooting fish in a bucket. A little more trouble, but not much. In fact, I would venture that fish would have had more brain matter."*

Even in the moonlight he could see that her expression was more admiring than before; as though his honest candor created even more admiration.

"I thought you'd say something like that!" she said contentedly. *"Go on!"*

"That's all," said Vash.

"Quite all?" she asked, unsatisfied.

"I can't think of anything else," he told her. He then added somewhat drearily: *"I rode a horse for three hours today. I'm not used to it. I ache. Your father is thinking of putting me in a dungeon until some scheme or other of his goes through. I'm disappointed. I'm worried about three lights that went across the sky at sundown and I'm simply too tired and befuddled for normal conversation, so please forgive me for my abruptness to your inquiries."*

"Oh," said Adeline.

"If I may take my leave," asked Vash in a petulant tone, *"I'll get some rest and do some thinking when I get up. I'll hope to have more entertaining things to say in the morning."*

He got to his feet and picked up his bag.

"Where do I go?" he asked.

Adeline regarded him enigmatically as Bazil squirmed and winced at Vash's candor.

"Bazil will show you the way." Then Adeline said deliberately, *"Vash Rayburn, will you fight for me?"*

Bazil plucked anxiously at his arm as if caught in the middle of an awkward situation. Vash said politely:

"If my lady should find it at all desirable for me to do so, then yes," tipping the brim of his bowler hat to her, *'but now I must get some sleep."*

"Thank you," said Adeline. *"I am sorely troubled by the Lord Seymour."*

She watched him move away. Bazil, muttering softly, went with him down another monstrosity of a stone stairway that made every muscle in Vash's body curse his very existence.

"Oh, what folly!" lamented Bazil, rubbing his temples with the thumb and middle finger of his right hand while patting Vash on the shoulder with his left hand. *" You did not pay me attention... I tried to warn you! You simply would not pay me heed!"* Leaning in and speaking more softly, *"when the Lady Adeline asked if you would fight for her, you should have said if her father permitted you that honor. But instead, you said yes! The spearmen heard you! Now you must either fight the Lord Seymour within a night and day or bring disgrace upon Lord Fairbeard, the Lady Adeline and yourself!"*

"I doubt," said Vash tiredly, *"that the obligations of Toffpointian gentility apply to the grandson of a pirate or an escap.... To me."*

He'd been about to say an escaped criminal from Nemo Vesta, but caught himself in time.

"But they do apply!" said Bazil, shocked. *"A man who has been disgraced has no rights! Any man may plunder him, any man may kill him at will. But if he resists plundering or kills anybody else in self-defense, he is hanged on the spot!"*

Vash stopped short in his descent of the uneven stone steps.

"That's ridiculous?" he said sardonically. *"Surely the Lady Adeline didn't mean to put me in such a position!"*

"You weren't very polite to her," explained Bazil. *"She'd persuaded her father out of putting us in a dungeon until he thought of us again. You should at least have shown good manners! You should have said that you came here across deserts and flaming oceans because of the fame of her beauty. You might have said you heard songs of her sweetness beside campfires half a world away. She might not have believed you, but she may not have put you in that situation."*

"Wait!" said Vash. *"That's just manners to you? What would you have said to a girl you really liked?"*

"Oh, then," laughed Bazil, *"I would get complimentary!"*

Vash went heavily down the rest of the steps. He was not in the least pleased. On a strange island, with strange customs, and with his weapons losing their charge every hour, he did not need any handicaps. But if he got into a worse-than-outlawed category such as Bazil described—

Near the last step, finally reaching the bottom he said, seething:

"When you've tucked me in bed, go back and ask the Lady Adeline to arrange for me to have a horse and permission to go fight this Lord Seymour right after breakfast in the morning!"

He was too much enraged and exhausted to think further. He let himself be led into some sort of quarters, which at best could probably be best described as a sort of a cozy dungeon. Bazil vanished and came back with ointments for Vash's blisters, but no food. He explained once again that food given to Vash would make it disgraceful to cut his throat at which Vash waved him off with, "I know, I know, leave me be," as he stripped off his garments and smeared himself lavishly where he had lost skin. The ointment stung like wasp stings, and he presently lay awake in a sort of suspended unrest as he was sore and he was ravenous to boot!

It seemed to him that he lay awake for something shy of an eternity, but he must have dozed off at some point in the night because he was awakened by a shrill yell. It was not a complete yell; only the first part of one. It stopped in a particularly unpleasant fashion, and its echoes went reverberating through the stony walls of the castle. Vash was out of bed with a stun-pistol in his hand before his feet hit the floor, then the first yell was followed by other outcries of lament, by the clashing of steel upon steel, and all the frenzied tumult of combat in the dark. The uproar moved. In seconds the sound of fighting came from a different direction, as if a striking force of some sort went rushing through specifically defended corridors as if looking for something or someone.

It did not seem that the turmoil would pass before Vash's door, but he growled to himself knowing that, on a feudal world, presumably one might expect just about anything and anything meant that there was a situation in being here, a situation in which etiquette required a rejected suitor to carry off a certain scornful maiden by force. Some young lordling named Seymour had to carry off

Adeline or be considered a man of no spirit. So, if this were the case, Vash was compelled by the promise that he had hastily made to Lady Adeline and would have to leave the security of his cell to hunt down the culprits or be, himself, disgraced.

A gun went off somewhere. It was the sound of a powder musket, exploding violently to send a metal bearing somewhere. It went off again. There was an instance almost of silence. Then an intolerable screeching of triumph, and shrieks of another sort entirely, and the excessively loud clash of arms began once more.

Vash was now clothed, well enough to have places to stick stun-pistols. He jerked on the door to open it, irritably demanding of himself how he would know which side was which, or for that matter which side he should fight on.

Shockingly, the door was locked. He fumed to find that they had locked him in. He flung himself against it and it barely quivered. It had been barred from the outside. He yelled in highly indecorous terms, and tore his bedstead apart to make a battering ram.

The fighting reached a climax. He heard a girl scream, and without question knew that it was the Lady Adeline, and equally without question knew that he would fight to keep any girl from being abducted by a man she didn't want to marry. Vash swung the log, which was previously the corner post of his bed. Something cracked. He swung again.

The sound of battle changed to that of a running fight. The objective of the raiders had been reached. Having gotten the prize in which they came for—and it could only be Adeline—they retreated swiftly, fighting only to cover their retreat. Vash swung his bed leg with furious anger. He heard a flurry of yells and sword strokes, and a fierce, desperate cry from Adeline among them, and a plank in his guest-room-dungeon door began to give way. He struck again. The running raiders poured past a corner merely yards from his cell. He swung at the door another time. Again, and again and again, Vash swung as the tumult moved away, and he suddenly heard a scurrying thunder of horses' hoofs outside the castle altogether. There were yells of derisive triumph and the pounding, rumbling sound of horses headed away in the night until it was lost in the silence of the blackness.

Still raging inarticulately to himself, Vash crashed his small log at the door. He was not consciously concerned about the distress Fairbeard might feel over the abduction of his daughter. But there is an instinct in most men, no matter where you were brought up, against the forcing of a girl to marriage against her will. Vash battered at his door.

Around him the castle began to hum like a hive of bees. Women cried out, and men shouted furiously to one another, and off-duty fighting men came belatedly looking for somebody to fight, dragging weapons behind them and not knowing where to even find enemies.

Vash probably made as much noise as any of them. Somebody brought a light somewhere nearby. It shone through the cracks in the splintered planks. He could see to aim. He smote savagely and the door finally came apart well enough that he could escape his captivity. He pushed himself outward through the loosely battered planks and found himself in the corridor outside, being stared at by a handful of complete strangers.

"It's the engineer," a scullery maid explained to another. *"I saw him when he rode in with Bazil, I did."*

"I want Bazil," said Vash coldly. *"I need a dozen horses and men to ride with me."* He pushed his way forward. *"Which way to the stables?"*

He then went back in his cell and picked up his bag of stun-pistols. His air was purposeful and his manner furious. The retainers of Fairbeard were in an extremely apologetic frame of mind. A raiding party undoubtedly led by Lord Seymour had carried off the Lady Adeline into the night. The defenders of the castle hadn't prevented it. So, there was no special reason to obey Vash, but there was every reason to be doing something useful, so a few pointed him in the right direction toward the stables.

He found himself almost swept along by agitated retainers trying to look as if they were about a purposeful affair. They went down a long ramp, calling uneasily to each other. They came around a place where two men lay quite still on the floor. Then there were shouts of, *"Bazil! This way, Bazil!"* and Vash found himself in a small stone-walled courtyard doubtless inside a sally-port. It was filled with figures aimlessly milling around and many waving torches. And there was Bazil, desperately pale and frightened. Behind him there was Fairbeard, his eyes burning and his hands twitching, literally speechless from fury.

Without cordialities, Vash yelled to Bazil, *"Pick a dozen men! Get 'em on horses! Get a horse for me as well! I'll show all of them how to use the stun-pistols as we ride!"*

Bazil panted, and shakingly responded, *"They ... hamstrung most of our horses in order that we could not pursue them!"*

"Then go get me all that are left!" barked Vash with impatience. He suddenly raged at Lord Fairbeard. *"Here's another time stun-pistols get used on Toffpoint! Object to this if you want to!"*

Hoof beats began to grow louder. Bazil, on horseback of a midnight-colored beast that shielded and reared at the flames and confusion around him. Other horses, followed; all with the smell of spilt blood in their nostrils, fighting against the men who led them, and followed reluctantly to the center.

Bazil called names as he looked about him for those called. There was plenty of light. As he called names, each man mounted a horse. Men on the ground thrust swords, spears—all manner of weapons upon them as soon as each found his mount stable. Some of the chosen men swaggered with pride as to have been chosen for this mission while others looked woefully unhappy. But with Fairbeard glaring frenziedly upon them in the smoky glare, no man refused for fear of retaliation and dishonor.

Vash climbed ungracefully upon the mount that four or five men held for him. Bazil, with a fine sense of drama, seized a torch and waved it above his head. There was a vast creaking, and an unsuspected gate opened, and Bazil rode out with a great clattering of hoofs as the others followed suit and rode out after him.

There were lights everywhere about the castle, now. All along the battlements men had set light to fire-baskets and lowered them partway down the walls, to disclose any attacking forces, which might have stayed behind with dishonorable intentions toward the stronghold. Others waved torches from the battlements.

Bazil swung his torch and pointed to the fresh hoof prints dug into the ground.

"They rode this way!" he called to Vash. *"They ride for Seymour's castle!"*

Vash said angrily:

"Put out that light you imbecile! Do you want to advertise how few we are and what we're doing? Here! Ride close!"

Bazil flung down the torch and glances down as the horses trod it underfoot as the knot of men rode on. Bazil beat forward as Vash waved him up:

"The pickings should be good, eh? Why do you want me?"

"You've got to learn something here," snapped Vash. *"Here! This is a stun-pistol. It's set for single-shot firing only. You hold it like so, with your finger along this rod. By keeping your finger along this rod"* he stressed, *"you merely have to point your finger at a man and pull this trigger with your middle finger. The pistol will buzz briefly. You let the trigger loose and point at another man and pull the trigger again. Understand? The next thing you need to know, don't try to use it over ten yards from your target. You're not a marksman, it will only cause you the waste of a good shot."*

There on a galloping horse beside Vash in the darkness, Bazil zestfully repeated his lesson.

"Show the others on your flank and then send them to me for a pistol," Vash commanded curtly. *"I'll be showing others on my flank."*

He turned to the man who rode closest to his left. Before he had fully instructed that man, another clamored for a weapon on his right.

This was hardly adequate training in the use of modern weapons. For that matter, Vash was hardly qualified to give military instruction. He had only gone on two pirate voyages himself. But little boys on Gibbit Cove played at pirate, in dutiful emulation of their parents. At least the possibilities of stun pistols were envisioned in their childish games. So Vash knew more about how to fight with stun-pistols than anyone save his grandfather.

The band of pursuing horsemen pounded through the dark night under strangely patterned stars. Vash held on to his saddle and barked out instructions to teach the Toffpointians how to shoot. He felt very uneasy about the whole matter and began to worry. With the lights of Lord Fairbeard's castle long vanished behind them, he began to realize how very small his troop was.

Bazil had said something about horses being hamstrung. There must, then, have been two attacking parties. One swarmed into the stables to draw all defending retainers there, then the other poured over a wall or in through a bribed-open sally-port, and rushed for the Lady Adeline's bed chamber. The point he was mulling over in his mind was that the attackers had made sure there could be only a token pursuit. They knew they were many times stronger than any who might come after them. It would be absurd for them to flee....

Vash kicked his horse and got up to the front of the column of riders in the night.

"Bazil!" he snapped. *"They'll be idiots if they keep on running away, now they're too far off to worry about men on foot. They'll stop and wait for us—most of them anyhow. We're riding into an ambush!"*

"Good pickings, eh?" said Bazil.

"Idiot!" yelped Vash. *"These men know you. You know what I can do with stun-pistols! Tell them we're riding into an ambush. They're to follow close behind us! Tell them they're not to shoot at anybody more than five yards off and not coming at them, and if any man stops to plunder, I'll kill him personally!"*

Bazil gaped at him. *"Not stop to plunder?"*

"Seymour won't!" snapped Vash. *"He'll take Adeline on to his castle, leaving most of his men behind to massacre us!"*

Bazil reined aside as Vash pounded on to the lead of the tiny troop. This was the second time in his life he'd been on a horse. It was two too many for his liking. This adventure was not exhilarating. It came into his mind, depressingly, that supposedly stirring action like this was really no more satisfying than piracy. Adeline had tricked him into a fix in which he had to fight Seymour or be disgraced to all—and to be disgraced on Toffpoint was equivalent to suicide.

His horse came to a gentle rise in the ground. The horse slacked in its galloping as the incline grew ever steeper. The horse slowed to a walk, which it pursued with a rhythmically tossing head. It was only less uncomfortable than a gallop. The dim outline of trees appeared overhead.

"*Perfect place for an ambush,*" Vash reflected suspiciously.

He pulled out a stun-pistol. He set the stun control of his pistol to continuous fire—this was information that he hadn't dared trust to the others.

His horse breasted the rise. There was a yell ahead and dim figures plunged toward him.

He painstakingly made ready to swing his stun-pistol from his extreme right, across the space before him, and all the way to the extreme left. The pistol should be capable of continuous fire for four seconds. But it was operating on stored charge. He didn't dare count on more than three.

He pulled the trigger. The stun-pistol hummed, though its noise was inaudible through the yells of the charging partisans of the Lord Seymour.

Chapter 5

Vash roared at the men who did not heed his earlier command of not plundering. *"Get back up on your horses now or I will blast you and leave you here for Seymour's men to handle when they're able to move about again! Get back on that horse! One—two—"*

The men reluctantly got back on their horses.

"I want every one of you to go on ahead," rasped Vash, waving his arm that held the stun pistol. *"All of you! I'm going to count you that way I know there is no one behind wasting time plundering!"*

The dozen horsemen retained by the auspicious Lord Fairbeard's stronghold rode on ahead as instructed with scowls and disdain to the prospect of missing such good plunders. And count them he did, out loud as they rode by him, as if to insure them that he was not joking and might very well shoot them if caught lagging behind. He rode on, shepherding the disgruntled flock before him.

"Lord Seymour," he told them in a chilled, hair-raising tone *"has a much bigger prize than any cash or bobbles you'll plunder from one of those shot-down retainers of his! He has the Lady Adeline! He won't stop before he has her behind castle walls! We've got to catch up with him before he gets that chance! Do you want to try to climb into his castle by your fingernails and defend yourself against his castle's battlement brigades? You'll have to do that very thing should he reach there first!"*

The horses moved a little faster now at the thought of less work for more plunder. Bazil said with surprising humility:

"If we force our horses too much, my good Lord Rayburn, they'll be exhausted before we can catch up and thus no good to us in our exit."

"No time for that," snapped Vash, currently ignoring the reference to him as a lord; a reference that he would have been intoxicated to here on Nemo Vesta." *We must catch up! Time is our surprise"*

Forever moving forward in his thoughts, his mind currently pondered over the ambush that had just occurred and then moved on to the next unfolding chapter of events; it had happened, and it had failed, leaving a pile of Seymour's men huddled up to nurse their wounds; there was no since in mulling over past events, for the huddled mass was but a small fraction of the raiding party, which meant another ambush must be set somewhere.

Four-fifths or so of Seymour's raiding party, which had fought its way into the stronghold and out again with the Lady Adeline, had now positioned themselves, waiting for their pursuers atop a certain bit of rising ground. They'd known their pursuers must come this way as there were certain passes through the low but rugged hills, but one went this way or that, yet none of the others were a direct route to Lord Seymour's castle.

Their blood already warmed by past fighting, left them ready and armed for the fight that was mere moments away as Vash and his paltry dozen seemed to ride right into destruction.

The hidden force flung themselves into a full charge at Vash and his men.

But little did they know that this ragtag team had stun pistols or that Vash, himself, had a stun-pistol set for continuous fire. He used it as if it were the Mitrailleuse, the automata rifle often found on the ports and starboards of the sky marshal vessels, painstakingly sweeping it across the night before him, neither too fast nor too slowly. It affected the rushing followers of Lord Seymour exactly as if it had been an oversized meat-chopper.

They went down, folding over in pain as if struck by an iron beam to the gut. Only three men remained in their saddles—they'd probably been sheltered from the blast by the bodies of men who rode ahead. Vash attended to those three with individual, personalized stun-pistol bolts—and immediately had trouble with his men, who wanted to dismount and plunder their fallen enemies.

He refused to even let them collect the horses of the men now out of action. It would cost time, and Seymour wouldn't be losing any that he could help. With a feared, trembling girl as prisoner, most men would want to get her behind battlements as soon as possible.

But Vash knew that his party was slowing him down at present and he began to think bitterly that Seymour would reach his stronghold before they would be able to overtake him.

"This place he's heading for," he said discouraged in the direction of Bazil. *"Any chance of our rushing it?"*

"Oh, no!" said Bazil, somewhat mournfully. *"Ten men could hold it against a thousand!"*

"Then can't we make better time?" Beseeched Vash.

Bazil said resignedly, *"Seymour probably had fresh horses waiting, so he could keep on at top speed in his flight. I doubt we will catch him, now."*

"The Lady Adeline," said Vash bitterly, *"has put me in a fix so if I don't fight him, I'm ruined!"*

"Disgraced," corrected Bazil. Vash said woefully, *"It's the same thing."*

Gloom descended on the whole party as the prospects of not achieving their mission filled their minds. Insensibly, the pace of the horses slackened still more. They had done well. But a horse that can cover fifty miles a day at its own gait can be exhausted in ten or less, if pushed too hard. By the time Vash and his men were within two miles of Lord Seymour's castle, their mounts were extremely reluctant to move faster than a walk. At a mile, they were kept in motion only by the repeated kicks of the men.

The route they followed was specific. There was no choice of routes here in the hills. They could only follow the ever-winding twists and turns of the trail that lay before them among steep mountain-flanks and minor peaks long since carved out by the receding waters. But suddenly the path opened to clear wide valley, yellow cressets burned at its upper end, no more than half a mile distant. The star draped night burned with path lights giving dimension to a castle gate, open, with the last of Lord Seymour's party of horsemen filing into it. Even as Vash momentarily regained a Vestibule of hope, the gate closed. Faint shouts of triumph came from inside the castle walls to the completely frustrated pursuers who watched from outside.

"I should have bet that this would happen, the way things have played out thus far," said Vash miserably as he struck the top of his saddle horn. *"Stop here, Bazil. Pick out a couple of your more hangdog, more browbeaten characters,"* remembering a story of a valiant Trojan horse move that Vash had heard his grandfather

recant many times, *"and fix them up so as to appear that their hands are apparently tied behind their backs. We take a breather for five minutes—no more."*

He would not let any man dismount, save the ones being outfitted for the stratagem, which he had developing in his mind. He shifted himself about on his own saddle, trying to find a comfortable way to sit so as to give some level of relief to the ever-growing blisters. He failed. At the end of five minutes, he gave his orders. There were still shouts occasionally from within Lord Seymour's castle. They had an almost eurhythmic frequency, which suggested that they were in response to a speech. Seymour was obviously making a fine, dramatic spectacle of his capture of an unwilling bride. He must be pompously addressing his retainers and saying that through their fine loyalty, co-operation and willingness to risk all for their chieftain, they now had the Lady Adeline to be their chatelaine. He must surely be thanking them from the bottom of his heart and they would all be invited to the official wedding, which would take place sometime tomorrow, most likely. Vash's thoughts immediately moved to getting behind the walls before that happened.

Before the speech was quite finished, however, Vash and his weary following rode up into the patch of light cast by the cressets outside the walls. Bazil bellowed to the battlements.

"Prisoners!" he roared, according to instructions from Vash. *"We caught some prisoners in the ambush! They got fancy news! Tell Lord Seymour he'd better get their story right away! No time to waste! Urgent!"*

Vash played the part of one prisoner, just in case anybody noticed from above that one man rode as if either entirely unskilled in riding or else injured in a fight.

He heard shoutings, over the walls. He glared at his men and they drooped in their saddles. The gate creaked open and the horsemen from Lord Fairbeard's castle filed inside single file. They showed no elation, because Vash had promised to ram a spear-shaft its full length down the throat of any of the men who gave away his stratagem ahead of time. The gate closed behind them then men appeared from the gloom to take their horses. This could have revealed that the newcomers were strangers, but Seymour would have recruited new and extra retainers for the emergency of tonight. There would be many strange faces in his castle at this point.

"Good fight, eh?" bellowed an ancient, long-retired retainer with a wine bottle in his hand.

"Good fight!" agreed Bazil.

"Good plunder, eh?" bellowed the ancient above the heads of younger men. *"Like the good old days?"*

"Even better!" boomed Bazil.

At just this instant the young Lord Seymour appeared. There were scratches on his cheek, acquired during the ride with Adeline forcibly held down across his saddlebow. He looked thrilled by his victory but a little uneasy about his prize.

"What's this about prisoners with fancy news?" he demanded. *"Well, what is it?"*

"Emory Demetrius Fairbeard!" whooped Bazil. *"Long Live the Lady Adeline!"*

At that, Vash painstakingly opened fire; with the continuous-fire stud of this pistol—his third tonight—pressed down. The merrymakers in the courtyard wavered and went down like windrows in the field in an impeding storm. Bazil then opened fire with yet another stun-pistol. The others bellowed and began to fling bolts at every living thing they saw.

"To the Lady Adeline!" rasped Vash, getting off his horse with as many creakings as the castle gate.

His followers now rushed, dismounting where they had to. They fired with reckless abandon. A stun-pistol, which does not kill, imposes few restraints upon its user. If you shoot somebody who doesn't need to be shot, he may not like it but he isn't permanently harmed. So, the twelve who'd followed Vash poured in what would have been a murderous fire if they'd been shooting bullets, but as it stands was no worse than a murderous vindication on their pride…with a slight blistering.

There were screams and flight and utterly hopeless defiance by sword-armed and spear-armed men. In an instant Vash went limping into the castle with Bazil close by his side, searching for

Adeline. Seymour had not fallen at the first fire. He vanished, and the castle was plainly fallen whereby he made no attempt to lead resistance against its invaders.

Vash's men went raging happily through corridors and halls as they came to them. They used their stun-pistols with zest and at such close quarters with considerable effect. Vash heard Adeline scream angrily leading both he and Bazil swiftly in the direction of the scornful cry. They came upon the young Lord Seymour trying to let Adeline down out of a window on a rope. He undoubtedly intended to follow her and complete his abduction on the run. But in the ill-tempered flight, Lady Adeline bit him, as Vash said somewhat vexed:

"Look here! It seems that I'm disgraced if I don't fight you somehow—"

The young Lord Seymour rushed him with absolute impunity, sword outstretched, eyes blazing in a fiery frenzy of despair and anger. Vash brought him down with a single buzz from his stun pistol.

One of Vash's followers came hunting for him.

"Sir," he sputtered, *"the garrison is cornered in their quarters, and we've been picking them off one by one through the windows, now those left thinks that we are dropping them dead like horseflies on a wall and wish to surrender before the same fate befalls them... Shall we let 'em?"*

"By all means," Vash said with a smirk of accomplishment. *"And Bazil, go get something heavier than a nightgown for the Lady Adeline to wear, and then do what plundering you feel is practical for such an occasion. But I want to be out of here in half an hour. Understand?"*

"I'll attend to my own clothing thank you very much," said the Lady Adeline vengefully. *"You cut his throat while I'm getting dressed."*

She kicked at the unconscious Lord Seymour as he lay on the pavement. She disappeared through a door nearby. Vash could guess that Seymour would have prepared something elaborate for his reluctant bride, so she would probably have an enjoyable time plundering the wears that were meant to accompany the forced name of Seymour.

"Bazil," said Vash, *"help me get this character into a closet somewhere. He's not to be killed. I don't like him, but at this moment I don't like anybody very much, and don't wish to play favorites with anyone."*

Bazil helped dragged the unconscious young nobleman into the next room. Vash locked the door and pocketed the key as Adeline came into view again. She was splendidly attired, now, in brocade and jewels. Seymour had evidently hoped to placate her after marriage by things of that sort and had spent lavishly for them.

Now, throughout the castle there were many and diverse noises coming from every corner. Sometimes you could still hear the crackling hum of a stun-pistol followed by a writhing sound of pain. Most often, these were muffled by the sounds of shouting and merriments caused by the finding of a worthy cash of loot to be plundered. There were some giddy squeals in female fashion followed by more giggling and yells of excitement.

"I need not say," said the Lady Adeline with as much dignity as she could muster, *"that I thank you so very much. But I do and my appreciation has no limits."*

Tipping his hat as he customarily did often in greeting and gratitude, giving way to a slight adjustment forward of the old black Fedora given to him by his grandfather, *"You're quite welcome,"* said Vash politely.

"And what are you going to do now?" inquired Adeline in a sheepishly concerned voice.

"I would imagine," said Vash, *"that we'll go down into the courtyard where our horses are. I gave my men half an hour for looting; we must keep up with tradition you know"* he grinned. *"During that half hour I shall sit down on something with a cushion, which will, I hope, remain perfectly still. And I may,"* he added with hopeful anticipation as he glanced into the Lady Adeline's eyes, *"eat something from that reception table laid out in the next room. I've had nothing to eat since I landed on Toffpoint, as no one could decide whether to feed me or slit my throat. I*

mean, heaven forbid a person to commit him or herself to not cutting my throat. But after half an hour we'll mount and leave."

The Lady Adeline looked at Vash sympathetically.

"But the castle is now surrendered to you," she protested. *"You now hold it! Aren't you going to try to keep it?"*

"Look out there." Casting out his hand at the vast expanse of land which could now be seen as the sun began to rise. *"There are a good many unpleasant characters out there,"* said Vash, *"who have reason to dislike me very much. They would have no hesitation to express these emotions, when they feel up to it. I want to dodge them if I can. And presently the people in this castle will realize that even stun-pistols can't keep on shooting indefinitely. I don't want to be around when that thought occurs to them, or worse, when the charge does deplete."*

He offered his arm with a reasonably grand air and went limping with her down to the courtyard just inside the gate, but not before stopping at a lavishly decorated reception table to pick up something in the way of a light snack for the journey. Two of Emory Fairbeard's retainers staggered into view as they arrived, barely able to effectively move under the plundered loot that they had acquired, which ranged from a quarter keg of wine to a mass of frothy stuff which must have been female garments. They went away and other men arrived loaded down with their own accumulations of loot. Some of the local inhabitants looked on with uneasy indignation.

Vash found a bench and sat down. He conspicuously displayed one of the weapons, which had captured the castle. Seymour's defeated retainers looked at him with dark intent.

"Bring me something to drink," commanded Vash. *"Then if you would be so kind as to bring fresh horses for my men and I, as well as tend to the horses we came in on so they will be ready to pack the loot my men have gained and then I'll take them off of your hands. I'll even throw in the Lord Seymour as a parting gift for your service, who is now unharmed but with his life in the balance.*

He moved the pistol suggestively. The normal inhabitants of Seymour's castle moved away, discussing the situation in subdued voices as they began to tend to the horses.

The Lady Adeline sat down proudly on the bench beside him.

"You are absolutely wonderful!" she said with the utmost conviction.

"I've been known to fancy that illusion myself from time to time, but then reality sets in," said Vash as he bit into a piece of fruit.

"But nobody before in all Toffpointian history has ever fought twenty men, and then thirty men, destroyed an ambush, and captured a castle, all in one day!"

"And on an empty stomach mind you," added Vash slyly, *"and we mustn't forget the blisters, lots and lots of blisters!"*

Somebody came running with bread and cheese and wine. He bit into the bread and cheese. After a moment he said with his mouth full:

"Personally, I have never especially wanted to fight other men or set out to break up ambushes or capture castles. I want to do what I want to do, what I feel to be right for me and not what other people happen to admire."

"Then what do you want to do?" she asked admiringly.

"I'm not quite sure now," said Vash gloomily. He took a fresh bite. *"But a little while ago I wanted to do some interesting and useful things in mechanics, and get reasonably rich, and marry a delightful young girl, and become a prominent citizen on Nemo Vesta. I think I'll settle for another Colony now, however."*

"For what you have done, my father will make you rich," said the girl proudly. *"You saved me from being married to that scoundrel Lord Seymour!"*

Vash just shook his head.

"Forgive me, but I have my doubts," he said. *"He had a scheme to import a lot of stun-pistols and arm his retainers with them. Then he meant to rush the port and have me set up a broadcast-power unit that would keep them charged all the time. Then he'd sit back and enjoy life. Holding the sky port, nobody else could get stun-weapons, and nobody could resist his retainers who had them. So, he'd be top man on Toffpoint. He'd have exactly as much power as he chose to seize. I think he cherished that little idea, —and I've*

given advance publicity to stun-pistols. Now he hasn't a ghost of a chance of pulling it off. I'm afraid he might be displeased with me."

"You may have a good read on my father, not sure I can help you with that," said Adeline confident in the knowledge that her father was good at holding grudges. She did not question that her father would be displeased and therefore was uncertain how he would receive Vash even though they had saved her.

"Hmmmmm, maybe you can," said Vash, *"he's kept a daughter and lost a dream. And that's bereavement! I know! Let me think on it and I shall plot more with you later on the matter."*

The horses came plodding into the courtyard with Seymour's retainers driving them. They were anxious to get rid of their conquerors. Vash's men came trickling back, with armfuls of plunder to add to the piles they'd previously gathered. Bazil took charge, commanding the exchange of saddles from tired to fresh horses and that the booty be packed on the old mounts. It was now time to begin the journey back. Nine of the dozen looters were at work on the task of getting things ready to leave when there was a loud sudden tumult back in the castle; yelling and the clash of steel. Vash just looked at the ground and shook his head.

"Bad! Bad! Bad! Someone's stun pistol obviously went empty and the local boys figured it out. Now we'll have to fight some more—I have no more time for such matters," Vash thought.

He beckoned over a resentful inhabitant of the Lord Seymour's castle. He held up the key of the room in which he'd locked young Seymour.

"Now open the castle gate," he commanded, *"and fetch out my last three men, and we'll leave without setting fire to anything. I believe that the Lord Seymour would like it that way. He's locked up in a room that's particularly flammable."*

Vash had only guessed as to the flammability of the room, but Seymour's retainer looked horrified at the thought and bellowed with lament. There was an instantaneous change in the bitterly hostile atmosphere of the castle. Though still with scowled faces, there were men of Seymour's who, at present, came angrily to help load the spare horses. Vash's last three men came out of a corridor, wiping blood from various scratches and complaining plaintively that their pistols had shot empty and they'd had to defend themselves with knives.

Three minutes later the cavalcade rode victoriously out of the castle gate and away into the now bright magenta hue of the morning light. Vash had arrived here when Seymour was inside with Adeline as his prisoner, when there were only a dozen men without and at least a hundred inside to defend the walls. And the castle was considered impregnable.

In just over an hour Vash's followers had taken the castle, rescued Adeline, looted it quite thoroughly, gotten fresh horses for themselves and the old ones set up to handle their plunder, and were headed away again. In only one respect were they worse off than when they arrived. Some stun-pistols were now empty and useless.

"Hold it!" he said sharply to Bazil. *"We don't go back the same way we came! The gang that ambushed us will be stirring around again by now, and we are without full stun-pistols! We make a wide circle and go around the obvious path where they will be surely waiting for a second attempt on us!"*

"Why?" demanded Bazil. *"There are only so many passes. The only other one is three times as long. Besides it is disgraceful to avoid a fight"*

"Bazil!" snapped an icy voice from beside Vash, *"you have an order! Obey it!"*

Vash could see Bazil jump to attention in his saddle.

"Yes, my Lady Adeline," said Bazil shakily. *"But we go a long-distance roundabout, it may take as much as a day to make it back with our haul."*

"That will be fine," Vash retorted back. "It gives me time to take in the scenery."

The long line of horses moved in and out of valleys as the new winding path seemed to go on and on, lessened only by the occasional topside bend that allowed for a vast view of the upcoming valley. The spectacle of twenty-eight beasts moving through dark defiles and over steep passes among the rugged, ragged hills was truly a sight to behold. From any one spot they seemed at once to swagger and to slink, swaying as they moved on and vanished into obscurity. The small wild things in the surrounding brush and trees would take paused affrightedly in their scurries until they had gone far from view.

Adeline said in a soft voice:

"This is nice!"

"What's nice about it?" Vash inquired with a soft tone as he readjusted himself to minimize blister awareness.

"Riding like this," said Adeline enthusiastically, *"with men who have fought for me to guard over me as we make it back, alongside the leader who has rescued me, grazed by a cool fresh breeze— It's a delicious feeling!"*

"Ahhh! But you're used to riding horseback," said Vash dourly as he shifted in his saddle again.

They rode on, while mountains stabbed upwards to connect with the sky and the pass they followed danced this way and that, he was now more than 'painfully' aware of how roundabout this way to the castle truly was indeed.

But they came, at last, to a narrow defile which opened out before them and there were no more mountains ahead, but only foothills. And there, far off in the distance, they could see the sky get brighter and the surrounding landscape become crisper. As they went on, indeed, a glory of red, magenta and deep orange colorings appeared at the horizon as the sun began to steadily move across the sky on their second day of travel.

Suddenly, out of that magnificence three bright lights suddenly darted. In a strict V-formation, they flashed from where the sun had just begun to rise and over the mountains toward the west until they disappeared. They went overhead, more brilliant than the brightest stars, and when partway down to the horizon, as if kissing the mountain peaks, they suddenly winked out.

"What on Earth were those?" demanded Adeline. *"I never saw anything like that before!"*

"They're sky marshal Aeronef pursuers," said Vash. He was as astounded as the girl, but for a different reason. *"I thought they'd be landed by now!"*

It changed everything. He couldn't be for certain as to what the change amounted to, but change there was, and change they were going to have to face.

"We're going to the sky port before we go back to the castle," he told Bazil curtly. *"We'll recharge our stun-pistols there. I thought those ships had landed. They haven't. Now we'll see if we can keep them aloft! How far to the landing grid from here?"*

"You are the one who insisted," complained Bazil, *"that we not go back to the castle the same way we left. There are only so many passes through the hills that we can take. The only other one is very long. We are only four miles from the cas..."*

"Then we head there right now!" snapped Vash, cutting off Bazil's complaint. *"And we step up the speed!"*

He barked commands to the line of followers. Bazil, puzzled but in dread of an acid comment from Adeline if he didn't follow commands, bustled up and down the line of men, insisting on a faster pace. And the members of the cavalcade had not pushed these animals as they had their first trip so even the lead horses, loaded with loot, managed to get up to a respectable ambling trot. The detour to the landing grid was long and stretched into another night as sunset proceeded into dusk. As dusk started to become night once again, the band of riders made way around a bend where then the angular metal framework of the landing grid rose dark against the ever-darkening sky.

When they rode up to it. Vash reflected that it was the only really civilized structure on the colony. Architecturally it was surely the least pleasing. It had obviously been built when Toffpoint was first settled on or possibly right before Halley's disaster and was able to survive, and when ideas of commerce and intercolonial trade seemed more affluent and viable. It was half a mile high and built of massive metal beams. It loomed hugely overhead as the double file of loot-weighed horses trotted under its lower arches and across the grass-grown space within it. Vash headed purposefully for the control shed. There was no sign of movement anywhere. The steeply gabled roofs of the nearby town showed only the fluttering of tiny birds. No smoke rose from chimneys. Barely a light could be seen in windows even though it was nightfall.

As Vash actually reached the control shed, he saw a sleepy man in the act of putting a key in the door. He dismounted within feet of the briskly bearded man, who turned and blinked sleepily at him, and then immediately looked the reverse of cordial. It was the redheaded man he'd stung with a stun-pistol the day before.

"I've come back," said Vash, *"for a few more kilowatts."*

The redheaded man angrily began to announce that he was under orders to make sure that no one accesses the control shed.

"Just be quiet!" said Vash gently. *"The Lady Adeline is with us."*

The redheaded man jerked his head around and lost all color in his face. Bazil glared down at him from his mount. Others of Lord Fairbeard's retainers shifted their positions significantly as to make their oversized belt-knives handier.

"Well since you seem to have permission this time," said the redheaded man, *"I guess you can go on in."*

"Bazil, collect all of the pistols and bring them inside."

Adeline swung lightly to the ground and followed him in. She looked curiously at the cables and instrument boards with knobs and switches inside. On one wall a red light pulsed, and went out, and pulsed again. The redheaded man looked at it.

"You're being called," said Vash. *"Don't answer it."*

The redheaded man just seethed and scowled. Bazil came in with an armful of stun-pistols in various stages of discharge. Vash briskly broke the butt of one of his own and presented it to the terminals he'd used the day before. Again, the open port of the stun pistol accepted an arch that gave semblance to that of a Tesla coil.

Looking in the direction of the redheaded man, *"He's not to touch anything, Bazil."* said Vash. *"I suspect that call's been coming in all night. Something was patrolling the skies at sundown. You closed up shop and went home early, eh?"*

"Why wouldn't I?" rasped the redheaded man. *"This is Toffpoint, there's only one ship a month that ever comes through here!"*

"Sometimes," said Vash as he cracked open another stun pistol, *"there are specials. But I commend your negligence. It was probably a good thing for us that you did."*

He finished the charge on that pistol, and snapped its butt shut, and snapped open another, and charged it. There was no difficulty, of course. In minutes all the pistols he'd brought from Nemo Vesta were ready for use again.

He tucked away as many as he could conveniently carry on his person. He handed the rest to Bazil. He went competently to the pulsing call-signal. He put headphones to his ears and listened. His expression became extremely strange, as if he did not quite understand nor wholly believe what he had heard.

"How odd," he said mildly. He considered for a moment or two then he rummaged around in the drawers of the desks. He found wire clips. He began to snip wires in half.

The redheaded man started forward automatically to defend the materials that Vash was seemingly destroying.

"Take care of him, Bazil," said Vash.

He cut the microwave receiver free of its wires and cables. He lifted it experimentally and opened part of its case to make sure the thermo battery that would power it in an emergency was there and in working order. He was relieved to find that it was.

"Here Bazil, put this on a horse," commanded Vash. *"We're taking it up to the Lord Fairbeard's castle with us."*

The redheaded man's mouth dropped open as he said stridently:

"Hey! You can't do that!" Vash turned to him and said sourly: *"Why not, it's not like you don't have more of these stacked away in those hard cases that we passed on our way in here."*

"You can build another in a week," said Vash kindly. *"You must have spare parts around here."*

Bazil carried the dismantled communicator outside. Vash opened a cabinet, threw switches, and painstakingly cut and snipped and snipped at a tangle of wires within.

"Look, it's just your instrumentation," he explained to the now appalled redheaded man. *"You won't be able to use the grid until you've got this fixed, too. A few days of harder work than you're used to. That's all!"*

He led the way out again, and on the way explained to Adeline:

"Pretty old-fashioned job, this grid. They make simpler ones nowadays. They'll be able to repair it, though, in time. Now we go back to your father's castle. He may not be pleased, but he should be somewhat mollified when he sees that you are safe."

He saw Adeline mount lightly into her own saddle and shook his head gloomily as he climbed clumsily into his own. They moved off to return to Fairbeard's stronghold with Vash feeling every blister the entire way, now exacerbated by fatigue.

They reached the castle before rising dawn of the third day, and the entire troop was worn and tired, but the sight of the Lady Adeline riding beside a worn-out Vash was paramount for cheers of enthusiasm from the group as they came upon the gate. The loot displayed by the returned wayfarers increased the rejoicing of those on the battlement walls. There was envy among the men who had stayed behind. There were respectfully admiring looks cast upon Vash. He had displayed, in furnishing opportunities for plunder, the most-admired quality a leader of feudal fighting men could show.

The Lady Adeline beamed as she, Bazil and Vash, all very dusty and travel-stained, presented themselves to her father in the castle's great hall.

"Here's your daughter, sir," said Vash with a yawn. *"I hope there won't be any further trouble with Seymour. We took his castle and looted it a little and brought back some extra horses. Then we went to the sky port. I recharged all of the stun-pistols and put the landing grid out of order for the time being. I brought with us the communicator from there."* He yawned again. *"There's something highly improper going on, up just beyond the atmosphere. We counted three Aeronef vessels up there patrolling, and they were trying to call the sky port in a non-regulation fashion, and it's possible that some of your neighbors might be interested. So, I postponed their plans until I could get some sleep. It seemed to me that when skullduggeries are concocted, that the good Lord Fairbeard and his associates ought to be the one concocting them, don't you agree?"* Vash looked at Fairbeard. *"so now, if you'll excuse me—"*

He moved away, practically dead on his feet. If he had been accustomed to horseback riding, he wouldn't have been so exhausted. But, as it were, the horseback ride was an added extra that took the life out of Vash and Bazil took him to his room. This time, the room was quite different from the "guest room" dungeon to which he'd been taken just two nights before. He noted that the door, this time, opened inward. He braced chairs against it to make sure that nobody could open it from without. He lay down and slept heavily, deeper than he had slept since the supply ship ride he had taken from Nemo Vesta.

He was awakened by loud poundings. He roused himself enough to say sleepily:

"Whaddyawant? State your business."

"The lights in the sky!" cried Adeline's voice outside the door. *"The ones you say are sky marshals! It's sunset again, and I just saw them again, but there aren't three now. Now there are nine!"*

"All right," said Vash. He lay down his head again and thrust it into his pillow. Then he was suddenly very wide-awake indeed. He sat up with a start.

"Nine spaceships? That wasn't possible!" He thought to himself. That would be an entire fleet! And there were no fleet ports around! Nemo Vesta would certainly have never sent more than one ship to demand his surrender to the marshals. The Sky Marshal Patrol never needed more than three ships anywhere, even in dealings with his grandfather. Commerce wouldn't cause ships to travel in company. Piracy? No, they couldn't be a pirate fleet! There'd never be enough loot anywhere to keep it in operation. Nine Aeronef vessels at one time—traveling in a patrol pattern around a non-commercial colony like Toffpoint just didn't make since.

It couldn't happen! Vash couldn't conceive of such a thing. But a recently developed pessimism suggested that since everything else, to date, had been to his disadvantage, that this, too, was probably a catastrophe in the making. Again, Vash snarled at the belief that he was fate's personal pet project.

He groaned and lay down to try and sleep again.

Chapter 6

When frantic banging on his propped-shut door awakened him later that morning, he, being half-dazed, imagined that they were noises in the communicator headphones, and until he heard his name called tried drearily to make sense of them.

But suddenly he opened his eyes. Somebody banged on the door once more. A voice cried angrily:

"Vash Rayburn! Wake up or I'll go away and let whatever happens to you happen! Wake up now!"

Again, it was the voice of the Lady Adeline, at once indignant and tearful and solicitous and angry all at once.

He rolled out of bed and reached for his clothes only to find that he had been so tired he never undressed, but fell fast asleep upon reaching his room. He hadn't slept the full night though. One time he woke for thinking about the sounds in the communicator when he listened at the sky port. He recalled distinctly hearing a Nemo Vestaian voice, speaking communications speech with crisp distinctness, calling the landing grid. The other voices, however were not natives of Nemo Vesta and made him dizzy trying to figure them out. He'd gone back to sleep while he tried to make sense of things. Now, long after daybreak, he shook himself and made sure a stun-pistol was handy. Then he said:

"Hello. I'm awake. What's up? Why all the noise?"

"Come out of there!" cried Adeline's voice, simultaneously exasperated and filled with anxiety. *"Things are happening! Somebody's here from Nemo Vesta! They are demanding to speak with you!"*

Vash could not believe it. It was too unlikely. But he opened the door and Bazil came in with Adeline following close behind.

"Good morning," said Vash automatically.

Bazil said mournfully:

"No, it's a bad morning, Vash Rayburn! A bad morning indeed! Men from Nemo Vesta came riding over the hills—"

"How many?" asked Vash.

"Two," said Adeline angrily. *"A fat man in a uniform, and a young man who looks like he wants to cry. They had an escort of retainers from one of my father's neighbors. They were stopped at the gate, of course, and they sent a written message in to my father, and he had them brought inside right away!"*

Vash shook his head.

"They probably said that I'm a criminal and that I should be sent back to Nemo Vesta. How'd they get down? The landing grid isn't working."

Adeline said viciously: *"They landed in something that burned aether. It came down close to a castle over that way—only six or seven miles from the sky port. They asked for you. They said you'd have landed from the last liner from Nemo Vesta. And because you and Bazil fought so splendidly—why, everybody's talking about you. So, the chieftain over there accepted a present of money from them, and gave them horses as a return gift, and sent them here with a guard. Bazil talked to the guards. The men from Nemo Vesta have promised huge gifts of money if they help take you back to the contraption that burned aether."*

"I suspect," muttered Vash, *"that they came down in a lifeboat. Hm-m-m.... Yes. With a built-in tool-steel cell to keep me from telling anybody how to make—"* He stopped and grimaced. *"If they had time to build one onboard, that's certainly what they would have done! They'd take me to the sky port in a sound-proofed can and I'd be hauled back to Nemo Vesta in it!"*

"What are you going to do?" asked Adeline anxiously.

Vash didn't make his ideas clear to the others, but Toffpoint was obviously not a healthy place for him. It was extremely likely, for example, that the honorable Emory Demetrius Fairbeard, lord of this and baron of that, though holding better feelings now for the rescue of his daughter, could still not be counted on as an ally and definitely not a warm personal friend that he could rely on.

On the other hand, the social system of Toffpoint did not look favorable toward a stranger with an already lurid reputation for fighting, so that would also be a strike against him.

As a practical matter, his best bet was probably to investigate the nine inexplicable ships overhead. They hadn't co-operated with the Nemo Vesta authorities. It could be inferred that no confidential relationship existed up there. It was possible that the nine ships and the Nemo Vestaians didn't even know of each other's presence. There is a lot of room in the sky. If both called on ship-frequency and listened on ground-frequency, they would not have picked up each other's summons to the ground.

"You've got to do something!" insisted Adeline. *"I saw Father talking to them! He looked happy, and he never looks happy unless he's planning some level of skullduggery!"*

"I believe," said Vash, *"that I'll have some breakfast, if I may. As soon as I fasten up my ruck sack."*

Bazil said mournfully: *"If anything happens to you, something will happen to me too, because I helped you."*

"Breakfast first," said Vash. *"That, as I understand it, should make it disgraceful for your father to have my throat cut. But beyond that—"* he said gloomily. *"Bazil, get a couple of horses outside the wall. We may need to ride somewhere. I'm very much afraid we will. But first I'd like to have some breakfast. I am tired of plotting on an empty stomach."*

Adeline said somewhat disappointedly: *"But aren't you going to face them; the men from Nemo Vesta? You could shoot them!"*

Vash just shook his head.

"It wouldn't solve anything. Anyhow a practical man such as your father won't sell me out before he's sure that I can't make a better pay off. I'll bet he will set up a conference with me before he makes a final deal with them."

Adeline stamped her foot at him.

"Outrageous! Think what you saved me from!"

But she did not question the possibility. Vash observed:

"A practical man can always make what he wants to do look like a noble sacrifice of personal inclinations to the welfare of the community. I've decided that I've got to be practical myself, and that's one of the rules, so how about breakfast?"

He strapped the ruck sack shut on the stun-pistols his pockets would not hold. He made a minor adjustment to the communicator that he had 'barrowed' from the sky port. It was not ruined, but nobody else could use it without much labor finding out what he'd done to it exactly. This was the sort of thing his grandfather on Gibbit Cove would have advised.

His grandfather's views were explicit.

"Helping one's neighbor," he'd said frequently to Vash in his youth, *"is all right as a two-way job. But maybe he's laying for you. You get a chance to fix him so he can't do you any harm and you're a lot better off and he also becomes a lot better neighbor!"*

This was definitely true of the men from Nemo Vesta. Vash guessed that Derk was one of them. The other would represent the police or the intercolonial government. It was probably just as true of Fairbeard and others.

Vash found himself disapproving of the way that fate had designed his life. Even though presently he sat at breakfast high up on the battlements, and Adeline looked at him with interesting anxiety, he was filled with forebodings. The future looked dark. Yet what he asked of fate and chance was so simple! He asked only a career and riches and a delightful girl to marry as well as the admiration of his fellow-citizens. Trivial things! But it looked like he'd have to do battle for even such minor gifts of destiny!

Adeline watched him as he ate his breakfast.

"I don't understand you," she complained. *"Anybody else would be proud of what he'd done and angry with my father. Or don't you think he'll act ungratefully?"*

"Of course, I do!" said Vash, "*but I'm hungry,"*

"And you take it for granted that I want to be properly grateful," Adeline exclaimed, *"and yet you haven't shown the least appreciation of my getting two horses over in that patch of woodland yonder"*—she pointed and Vash nodded as he continued

to eat—*"and having Bazil there with orders to serve you faithfully—"*

She stopped short. Her father appeared, beaming, at the top of the steps leading here from the great hall where the conferences took place. He regarded Vash rather benignly.

"This is a very bad business that you are in, my dear fellow," he said benevolently. *"Has my daughter told you of the visitors who arrived from Nemo Vesta in search of you? They told me many terrible things about you!"*

"Yes," said Vash as he prepared another roll for eating. He said: *"One of them, I think, is named Derk. He's to identify me so good money isn't wasted paying for the wrong man. The other man's an officer of Nemo Vesta, isn't he?"* He reflected a moment. *"If I were you, I'd start talking at a million credits. You might get them to fork over half that."*

He bit into the roll as Lord Fairbeard looked at him in shock and amazement.

"Do you think," he asked indignantly, *"that I would give up the rescuer of my daughter to emissaries from another colony, to be locked in a dungeon for life?"*

"I wouldn't have put it in those words," conceded Vash. *"But after all, despite your deep gratitude to me, there are such things as one's duty to humanity as a whole. And while it would cause you bitter anguish if someone dear to you represented a danger to millions of innocent women and children—still, under such circumstances you might feel it necessary to wage a battle against your own emotions for the greater good."*

Fairbeard looked at him with abrupt suspicion. Vash then waved the roll as if physically trying to formulate a sentence.

"Moreover," he continued, *"gratitude for actions done on Toffpoint does not entitle you to judge my actions on other colonies. While you might and even should feel obliged to defend me in all things that I have accomplished on Toffpoint, your obligation to me does not let you deny that I may have acted less defensibly elsewhere."*

Fairbeard looked extremely uneasy as Vash continued to paint reason that he should make a deal with the visitors.

"I may have thought something of sorts in all honesty," he admitted. *"But—"*

"So then," interrupted Vash, *"while your debt to me cannot and should not be overlooked, nevertheless"*—Vash put the roll into his mouth and spoke less clearly—*"you feel that you should give consideration to the claims of those from Nemo Vesta to inquire into my actions while there."*

He chewed, and swallowed, and then said gravely:

"And the question must be asked for safety's sake, can I make death rays?"

Fairbeard's face brightened. He drew a deep breath of relief. He said in the form of a slighted complaint:

"I don't see why you have to be so sarcastic about the matter! Yes. That is a rather important question. You see, on Nemo Vesta they don't know how to. They say you do. They're very anxious that nobody should be able to. But while in unscrupulous hands such an instrument of destruction would be most unfortunate ... ah ... under proper control however—"

"Yours," interrupted Vash once again.

" Let's say—ours for argument's sake," said Fairbeard hopefully. *"With my experience of men and affairs, and my loyal and devoted retainers—"*

"And cozy dungeons," said Vash with a scrupulous expression. He wiped his mouth. *"No."*

Fairbeard started violently.

"No, what?"

"No death rays," said Vash. *"I can't make 'em. Nobody can. If they could be made, some power-hungry dictator somewhere would be turning them out, or some natural phenomenon would let them loose from time to time. If there were such things as death rays, all living things would have died, or else would have adjusted to their weaker manifestations and developed immunity so they would no longer be death rays. As a matter of fact, that's probably been the case, sometime in the past. So far as the gadget goes that they're talking about, it's been in use for half a century in the Cetus Colony. Nobody's died of it yet."*

Fairbeard looked bitterly disappointed.

"That's the truth?" he asked unhappily. *"Honestly? That's your last word on it?"*

"Much ado about nothing I am afraid," said Vash, *"as much as I hate to spoil the prospects of profitable skullduggery on your part, that's my last word and it's true."*

"But those men from Nemo Vesta are very anxious!" protested Fairbeard. *"There was no ship available, so their government got an airliner that normally wouldn't stop here to take an extra lifeboat aboard. It circled Toffpoint and then let out the lifeboat, and went on its way again. Those two men are extremely anxious—"*

"Ambitious, maybe," said Vash. *"But they're prepared to pay to overcome your sense of gratitude to me. Naturally, you want all that this traffic will bear. I think you can get half a million."*

Fairbeard, once again, looked suspiciously at Vash.

"You don't seem too worried about the situation in front of you," he said fretfully. *"I don't understand you at all!"*

"Ahhhh, see, I have a secret," said Vash.

Fairbeard looked at him curiously; *"What is it?"*

"Not now, it will develop in time," said Vash, popping the last piece of a roll in his mouth...

His majesty of so many things on Toffpoint was taken back and hesitated, tempted to speak further on the topic, but then thought better of it. He shrugged his shoulders and went slowly back to the flight of stone steps. As he descended, leaving Vash to finish his breakfast, the Lady Adeline started ringing her hands with worry, but then she asked with a slight tone of hopefulness:

"What's your secret?"

"That your father thinks I have one," said Vash. *"Thanks for the breakfast. Should I walk out the gate, or—"*

"It's closed," said the Lady Adeline forlornly. *"But I did manage to have a rope for you. You can go down over the wall."*

"Thanks," said Vash. *"It was truly a pleasure to rescue such an amazing and captivating young lady as yourself. The blisters were worth it."*

"Will you—" Adeline hesitated. *"I've never known anybody like you before. Will you ever come back? Will I— Will we ever see you again?"*

Vash shook his head at her.

"Once you asked me if I'd fight for you, and look what it got me into! To stay would only insure more of the same, I fear."

He glanced down along the battlements. There was a fairly large coil of rope in view. He picked up his bag and went over to it. He checked the fastening of one end and tumbled the other over the wall.

Ten minutes later he was trudging up to Bazil who had been waiting in a nearby wooded area with two horses.

"The Lady Adeline," he said, *"has the kind of brains I like. She pulled up the rope and placed it out of sight after I descended, so as not to draw attention to the escape."*

Bazil did not comment. He simply watched in blank silence as Vash fastened his ruck sack to the horse and mounted.

"What are you going to do now?" asked Bazil unhappily. *"I didn't give a parting-present to Lord Emory Fairbeard before leaving my retainership, so I'll be disgraced if he finds out I helped you. And I don't know where to take you."*

"Where," asked Vash, *"did those characters from Nemo Vesta come down?"*

Bazil told him. *"At the castle of a considerable feudal chieftain, on the plain some four miles from the mountain range and six miles this side of the sky port."*

"Then that is where we ride to," said Vash. *"A man once said that Liberty is sweet, but the man who said that obviously didn't gain his with blisters from a saddle. Let's ride."*

They rode away post haste. There would be no immediate pursuit, and possibly none at all. Fairbeard had left Vash at breakfast on the battlements. The Lady Adeline would make as much confusion over his disappearance as she could. But in any case, there'd be no search for him until after Fairbeard had made his deal with the two men from the lifeboat.

Vash was sure that Adeline's father would have an enjoyable morning. He would relish the bargaining session. He'd explain in great detail how valuable had been Vash's service to him, in rescuing Adeline from an abductor who would have been an intolerable son-in-law. He'd grow almost tearful as he described his affection for Vash as the son he never had—how he loved his daughter—as he observed aggrievedly that they were asking him to betray the man who had saved for him the solace of his old age. He would mention also that the price they offered was an affront to his paternal affection and his dignity as prince of this, baron of that, lord of the other thing and claimant to the dukedom of something-or-other. Either they'd come up with what he asked or the deal was off!

But meanwhile Vash and Bazil rode industriously toward the place from which those emissaries had come.

All was tranquil. All was calm. Once they saw a dust cloud, and Bazil turned aside to a providential wooded copse of Birch and high undergrowth, in which they laid low while a cavalcade from the Chieftain's castle went by. Bazil explained that it was a feudal chieftain on his way to the sky port town. *"It's not for fear of capture, mind you, that I think it's best to lay low as they pass"* He directed at Vash as he watched them ride by, *"but simple discretion for us not to be observed."* He loosened his tense stance as the clan of riders past, *"...because we now have reputations as great fighting men. Whoever defeats us would surely become prominent at once. So, somebody might try to pick a quarrel under one of the finer points of etiquette when it would be disgrace to use anything but standard Toffpointian implements for massacre."* Vash nodded his head in agreement, silently admitting to Bazil that he did not feel quarrelsome right at that particular moment.

They rode on after a time, and in late afternoon the towers and battlements of the castle they sought appeared on the horizon. The ground here was only gently rolling, covered with yellow furrows of wheat crop ready for harvesting. They approached it with caution, following the reverse slope of hills, and dry streambeds, and at last penetrating horse-high brush to the point where the castle gates were clearly in view.

If Vash had been a student of early terrestrial history, he might have remarked upon the re-emergence of ancient architectural forms to match the revival of primitive social systems. As it was, he noted in this feudal castle the use of bastions for flanking fire upon attackers, he recognized the value of battlements for the protection of defenders while allowing them to shoot, and the tricky positioning of sally ports. He even grasped the reason for the massive, stark, unornamented keep. But his eyes did not stay on the castle for long. He saw the lifeboat in which Derk and his more authoritative companion had arrived.

It lay on the ground a half-mile from the castle walls. It was a clumsy, obese, flattened shape some forty feet long and nearly fifteen feet wide. The ground about it was scorched where it had descended using its rocket flames. There were several horses tethered near it, and men who were plainly retainers of the nearby castle reposed in its shade.

Vash reined in his horse as he leaned in to face Bazil.

"Here we part," he told Bazil. *"When we first met, I enabled you to pick the pockets of a good many of your fellow-countrymen. I never asked for my split of the take. I expect you to remember me with affection."*

Bazil clasped both of Vash's hands in his own.

"If you should ever return," he said with mournful warmth, *"Do not look at me as a retainer for I am your friend!"*

Vash nodded and rode out of the brushwood toward the lifeboat which had landed the emissaries that would very soon, be finding out the news that he was no longer under the protection of the Lord Fairbeard.

The fact that the lifeboat had touched down so close to the sky port, of course, was no accident. It was plainly obvious that they knew Vash had taken sky passage to Toffpoint. He had only landed but two days prior before his pursuers could realize and then get passage themselves that distance. And on a more primitive colony such as Toffpoint, he couldn't have gotten too far from the sky port. So, his pursuers, aware of this, would have landed close by, as well.

It must have taken considerable courage on their part to land at all when the landing grid failed to answer their communication, it must have seemed likely that Vash's death rays had been hard at work.

At present, Vash remained casual and unassuming as his horse made slow gait of reaching his destination. He knew that he had been seen from a distance and was being watched without much apprehension by the loafing guards about the boat. He looked hot and thirsty which was an easy performance for him to do since he was, in fact, both. The posted guard merely looked at him without too much interest when he brought his dusty mount up under the shadow the lifeboat cast, and apparently decided that there wasn't room to get into it.

He grunted a greeting and looked at them speculatively.

"Those two characters from Nemo Vesta," he observed, *"sent me to get something from this thing, here. Lord Emory Fairbeard told 'em I was a very honest man."*

After a moment there were responsive grins. *"If there's anything missing when I start back,"* said Vash, *"I can't imagine how it happened! None of you would take anything. Oh, no! I bet you'll blame it on me!"* He shook his head and said *"pity."*

One of the guards sat up and said unappreciatively toward the insinuation that they themselves were dishonest:

"But it's locked up good and tight."

"Being an honest man," said Vash amiably, *"of course they told me how to unlock it."*

He got off his horse, removed the bag from his saddle, then went into the cool welcoming shadow of the metal hull. He then paused and mopped his face with a handkerchief that he removed from his breast pocket and made his way to the entrance port of the lifeboat. He put his hand on the turning bar. Then he painstakingly pushed in the locking-stud with his other hand.

Of course, knowing how these lifeboats like the back of his hand, the handle turned. The boat port opened. The two from Nemo

Vesta, not knowing the culture of Toffpoint, would have thought everything safe because it was under guard. On Nemo Vesta, that protection would have been enough. On Toffpoint however, the only reason the lifeboat had not been looted was simply because the guards did not understand that the locks were made with separate vibration-checks to keep vibrations from take offs and landings from loosening them, leaving the men to think that the port was locked.

"Give me two minutes," said Vash over his shoulder. *"I have to get what they sent me for. After that everybody starts even."* Knowing that they would do exactly what he had made accusation of.

He entered and closed the door behind him. Then he locked it. By the nature of things, it is as needful to be able to lock a lifeboat from the inside, as it is unnecessary to lock it from without.

He looked things over; standard equipment everywhere. He checked everything, even to the fuel supply. There were knockings on the port. He continued to inspect. He turned on the vision screens, which provided the control room—indeed, all the boat—with an unobstructed view in all directions. He was satisfied.

The knocks became bangings. Something approaching indignation could be deduced. The guards around the lifeboat felt that Vash was taking an unfair amount of time to pick the cream of the loot inside.

He got a glass of water. It was excellent; how he missed the sterile water of Nemo Vesta. Being a sky city, the water was collected from surrounding vapor condensers placed directly in surrounding clouds, untouched by contaminants of any type.

The bangings became violent hammerings now.

Vash seated himself leisurely in the pilot's seat and turned small knobs. He waited. He touched a button. There was a mildly thunderous bang outside, and the lifeboat reacted as if to a slight shock. The visionscreens showed a cloud of dust at the lifeboat's stern, which was roused by a deliberate explosion in the rocket tubes. It also showed the retainers in full flight, going in every direction.

Not wishing to harm anyone unnecessarily, Vash cordially waited until they were safe from the blast zone and made the standard take-off preparations. With the maneuverings of a few more knobs and switches, there came a horrific roaring outside. He touched controls and a monstrous weight pushed him back in his seat. The rocket swung, and lifted, and shot skyward with greater acceleration than before.

It went up at a lifeboat's full rate of climb, leaving a trail of blue-white flame behind it. All the surface of Toffpoint seemed to contract swiftly below him. The sky port and the town quickly shrank into a spot beneath the sky boat's tail.

They shrank and shrank. He saw other places. Mountains. Castles. He saw Fairbeard's stronghold and comically waves as if he were saying good bye to the two men sent to take him back. Higher, he saw the sea.

The sky turned purple. Almost in the outer orbit where the stellar stations keep ever vigilant for future anomalies, Vash swung to a westward course and continued to hold a steady orbit, watching the seascapes and bits of land move by as they shifted on the surrounding visionscreens. The rockets continued to roar, though in a minor fashion.

Vash, not completely familiar with all of the gauges, made use of those rule-of-thumb methods of astrogation, which his piratical forebearers had developed, which boys on Gibbit Cove absorbed without being aware.

Presently, feeling confident that he was in a good position, he relaxed. He sped swiftly back past midday and toward the sunrise line.

He turned on the communicator. Its reception-indicator was piously placed at "Ground." He shifted it to "Air," so that it would pick up calls going upward, instead of listening vainly for replies from the now non-operative landing grid he had previously disabled.

Instantly voices boomed in his ears. Many voices. An impossibly large number of voices now made it obvious that there were more than the nine ships previously counted.

"Idiot!" said a voice in quiet passion, *"sheer off or you'll get in our drive-field!"* A high-pitched voice said; *"... And group two take second-orbit position—"* Somebody bellowed: *"But why don't they*

answer?" Said yet another voice formally: *"Reporting group five, but four ships are staying behind with sky tanker Maelstrom, which is having some stabilizer trouble...."*

Vash's eyes opened very wide. He turned down the sound while he tried to think. But there wasn't anything to think. He'd come aloft to scout three ships that had turned to nine, because he was in such a fix on Toffpoint that anything strange might be changed into something useful. But this was more than nine vessels—itself an impossibly large fleet. There was no reason why this many flying vessels should ever travel together. There were innumerable reasons why they shouldn't. There was a limit to the number of ships that could be accommodated at any one sky port in any area of the planet, sky ground or sea. There was no point, no profit, no purpose in a number of ships traveling together—

The lightening of the horizon appeared far ahead. The lifeboat would soon cease to be a bright light in the sky, now. The boat went hurtling onward towards the horizon, just hiding in the shadows of dawn.

Vash could still hear the voices squabbling, and wrangling, with the occasional superior admonishing disputants to a proper discipline of radio protocol.

During the period of early dawn, Vash racked his brains for the vaguest of ideas on why so many ships should appear about an obscure and unimportant colony like Toffpoint.

Presently as the sun appeared ahead, far away he saw moving reflections of the sun's rays, which were the hulls of the rather volubly communicating vessels. He stared, blankly with his mouth open wide at the spectacle. There were tens, no scores. He was forced to guess at the stark impossibility of more than a hundred crafts in view. As the boat rushed onward, he had to raise the guess. It couldn't be, but—

He turned on the lifeboat's outside telescopic visionscreen, and the image on its screen was more incredible than the voices and the existence of the fleet itself. The scope focused first on a bulging, monster, antiquated freighter of a design that, in his years of living on a pirate colony and seeing every vessel ever created, had never seen before except that of history screens.

The second view was of, what appeared to be a passenger liner with the elaborate ornamentation that in past generations might have been considered suitable for royal travel. There was a bulk-cargo ship, with no emergency rockets at all and crews' quarters in long blisters built outside the gigantic tank, which was the ship itself. There was a needle-sharp Dirigible yacht that caught Vash's fancy right quick. There were more freighters, with streaks of rust on their sides where they had lain aground for some time, as well as other lifeboats and independent transport congesting the skies.

The fleet was an anomaly, and each of its component parts were separately a freak of flying scrap. It was a gathering-together of antique, outmoded and obsolete hulks as well as monstrosities of past sky travel. Vash wondered how many of these relics had actually survived the flooding. One would have to scavenge half the entire planet to bring together so many crazy, over-age derelicts that should have been in junkyards or the bottom of the seas.

Then Vash drew an explosively deep breath. It was suddenly clear what the fleet was and what its reason must be. Why it stopped here could not yet be guessed, but—

Vash watched absorbed in the enormity of the fleet. He had no idea what this was all about, but there was some emergency afoot. It could be in the line of what a mechanical engineer could handle. If so—why—it could mean an opportunity to accomplish great things, grow rich, and probably marry some delightful girl and be a great man somewhere—an assortment of ambitions one could obviously not easily gratify on Gibbit Cove, or Nemo Vesta, or Toffpoint.

Chapter 7

The lifeboat hovered forward as if on a deliberate collision course with the arriving fleet. That would not mean, of course, actual contact with any of the goliath vessels themselves. It was more than likely that even with ten-mile intervals the ships would be considered much too crowded. But they came pouring out of emptiness to go into a swirling, plainly pre-intended orbit about the sky above Toffpoint from which Vash had risen less than an hour before.

There was an inevitable confusion, though, and the communicator proved it. There were disputes between freakish ships, when crafted with the astrogational qualities of washtubs, tried to keep assigned positions and failed, and there were squabbles when ships had to pass close together. One had to shut off its turbines to keep from blowing the other off of its designation orbit.

But there were some ships, which proceeded quietly to their positions, and others, which did the same after tumult amounting to mutiny and rebellion. And naturally there were a few others, which seemed incapable of co-operation with anybody. They went careening through the other ships' paths causing great unrest among those trying to keep the vessels aloft.

It was a gigantic traffic entanglement, and Vash's boat drifted right toward it. He'd counted a hundred ships before, but now his count now passed two hundred and continued. Before he gave up he'd numbered two hundred forty-seven antiquated dirigibles, sky liners, air tankers and even a Dreadnought or two, among others, swarming to make a whirling band—an attempt at what some might call a Dyson Sphere—around the Toffpoint skyline.

He was fairly sure that he knew what they were now, but he could not possibly guess where they came from or why. Most mysterious of all was the question of how did they all manifest so quickly to make of themselves a celestial feature in the outer orbit just over a land-based colony which had practically nothing to offer to anyone.

Presently the lifeboat was in the very thick of the fleet. His communicator spouted voices whose tones ranged from bass to high tenor, and whose ideas of proper astrogation seemed to vary more widely still.

"You there!" boomed a voice with deafening volume. *"You're in our clear-space! Sheer off! Sheer toward your port now!"*

The volume of a signal in the upper ionosphere varies as the square of the distance from that which is transmitting and this voice was thunderous. It came apparently from a nearby, pot-bellied Flocking of a very ancient empire vintage. Rows of ports in its sides had been welded over. It had rocket tubes whose size was indicative of the kind of long-obsolete fuel on which it once had operated. More slender nozzles now peered out where the originals had once been connected. It had been adapted to modern propellants by simply welding more modern rockets inside the old fittings. It was less than a half a mile away from Vash's vessel.

Vash's lifeboat floated on. The relative position of the two ships changed slowly. Another voice said indignantly:

"That's the same thing that missed us by less than a mile! You, there! Stop acting like a suicidal squib! Get on your own course!"

A third voice soon range out; *"What boat's that? I don't recognize it! I thought I knew all the freaks in this fleet!"*

Still yet, a fourth voice said sharply: *"That's not one of us! Look at the design! That's not us!"*

Other voices quickly broke in. There was babbling. Then a harsh voice roared:

"Quiet! I order all of you to be quiet!" There was instant silence. The harsh voice said heavily, *"Relay the image to me."* There was a pause. The same voice said grimly: *"It is not of our fleet."* Immediately, the voice boomed out an order directed at Vash's vessel. *"You, stranger! Identify yourself! Who are you and why are you trying to slip secretly among us?"*

Vash, now fully aware that he is being monitored, pushed the transmit button.

"My name is Vash Rayburn," he said. *"I came up to find out why three ships, and then nine ships, went into orbit around Toffpoint. It was somewhat alarming. Our landing grid's disabled, anyhow, and it seemed wisest to look you over before we communicated and*

possibly told you something you might not believe. But you surely don't expect to land all this fleet! For in actuality, you can't land any at the current moment."

The harsh voice said in an even grimmer voice than before: *"You come from the colony below us? It's called Toffpoint? Why is your ship so small? The smallest of ours is greater than that coffin that you are in."*

"This is generally referred to as a lifeboat, sir." said Vash pleasantly. *"It's supposed to be carried on larger ships in case of emergency."*

"If you will make your way to our lead ship," said the voice, *"we will answer all your questions. I will have a smoke flare set off to guide you."*

Vash thought to himself: *"No threats and no offers. I can guess why there are no threats. But they should offer something!"*

He waited. There was a sudden huge eruption of vapor in the upper atmosphere that could have easily been some twenty miles away due to the obstacle course of flying antiquities that lay between him and the beckoning ship. Perhaps an ounce of explosive had been introduced into a rocket tube and fired. The smoke particles, naturally ionized, added their self-repulsion to the expansiveness of the explosive's gases. A cauliflower like shape of filmy whiteness appeared and grew larger then thinner as it dissipated.

Vash drove toward the spot with very light touches of rocket power. He swung the boat around and killed its relative velocity. The lead ship was a sort of gigantic, shapeless, utterly preposterous ark-like thing. Vash could neither imagine a purpose for which it could have been used, nor a time when men would have built anything like it. Its huge sides seemed to be made exclusively of great doorways now tightly closed.

One of the doorways suddenly gaped wide with the churning of large gears. It would have admitted a good-sized modern ship. A nervous voice essayed to give Vash directions for getting the minuscule lifeboat inside what was plainly an enormous hold now pumped empty of air. He grunted and made the attempt. It was tricky. He sweated when he cut off his power. But he felt fairly safe. Rocket flames would burn down such a door, if necessary. He could wreak havoc if hostilities began.

The great cargo door swung shut behind him as he volleyed his vessel to a station inside the antique behemoth. The outside-pressure needle swung sharply up and stopped at thirty-five centimeters of mercury pressure as the breathable air refilled the bay. There was a clanging. A smaller door evidently opened somewhere. Lights came on; the old-fashioned glow tube style. Then figures appeared through a door leading to some other part of this ship.

Vash nodded to himself. The costume was odd. It was awkward. It was even primitive by the current standards of preening and fashion, but not in the fashion of the soiled but gaudily colored garments of Toffpoint. These men wore the opposite, unrelieved black, with gray shirts. There was no touch of color about them except the single scarlet band around their left arms. Even the younger ones were indistinguishable from a distance. And of all unnecessary things, they wore visored helmet—inside of the ship as if ready for an eminent crash.

Vash opened the boat door and said politely: *"Good morning. I'm Vash Rayburn. You were talking to me just now."*

The oldest and most fiercely bearded of the men said harshly:

"I am the leader of this fleet. We are the people of Ivoryhelm." He frowned when Vash's expression remained unchanged. *"The people of Ivoryhelm!"* he repeated more loudly. *"The people whose forefathers created the flying and floating cities and helped to re-colonize this planet after the flooding, and brought it back to a livable society before the independent power of feudalism took over and everyone decided to create their own independent systems of governance!"*

"Too bad," said Vash. He felt that he knew what these people were doing, and giving background of who they were told him nothing to solidify in his mind of what they wanted with Toffpoint.

"It was originally a fair world," said the bearded man fiercely. *"But it was my brother who destroyed it. He believed that we should share power. It was he who persuaded the intercolonial*

council to allow each colony to govern itself, believing that they would all live under the same rules and standards."

Vash nodded expectantly. These people were in some sort of trouble or they wouldn't have made themselves known so abruptly. But they'd talked about it until it had become an emotionalized obsession that couldn't be summarized. When they encountered a stranger, they had to picture their predicament passionately and at length as to how they would address the situation.

The bearded man looked at Vash with burning eyes. When he went on, it was with gestures as if he were making a heartened speech to a large crowd; it was a special sort of speech that warranted expressiveness. His first sentence told what type of speech it was to be.

"Each leader clung to his own sins and vices!" said the bearded man bitterly. *"They did not adopt our ways! Our example went for naught! They brought in their cultures and beliefs and discarded the protections afforded through assimilation. After a little they laughed at us as they flaunted their cultural differences, the very differences that had left their original societies in ruin after the flooding through poor development and planning; all the while condemning us as bigots if we spoke out against them or promoted assimilation over segregation. In a little more time, as the council allowed for more and more immigrants to settle in our society, they outnumbered us and we became the minority! Then, as they began to gain support for their causes through the effective use of cultural shaming through geopolitical and social norms manipulation, they ruled that the laws of Ivoryhelm should not govern them. And they lured many of our young people to imitate them—frivolous, sinful, riotous folk that they were!"*

Vash nodded again. He was reminded of elderly people on Gibbit Cove who spoke like this. Not his grandfather of course! If you listened long enough, they'd come to some point or other, but they had arranged their thoughts so solidly that any attempt to get quickly at their meaning would only produce confusion, so Vash patiently waited to receive the information that the man was trying to relay.

"Sixty years since," said the bearded man with an angry gesture, *"we finally made a bargain. We had held a third of all the new*

colonies on the planet that we had built, but our young men, through the steady bombardment of social shaming and geopolitical manipulations, were falling away from the ways of their fathers. We made a bargain with the interloper groups who abused our generosity, those whom we had cherished at one point and invited in with open arms. We would trade our lands, our sky cities, our floating colonies, and our civilization infrastructure, for the means to create flying vessels that would take us past the aether of this world. In the search for the ability to find another planet, we found something better, or worse, depending on your view; not a world, but an otherverse, a void in the aether that allows an object... a ship...us to pass in and out as easy as light through a pinhole in a sail."

Again, Vash had no reaction. Otherverse, the name meant nothing at present.

"We began to prepare," said the old man, his eyes fixed on Vash. *"Ten years since, we were ready. But we had to wait two more before the bargainers were ready to complete the trade that would allow us to finish our devices. Per their terms, they had to buy and collect the ships we would use. They would be responsible for acquiring the mechanisms used in the design and build of the machinery we would need. We would be responsible for collecting the food supplies and mainstay necessities needed."*

"One year ago, we received a good number of the ships promised, minus a couple that they said they compensated for with extra mechanical parts and survival gear, so we began moving our animals into the lower decks of the vessels, as well as our food and our furnishings, and took our places. Lastly, we loaded large crates with the mechanical devices needed to assemble the Ansiblary Resonance Modulation Units needed to take our fleet into the jump once we reached enough altitude to open a jump hole large enough without affecting the planet or its orbit; still concerned for those who took over our civilization, mind you. For months we have moved our fleet miles away from our homeland in order to find space open enough for the jump, during this time we journeyed in and out of this otherverse with an independent scout ship equipped with the smaller A. R. M. U., hoping to come out next to a new world that we could set up the New Ivoryhelm."

Vash felt an instinctive respect for people who would undertake such an arduous task of moving themselves, the third of the population of a planet, over a distance that meant, even if they could jump to their new location, as the old man said, they would still spend years rebuilding their new lives. They might have tastes in clothing that he did not share, and they might go in for elaborate oratory instead of matter-of-fact statements, but they had courage and that was appealing to Vash.

"Yes, sir," said Vash. *"I take it this brings us up to the present."*

"No," said the old man, his eyes beginning to flash with hot rage. *"two months ago we considered that we might well begin to train the vessel operators on how the devices worked, so that we could begin installing them into each vessel's power system. So, we uncrated the machines only to find that we had been cheated further by those who took over our property!"*

Vash found that he could make a fairly dispassionate guess of what had transpired simply because of his knowledge of people such as Jessica's father. For example, he would take great pleasures of people who would not check on his good faith for two years and until they were two years' journey away. The businessmen on Ivoryhelm would have had some sort of code to determine how completely one could swindle a customer. Even on a colony such as Gibbit Cove, there were codes of conduct, checks and balances, a time in which to check over the goods delivered...

"How badly were you cheated?" asked Vash, canceling the micro gesture of indignation he gazed upon the old man for taking someone at their word, especially someone who has already wronged them in the past.

"Of our lives!" said the angry old man. *"Do you know machinery?"*

"Some," admitted Vash, understating his abilities.

"Come," said the leader of the fleet.

With a sort of dignity that was theatrical only because he was aware of it, the leader of the people of Ivoryhelm showed the way. Vash had been admitted with his lifeboat into one of the gigantic cargo holds. He was now escorted to the next. It was packed tightly with cases of machinery. One huge crate had been opened and its contents fully disclosed. Others had been hacked at enough to show their contents.

The uncrated machine was a monstrosity of gears, gauges and tubes. It looked to be a powerful piece of equipment, which would be a site to behold if it, indeed worked. Such a machine would be a feat to build.

"We ran this for five minutes and it never gained any pressure before seizing," said the bearded man fiercely as Vash nodded approval. He lifted a side hood.

The steam engine boiler had been dried out and seal cracked. Worthless scrap metal at this point... Gears were splintered and smashed, low-grade metal castings, assembly bolts had separated from the housings and parted, resonance treads were bent and cracked and some of the geodode quartz fittings were missing. It was not really a machine at all except in shape. It was a mock-up in worthless materials, which probably cost its maker the twentieth of what was told.

Vash looked at the old man and felt the anger that any man feels when he sees betrayal of his honor in front of those who look up to him.

"It's not all like this, is it" he asked incredulously.

"Some are worse," said the old man, with mustered dignity and low tone. *"There are crates which are marked to contain turbines. Their contents are ancient, worn-out brick-making machines. There are crates marked to contain generators. They are filled with corroded irrigation pipe and broken castings. We have shiploads of crushed, rusted sheet-metal trimmings! We have been cheated of our lives!"*

Vash found himself sick with honest fury. The population of one-third of a planet, packed into a conclave of prehistoric air relics planning their voyage for years, would be appropriate subjects for sympathy at the best of times. Vash further found that when they tried to contact those who had duped them, they were responded with jeers and threats that if they came back, their vessels would be shot down to the depths of the seas.

Because of the size of the fleet, there was nowhere for the fleet to land. Many of these vessels were not equipped for water landing or maneuverings. The population of this undertaking was now starting to run low on supplies and no one was capable of taking all of them in. Because there was nowhere else that they could go, there was no new colony, which could absorb so many people, with only their bare hands for equipment to live by, there was no civilized, settled world that this patchwork or relics could make it too since none were outer-heavens worthy, which could admit so many paupers, there was nowhere for these people to go!

Vash's anger took on the feeling of guilt. He could do nothing, and something had to be done.

"Why ... why did you come to Toffpoint?" he asked. *"What can you gain by orbiting here? You can't expect—"*

The old man faced him.

"We are now diminished to beggars," he said with bitter dignity. *"We stopped here to ask for charity—the same charity we ask from all of the colonies that we have visited, donations for the old and worn-out machines the people of Toffpoint can spare us. We will be grateful for even a single rusty turbine. Because we have so many supplies that have gone and we are now perpetual nomads of the air, we have to go on. We can do nothing else. Our scout ship did find another planet; ironically two days after we made our discovery of deception and would have gone there immediately if not for the cheats that befell us. Since we do not have the materials or the capabilities of manufacturing the devices needed to open up a portal large enough, we are wonderers and one generator, a crate of grain, a cow still giving milk can mean that a few of us will live who otherwise would die with ... with the most of us."*

Vash removed his hat and ran his hand through his hair. This was not his trouble, but he could not thrust it from him.

"But again—why Toffpoint?" he asked helplessly. *"Why not stop at a world with riches to spare? Toffpoint's a poor place with barely the resources for itself."*

"Because we have found that it is the poor who are generous," said the bearded man with conviction in his voice. *"The rich might give us what they could spare; junk, discarded items and then send us on our way, but simple, people, close to the soil people, people who understand what it is to be without and to appreciate what you*

have, will give us from what they need themselves. They will share part of themselves with us, and accept a share of our need as their own. These are the people we trust."

Vash slowly paced up and down the ancient flooring of the cargo compartment of the ancient ship. Presently he said with cracked voice:

"With all the good will this colony can express.... the fact is Toffpoint is poverty-stricken. It has no industries. It has very little technology. It has no real roads! It is a small land base of little villages and tiny towns with a single sky port that juts out into the sea. A ship from elsewhere stops here only once a month. Ground communications are almost non-existent. To spread the word of your need over Toffpoint would require months. But to collect what might be given, without roads or even wheeled vehicles— No. It's impossible! And I have the only space vessel in the area, and it's not fit for a journey like you are looking at making."

The bearded man waited with a sort of implacable despair in his eyes.

"But," said Vash grimly, *"I have an idea. I ... uh ... have contacts on Nemo Vesta. Now the government of Nemo Vesta does not regard charity with favor. The need for charity seems a ... a ... a criticism of the Nemo Vestaian standard of living, you might say."*

The bearded man said coldly:

"I can understand that. The hearts of those who feel they deserve something because they were given it and did not earn it become hardened. The existence of someone needing something that they, in turn would have to give up is a reproach to them. The thought of gaining something because they breath excites their senses, while the thought of losing something that wasn't really theirs to begin with to help someone who disserves it more is sickening. Nemo Vesta, I regret to say, is one of the sky cities which we turned over to our deceivers."

With this, Vash started thinking back to the wrongs that Nemo Vesta had lay on him and now seeing further tumult caused to a third of the planet, began suddenly to see real possibilities. This was not a direct move toward the realization of his personal ambitions, but on the other hand, it wasn't a movement away from them either. Vash suddenly remembered an oration he'd heard his grandfather give many, many times in the past.

"Straight thinkin'," the old man had said obstinately, *"is merely an illusion. You think things out clear and simple, and you can see yourself ruined and your family starving any day! But real things aren't that simple! They just aren't as clear as we would like them to be! Any time you try to figure these things out so they're simple and straightforward, you're going against nature and you're going to get things mixed up! So, when something happens and you're in a straightforward, hopeless fix—why, you go along with nature! Make it as complicated as you can, and the people who want you in trouble will get hopelessly confused and eventually you can see the out!"*

Vash adverted to his grandfather's wisdom—not making it the reason for doing what he could, but accepting that it might apply to his advantage in the grand scheme of things. He saw one possibility right away. It looked fairly good. After a minute's examination it looked better. It was astonishing how plausible it actually was.

"Hm-m-m," he said. "I have planned work of my own, as you may have guessed. I am here because of ... ah ... people on Nemo Vesta. If I could make a quick trip there my ... hm-m-m ... present position might let me help you. I cannot promise very much, but if I can borrow even the smallest of your ships for the journey my lifeboat can't make ... why.... I may be able to do something. Much more than can be done on Toffpoint anyway!"

The bearded man looked at his companions.

"He seems frank," he said forbiddingly, *"and we can lose nothing more than what we already have. We have stopped our journey and are in orbit. We can wait. But ... our people should not go to Nemo Vesta. Should they find out it is us, they would surely be imprisoned or worse."*

"No need to worry about that, I believe that I can find a crew," said Vash cheerfully. Inwardly he was tremendously relieved. *"If you say the word, I'll go down to ground and come back with them. Er ... I'll want a very small ship though!"*

"It will be," said the old man. *"We thank you—"*

"Get it inboard, here," suggested Vash, *"so I can come inside as before, transfer my crew without pressured air suits, and just leave my lifeboat in your care until I come back."*

"It shall be done," said the old man firmly. He added gravely: *"You must have had an excellent upbringing, young man, to be willing to live among the poverty-stricken people you describe, and to be willing to go so far to help strangers like ourselves."*

"What?" Vash said somewhat enigmatically, *"What lessons I shall apply to your affairs, I learned at the knee of my grandfather."*

Of course, his grandfather was head of the most notorious gang of pirates on the disreputable colony of Gibbit Cove, but Vash found himself increasingly respecting the old gentleman as he gained experience of various colonies and history that the gentleman was bringing to light.

He went briskly back to his lifeboat. On the way he made verbal arrangements for the enterprise he had envisioned just minutes prior. It was remarkable how two sets of troubles could provide suggestions for their joint alleviation. He actually saw possible achievement before him. Even in a rusted hodgepodge of mechanics.

By the time the cargo space was again pressured down and the great door opened to the upper ionosphere, Vash had a very broad view of things. He'd said just the day before, to Adeline that a practical man can always make what he wants to do look like a sacrifice of his personal inclinations to others' welfare in order to instill their help, but now he began to suspect that the welfare of others can honestly often coincide with one's own.

He needed some rather extensive distances in between himself and Nemo Vesta and Nemo Vesta was prepared to pay bribes for him. Fairbeard felt it necessary to have him confined somewhere. There were a number of Toffpointian gentlemen who would assuredly like to slaughter him if he wasn't kept out of their reach in some cozy dungeon. But up to now there had not been even a practical thought as to how to leave Toffpoint, to act upon Nemo Vesta, or even to change his status in the eyes of the Toffpointians.

He backed out of the cargo hold and consulted the charts of the lifeboat. They had been left out from being consulted before by the previous captain in order to locate the landing grid, which did not answer calls. He found its position. He began to compare the chart with what he saw from out here above where Toffpoint would be in the mass of specs below. He identified a small ocean, with Toffpoint's highest mountain chain just beyond its eastern limit. He identified a river-system, emptying into that sea. And here he began to lessen the velocity of his vessel, as the landing grid was not but some twenty miles or so away.

To a scientific pilot, his maneuvering from that time on would have been a complex task. The advantage of computation over astrogation by ear, however, is largely a matter of saving fuel. A perfectly computed course for landing will get down to the ground with the use of the least number of centigrams of fuel possible. But fuel-efficient maneuvers are rarely time-efficient ones and for Vash, time was of the essence.

Vash hadn't the time or the data for computation. He swung the lifeboat end for end, making a very judgmatical use of his rocket power to slow himself to a suitable east-west velocity, and at the last and proper instant applied full-power for a deceleration and went down practically like a stone. One cannot really learn this. It has to be absorbed through the pores of one's skin as Vash had taken it all in on Gibbit Cove.

Within minutes, then, the stronghold of Lord Emory Fairbeard was startled by a roaring mutter in the sky overhead. Sentries posted on the battlements stared upward. The mutter rose to a howl, and the howl to the volume of thunder, and the thunder to a very great noise, which made loose pebbles dance and quiver with the sonic vibration.

Then there was a speck of white cloudiness in the late afternoon sky. It grew swiftly in size, as it winked of blue-white billows a light appeared in its center. That light grew brighter—and the noise managed somehow to increase—and presently the ruddy sunlight was diluted by light from the rockets with considerably bluer tint in it. Secondary, pallid shadows quickly appeared.

Then, abruptly, the rockets cut off, and something dark plunged downward, and the rockets flamed again, and a vast mass of steam arose from scorched ground—and the lifeboat lay in a circle of wildly smoking, carbonized Toffpointian soil. The return of tranquility after so much tumult was somewhat startling to those who observed it.

Absolutely nothing happened. Vash unstrapped himself from the pilot's seat, examined his surroundings thoughtfully before turning off the visionscreens. He went back and examined the feeding arrangements of the boat. He'd had nothing to eat since breakfast back before leaving this time-zone. The food in store was extremely easy to prepare and not especially appetizing. He ate with great deliberation, continuing to make plans which linked the necessities of the emigrants from Ivoryhelm to his relationship with the government of Nemo Vesta, the brief visit he'd made to Port Baragate, the ship the emigrants would lend him and his current unpopularity with Lord Emory Fairbeard. He also thought very respectfully about his grandfather's opinions on many subjects, including sky piracy. Vash, looking back on recent situations and predicaments, now found himself much more in agreement with his grandfather than he had ever believed possible.

Now, as the lifeboat was completely powered down and nature began to go back to the normal activities of the day; birds flying, horses eating, and so forth, there were now signs of human reactions. Fairbeard had been in an excessively fretful state of mind since the conclusion of his deal with the pair from Nemo Vesta. Vash had estimated that he ought to get a half-million credits for Vash to be delivered to Derk and the Nemo Vesta police. As Vash suggested, he started his bid at a million and, after some barter and bargain, the officer was able to convince Fairbeard to take half. But he closed the deal and sent for Vash—only to find Vash was now gone.

Now the landing of this lifeboat roused a lively uneasiness in Fairbeard. It might be new bargainers for Vash, it might be sky marshals looking to bring charges for the assistance in Vash's second escape, it could mean anything. Vash had said he had a secret. This might be it. Fairbeard, most assuredly vexed by his own thoughts at this point, tried to contrive some useful skullduggery without any true information to base it on.

Adeline looked at the lifeboat with bright eyes. Basil was back at the castle. He'd told her of Vash riding up to the lifeboat near another chieftain's castle, entering it, and that it then had taken to the skies in an aura of blue and white flames with much smoke and thunder. Adeline hoped that he might have returned here in it. But she worried while she waited for him to do something.

Vash did nothing. The lifeboat gave no sign of life, neither from the inside or out.

The sunset, and the sky twinkled with darting lights, which flew toward the west and vanished. Twilight followed, and more lights flashed across the heavens from the outer orbit vessels from the fleet moving as if pursuing the sun. These particular dirigibles needed solar rays to keep the aether in their bladders heated in order to stay aloft. Adeline had learned to associate three and then nine such lights with aircraft, but she could not dream of an entire fleet of hundreds. She dismissed the lights from her mind, being much more concerned with Vash. He would be in as bad a fix as ever if he came out of the boat now.

Twilight remained, a fairy dust half-light in which all things looked much more charming than they really were. Fairbeard, reduced to peevish sputtering by pure mystery, had summoned Bazil to him. It should be remembered that Fairbeard knew nothing of the disappearance of the lifeboat from his neighbor's land. He knew nothing of Bazil's journey with Vash, but he did remember that Vash had seemed unworried at breakfast and explained his calm by saying that he had a secret. The feudal chieftain worried that this lifeboat was Vash's secret; a secret that he was not made privy to.

"Bazil," said Fairbeard peevishly, sitting beside the great fireplace in the enormous, draughty hall, *"you know this Vash Rayburn better than anybody else I feel."*

Bazil breathed heavily as the blood began to rush from his face.

"Where is he? Where did he go?" demanded Fairbeard.

"I don't know," said Bazil. It was true. As far as he knew, Vash had vanished into the sky.

"What does he plan to do?" demanded Lord Fairbeard.

"I don't know," said Bazil helplessly.

"Where does that ... that thing outside the castle come from?"

"I am afraid that I don't know that either, Lord Fairbeard," said Bazil.

Fairbeard drummed on the arm of his intricately carved chair almost digging his nails into it.

"I don't like people who don't know things! I dislike, more, people who keep things from me deliberately" he said glaring intensely at Bazil as if to detect a lie in his eyes. *"There must be somebody in that—thing. Why don't they show themselves? What are they here for? Why did they come down—especially here? Because of Vash Rayburn?"*

"I don't know," said Bazil humbly.

"Then what are you waiting for? Go find out!" snapped Fairbeard. *"Take a reasonable number of guards with you. The thing must have a door. Knock on it and ask who's inside and why they came here. Tell them I sent you to ask."*

Bazil respectfully saluted. He then gathered a half-dozen of his fellows and went tramping out the castle gate. Some of the half dozen had been involved in the rescue of the Lady Adeline from Seymour. They were still in a happy mood because of the plunder they'd brought back. It was much more than a mere retainer could usually hope for in a year.

"What's this all about, Bazil?" demanded one of them as Bazil arranged them in two lines to make a proper military appearance, spears dressed upright and garrison-shields on their left arms.

"Atten Hut!" barked Bazil, and they swung into motion. *"Two, three, four, Hup, two, three, four. Hup, two, three—"* The cadence was now established.

Bazil said gloomily, *"Lord Fairbeard said to find out who landed that thing outside our gate and he keeps asking me about Vash Rayburn, too."*

He strode in step with the others. The seven men made an impressively soldierly-styled group, tramping away from the castle wall in lock step as they did.

"What happened to him?" asked a rear-file man. He marched on, eyes front, chest out, spear-shaft swinging splendidly in time with his marching. *"That lad has a nose for loot! Yet doesn't take any for himself, though. If he set up in business as a chieftain, now—"*

"Hup, two, three, four," muttered Bazil, trying to ignore the comment that would follow. *"Hup, two, three—"*

"Lord Fairbeard is a hard chieftain," growled the right-hand man in the second file. *"Plenty of grub and beer, but no fighting and no loot. I didn't get to go with you characters the other day, but what you brought back..."*

"Wasn't even half of what was there," mourned a front-file man. *"Wasn't half! Those pistols he issued got shot out and we had to get outta there fast!... Hm-m-m.... Here's this thing, Bazil. What do we do with it?"*

"Ready, halt!" barked Bazil. He stared at the motionless, seemingly lifeless lifeboat. He'd seen one like it earlier today and this could very well be the one and the same. That one spouted fire and went up out of sight. He was wary of this one. He grumbled: *"Those pipes in the back of it—steer clear of them. They spit fire. No door on this side. Lord Fairbeard said to knock on the door. We go around the front. March! two, three, four, hup, two, three, four. Left turn here and mind those rocks. It can be expected that Lord Fairbeard is watching us through his spy glass and we should not hear the end of it should somebody fall down. Left turn again, Hup, two, three, four..."*

"Here goes," rumbled Bazil. *"I tell you, boys, if she starts to spit fire, you get away fast, away I tell you. Don't look back!"*

He marched up to the lifeboat's port. He knocked on it. There was no response. He knocked again.

Vash opened the door. He nodded cheerfully to Bazil

"Good afternoon, Bazil! Glad to see you again. I've been hoping you'd come over this way. Who's with you?" He peered through the semidarkness. *"Some of the boys, eh? Come on in!"* He beckoned and said casually: *"Lean your spears against the hull over there."*

Bazil hesitated and was lost while the others obeyed without even thinking about it. All six of the retainers followed Bazil into the lifeboat's interior, amazed as they gazed at it with wonder that this fine vessel was that of the man who led them into a rescue mission which made some of them very rich men.

"Come, sit down!" said Vash cordially. *"If you want to feel what a sky vessel is really like, clasp the seat belts around you."*

You'll feel exactly like you're about to make a journey into the upper atmosphere. That's it. Lean back. You notice there are no viewports in the hull itself? That's because we use these devices known as visionscreens to look around with."

He then flicked on the screens. Bazil and his companions were charmed to see the landscape outside portrayed on screens. Vash then shifted the sensitivity-point toward a heat array level reader, and details came out that would have been invisible to the naked eye.

"With the port here closed," said Vash, *"like this—"* The port clanged shut and grumbled for half a second as the gear lockings disengaged. *"We're all set for take-off. I need only get into the pilot's seat,* throw on the fuel pump and then engage the steam burner" A tiny burn-off sounded as if a boiler had been engaged. *"And we move when I advance this throttle!"*

Vash then pressed the firing-stud. There was a soul-shaking roar. There was a terrific pressure. The seven men from Fairbeard's stronghold were pressed back in their seats with an overwhelming, irresistible pressure, which held them absolutely helpless to the backs of their seats. Their mouths dropped open as appalled protests tried to come out, but were pushed back by the seemingly ever-increasing acceleration.

The screens, showing the outside, displayed a great and confused tumult of smoke and fumes and dust toward the rear of the vessel. They showed only horizon ahead. The stars grew brighter and brighter in the now night sky as the roar of the rockets diminished to a slightly deafening roar.

Presently Vash turned off the fuel pump. He turned to look thoughtfully at the seven men. They were all very pale and unanimously sat very still, because they could see in the vision plates that a strange, mottled surface flowed past them with an appalling velocity; mountains, streams and sea all whirled across the screens. They were very much afraid that they knew what it was. They did. It was the surface of the planet and Toffpoint, well below them, was nothing more than a topographical picture.

"I'm glad you boys came along," said Vash. *"We'll catch up with the rest of the pirate fleet in a moment or two. You know, I'm very pleased with you. Not many groundlings like yourself would volunteer so quickly to join the ranks of sky piracy, not even with the loot there is in it!"*

Bazil choked slightly, but no one else made a sound. No one even protested. Protests would have been no use. There were just looks of anguish and shock, but nothing else, because Vash was the only one in the lifeboat who had the least idea of how to get it down again. His passengers had to go along for the ride he'd taken them for, no matter where it led.

Numbly, knuckle locked into their seats, they waited for the fate that would befall them momentarily.

Chapter 8

Vash did not worry about his followers, his captive guests as it were, noting the obsolescence of the sky fleet into which they presently drifted. Ancient hulks and impractical oddities did not seem antique or freakish to them. Lacking in knowledge of such machines, they had no standards by which to measure such matters.

In the screens, the land well underneath, and quite some distance away, moved visibly, while the lifeboat and the ships in orbit seemed merely to float in nearly fixed positions.

The spearmen were wholly subdued when their eyes fully focused to the lights of the oncoming fleet of ships and eccentric shapes around them. There was a ring-ship—the hull-like large metal beast resembled a wagon wheel with a huge tire at the outset and pipe passages converging toward a center hub that resembled spokes from that of a wagon's tire. This hub is where the control deck for that ship was located. It seemed unbelievable that such a relic could still exist, dating as it did from the period just after the flood or that it could be put into craft of such enormity in the first place. It would have provided a crazy sort of false gravity by spinning as it limped from one place to another. Vash had only seen pictures. Apparently, these were used to house the population that survived the flooding until more permanent systems of residence could be accomplished. Whoever had collected this fleet for the emigrants from Ivoryhelm must have required only one thing—that there be a hull that could sustain air within.

But Vash's involuntary crew could not appreciate the magnificence of each structure they passed. As they moved closer toward the center of the mass, the lifeboat drew up alongside the gigantic hulk, which belonged to the fleet's leader. The seven Toffpointians were still numbed by their kidnapping and the situation in which they currently found themselves. They looked with dull eyes at the mountainous object they approached. It had actually been designed as a fighter-carrier, intended to carry smaller craft to fight non-existent warships under conditions, which never came about. It must have been sold for scrap a good number of years since, and patched up for this emigration.

Vash waited for the huge door to open. It did. He headed into the opening, noticing as he did that an object two or three times the size of the lifeboat was already there. It cut down the room for maneuvering, but a thing once done seemed easier the second time around. Vash got the boat inside, and there was, once again, a very small grinding of gears sounding out behind them as the great door closed while the lifeboat began to drift once again.

Vash turned to his unwitting companions—followers—victims, once the lifeboat was still.

"This," he said in a manner, which could only be described as one of smiling ferocity, *"is a pirate ship, belonging to the pirate fleet that we passed through on the way here. Characters so murderous that their leaders don't dare land it anywhere away from their home colony, or the rest of the world's colonies would combine against them, to exterminate them or find their selves exterminated in the process. You've joined that fleet. You're going to get out of this boat and march over to that ship yonder. Then you're going to be official sky pirates under me."*

They quivered, but did not protest.

"I'll try you for one voyage," he told them. *"There will be plunder, lots of plunder. What you saw at Seymour's castle is nothing in comparison. There will be pirate revels. If you serve faithfully and fight well, I'll return you to Lord Fairbeard's stronghold with your loot after the one voyage. If you don't—"* He grinned mirthlessly at them—*"out the air lock with you, to free fall where you may. Do you understand?"*

The last comment was pure savagery on Vash's part. They cringed. The outside-pressure meter went up to normal. Vash turned off the visionscreens, so ending any view of the interior of the hold. He opened the port and went out. Sitting in something like continued paralysis in their seats; the seven spearmen of Toffpoint heard his voice in conversation outside the boat. They could catch no words, but Vash's tone was strictly businesslike. He came back.

"All right," he said shortly. *"Bazil, march 'em on over."*

Bazil gulped a hard gulp, trying to get his heart out of his throat. He loosened his seat belt. The enlistment of the seven in the pirate fleet was tacitly acknowledged. They were unarmed save for the conventional large knives at their belts.

"Ready, HUT!" rasped Bazil with the lump still in his throat. *"Two, three, four. Hup two, three, four. Hup—"*

The seven men marched dismally out of the lifeboat and down to the floor of the huge hold. Eyes front, chests out, throats dry, they marched to the larger but still small vessel that shared the hold compartment. They marched into that ship without a word.

Bazil barked, *"Halt!"* and they stopped and they waited.

Vash came in very matter-of-factly only moments later. He closed the entrance port, so sealing the ship. He nodded approvingly.

"You can break ranks now," he said. *"There's food and such stuff around. The ship's yours. But don't turn knobs or push buttons until you've asked me what for!"*

He went forward, and a door closed behind him.

He looked at the control board, and could have done with a little information himself. When the ship was built, obviously generations ago, there'd been controls installed which would be quite useless now. When the present working instruments were installed, it had been done so hastily that the wires and relays behind them were not concealed, and it was only for these exposed wires and switches to make-shift control panels that gave him the clues to understand them and what they were for.

The space ark's door opened. Vash backed his ship out. Its turbine propellers had surprising power for being spun using only one turbine. He reflected that the Lawlor Drive wouldn't have been designed for this present ship, either. There'd probably been a quantity order for so many Lawlor drives, and they'd been installed on whatever needed a modern drive-system, which was every ship in the fleet. But since this was one of the smallest craft in the lot, with its low mass, the rigged Lawlor Drive would have increased its mobility quite substantially. In short it should be fast… real fast.

"We'll see," he said to himself while rubbing the back of his neck.

Out in emptiness, far enough away from any of the other vessels to cause any damage should he make a bad maneuver, Vash tried out the rigged switches tentatively to see which ones worked and which ones didn't. He got the feel of it rather quick; picking up the operation of different ships was yet another talent taught to him by his grandfather.

Then as a matter of simple, rule-of-thumb astrogation, he got from a low orbit to a five-diameter height above any surrounding bodies that could become issues should they accidentally strike the hull when the rigged Lawlor drive would take hold by mere touches of turbine increases on the propellers. It was simply a matter of stretching the orbit to extreme eccentricity as all the ships went round the planet. After the fourth go round he was a full five diameters out at the left quadrant Aphelion Point, which gave him the most optimal views or the outside riggings as he toyed with the other controls. He touched the Lawlor drive button and immediately, the double bladders of the air vessel pulled in tight to the body, the rear propellers realigned vertically to allow space for the side rockets to project and then everybody had that very peculiar disturbance of all senses being tingled and jarred that accompanies going into a state of overdrive. The small craft sped through emptiness at a high multiple of shifting speeds.

Vash's knowledge of astrogation was strictly practical. Prior to taking off, he went over his ship, giving it a thorough look over and deduced from the outside that it had once been a sky yacht used by people like that of Nemo Vesta to enjoy leisurely trips away from the city; various touches inside added validity to his notion. There were two staterooms. All the hull-space was for living and supplies. None was for cargo. He nodded. There was a faint mustiness about it. But there'd been a time when it was some rich man's pride and joy.

He went back to the control room to make an estimate. From the pilot's seat one could see specks of brightness directly below. Almost infinitesimal dots of brightness from the ground and sea below, lights from colonized ground and floating cities grew swiftly brighter and then, as quickly as they grew, they shrank as they went past. There was no way to measure how fast they darted by. There were, of course, methods of measuring so that one could get an accurate picture of one's speed in overdrive; however, Vash had no functional instrument onboard for this purpose. But his previous experience and teaching of his grandfather had given him a good feel of things. This was a very fast ship indeed, at full Lawlor thrust he felt that he could beat the speed of sound from a blaster cannon that could allow him to be on a surprised mark before they even heard him.

Presently he went out to the central cabin. His followers had found provisions. There were novelties—hydroponic fruit that could be picked straight from the vine, for instance—and they'd begun to stuff themselves, more out of anxiety than hunger. They were almost resigned, now. Memory of the loot he'd led other men to at Seymour's castle inclined them to be hopeful. But they looked uneasy when he stopped where they were gathered.

"Well?" Vash inquired.

Bazil swallowed sharply. *"We have been companions, Vash Rayburn, on a few adventures thus,"* he said unhappily. *"We fought together in great battles, two against fifty, and we plundered the slain."*

"True enough," agreed Vash, if Bazil wanted to edit his memories of the fighting at the landing grid, that was all right with him and Vash wasn't going to make the effort to correct the facts. *"Now we're headed for something much better...but"*

"But what?" asked Bazil afraid of the catch that Vash was about to unleash; *"Here we are agreed on to help you in your quest against another chieftain?*

"Oh, no my friend!" said Vash. *"This has nothing to do with the chieftains of Toffpoint! You have no idea where we are heading."*

Bazil gulped. *"I ... do not understand what you want with us,"* he protested. *"We are not experienced in sky piracy! We are simple men—"*

"You're pirates now," Vash told him with a sort of genial bloodthirstiness in his voice. *"You'll do what I tell you until we fight. Then you'll fight well or die. That's all you need to know for now!"*

He left them again. *"When men are to be led"* Vash recalled his grandfather saying, *"it is rarely wise to discuss policy or tactics with them at the front. Most men work best when they know only what is expected of them. Then they can't get confused and they do not get ideas of how to do things better."*

Vash inspected the yacht more carefully. There were still traces of decorative embellishments, which had nothing to do with flight-worthiness. But the mere antiquity of the ship made Vash hunt more carefully. He found a small compartment packed solidly with supplies. A supply-cabinet did not belong where it was. He hauled out all of the items to make sure. It was ... or at least it had been ... a machine shop in miniature. In the early days, before ansibles could be used as long-range devices, a yacht or a ship that went beyond mid strata distance was strictly on its own. If there were a breakdown, it was strictly private. It had to repair itself or else fall into the sea and drift. So, all early craft carried amazingly complete equipment for repairs. Only liners and cargo supply vessels are equipped that way in recent generations, and it is almost unheard-of for their tool shops to even be used.

But there was the remnant of a shop on the yacht that Vash had in hand to use for his errand on Nemo Vesta. He'd told the emigrant leaders of Ivoryhelm that he went to ask for charity. He'd just assured his followers that their journey was for piracy. Now to make these two deceptions conjoin to create something that Nemo Vesta would not soon forget.

He began to empty the cubbyhole of all the items that had been packed into it for storage. It had been very ingenious, this miniature repair shop. The lathe was built in with strength-members of the walls as part of its structure. The drill press was recessed. The welding apparatus had its coils and condensers under the floor. The briefest of examinations showed the condensers to be in bad shape, and the coils might be hopeless. But there was good material used in the old days. Vash began to have quite unreasonable hopes.

He went back to the control room to meditate on how to use his newly appropriated ship and staff.

He'd had a reasonably sound plan of action for the pirating of a space-liner, even though he had no weapons mounted on the ship nor anything more deadly in hand than stun-pistols for his reluctant crew. But he considered it likely that he could make the same sort of landing with this yacht that he'd already done with the lifeboat. Which should be enough.

If he waited just off of Nemo Vesta outside of their visionscopes, until a liner went down to the sky city's grand sky port, he could try it. He would go into a close orbit around Nemo Vesta, which would bring him, very low, over the landing grid within an hour or so of the liner's landing. He'd turn the yacht end for end and apply full aether release on both bladders for deceleration. The yacht would drop like a stone into the landing grid. Everything would happen too quickly for the grid crew to think of clapping a force arm on it, or for them to even manage it if they tried. He'd be aground before they realized it.

The rest was simply fast action. Vash and his seven newly sworn pirates, stun-pistols humming, would tumble out of the yacht and dash for the control room of the grid where Vash would smash the controls. Then they'd rush the landed liner, seize it, shoot down anybody who tried to oppose them, tether the yacht to the liner and seal up the ship.

And then they'd take off using the liner's rockets, which were generally carried for emergency landing only, but, in this case, could be used for a single take-off. After one such use, they'd be exhausted and junk, but with the grid's controls smashed, nobody could even try to stop them, so it would work as long as they were able to get airborne before the local officials arrived on scene.

It wasn't a bad idea. He had a good deal of confidence in it. It was the reason for his Toffpointian crew. No one would expect such a thing to be tried, so it almost certainly could be done. But it did have the drawback that the yacht might have to be left behind, should they not get it tethered in time, after the seizing of the liner.

Vash thought it over soberly. Long before he reached Nemo Vesta, of course, he could have his own crew so terrified that they'd fight like fiends for fear of what he might do to them if they didn't. But if he could keep the sky-yacht also…it was, overall, a pretty fine vessel, it merely needed a little love by the right hands.

He nodded to himself gravely. He liked the new possibility. If it didn't work, there was the first plan in reserve. Worst-case scenario he'd get a modern sky-liner and a suitable cargo to present to the emigrants of Ivoryhelm. And afterward—

There were certain electronic circuits, which were akin to that of a Tesla work shop with the parts for creating induction motors, resonant transformers and much more. It is obvious that the interlopers who supplied the emigrants of Ivoryhelm with this ship did not thoroughly go through it before hand, lest they would have removed these items. Toward the back, there was a compartment that contained a code panel and a lever. *"Hmmm? Interesting. I wonder what that goes to*?" Vash thought before moving onto more important things.

The Lawlor drive unit formed a type of sonic field, a stress in the surrounding space if you will, into which a nearby ship could necessarily move with less resistance. The faster angle came from something likened to a donkey trotting after a carrot on a stick, changing the direction of the donkey by redirecting the carrot. With the Lawlor Drive engaged, it moved the stress away from the direction the vessel was being moved and applying it to the non-impacted field area, thus projecting the vessel in the direction the stressed area was moved from. The tractor fields of a landing grid on Nemo Vesta were similar. A tuning principle was involved, but basically a landing grid clamped an area of stress around the vessel trying to land, and the ship couldn't move out of it. When the landing grid moved the stressed area up or down, it was able to bring the ship down to the port of its choosing or project it up away from the grid enough that the ship did not need to use any of its own effort to take off or land.

Everybody who worked with, or around, landing grids knew all this, but the pirates on Gibbit Cove had evolved a third trick of which Vash was now happy to know of. It was based on the fact that a circuit fundamentally akin to the other two could generate ball lightning. Ball lightning was an area of space so stressed that its energy-content could leak out only very slowly, unless it made contact with a conductor, at which time all bets were off. It would blow and the sky pirates could then, by choosing the conductor, use the ball lightning to force the surrender of their victims as they could lock the vessel in a fixed position, plummet them to the depths of the sea, or discard them into the upper heavens beyond the aether of this world.

Vash began to draw diagrams. The Lawlor drive-unit had been installed long after the yacht was built. It would be modern, with no nonsense about it. With such-and-such of its electronic components cut out, and such-and-such other ones added in, it would become a perfectly practical ball lightning generator, capable of placing bolts wherever an industrious individual would have the passion to plant one.

This was a standard Gibbit Cove practice. Vash's grandfather had used it for years. It had the advantage that it could be used inside a tractor field, where a normally set Lawlor drive could not. It had the other advantage that commercial craft could not mount such gadgets for defense, because the insurance companies, being puppets to the power commission board, objected to meddling with Lawlor drive installations.

Vash set to work with the remnants of a tool shop on the ancient yacht and some antique coils and condensers and such.

He became filled with zest and vigor as he worked. He almost forgot that he was the skipper of an elderly craft, which should have been scrapped long before he was even born, but even he grew hungry, and he realized that nobody offered him food. He went indignantly into the yacht's central saloon where he found his seven crewmembers snoring torturously, sprawled in stray places here and there.

He woke them with a hostile sternness. He set them furiously to work on the housekeeping—including meals—which can be neglected in a feudal castle because strong outside winds blow smells away and dry up smelly objects, but this wasn't the case in tight, closed off spaces and must be practiced within an airtight vessel.

He went back to work, but suddenly stopped and began to meditated afresh, ceasing his actual labor to draw a diagram, which he regarded with great affection as his idea took physical shape. He returned to his adaptation of the Lawlor drive to aid in the production of ball lightning.

It was possible to wind coils for the stator needed to create the magnetic field. A certain percentage of the old condensers still held a charge. He tapped the drive-unit for brazing current, and the drill press became a die-stamping device for small parts. He built up the elements of a vacuum tube such as is normally found only in a landing grid control room. He set up a vacuum-valve arrangement in the base of a large glass jar he had found and emptied of its contents. He put that jar in the boat's air lock, bled the air to emptiness, and flashed the tube's quaint elements. He brought it back and went out of overdrive while he hooked the entire new assembly into the drive-circuit, with cutouts and switches so as to be able to operate the Frankenstein device from the yacht's instrument board.

"Finished!" he exclaimed with a great level of pride. He lined up the yacht again and went back into overdrive once more. Two hours later he came out again to get his bearings and determine exactly where he was before going into overdrive a third time.

He used the visionscope and quickly contemplated Nemo Vesta on its screen. The sky yacht moved briskly toward it. His seven Toffpointian crewmen, aware of coming action, dolefully sharpened their two-foot knives. They did not know what else to do, but they were far from happy and needed to do something productive.

Vash shared their depression. Such gloomy anticipations before stirring events are proof that a man is not a fool.

Vash's grandfather had been known to observe that when a man can imagine all kinds of troubles and risks and disasters that lay before him, he is usually right. Vash shared that view. But it would not do to back out now for Nemo Vesta was less than two miles away.

Bringing his vessel to a stop, he studied the flying city painstakingly while the yacht hovered just out of range of the city's detection. After a suitable and very long interval, passing by the many suburbia locations on the flying colony, the site of the capital city came around the southern edge exposing the gargantuan sky port, but not before passing the converter relay station that led to Vash's false accusation; surprisingly with his power unit still hooked in place, still functioning and still saving the Power board thousands of kilowatts. Vash wanted to blow it off of the roof, but refrained, keeping his disdain bottled for a later time.

From a bare hundred thousand feet, Vash stepped up magnification of the visionscope to its maximum limit and looked again. Then the landing grid more than filled the visionscope's screen. He had to hunt before he found the control room. Then it was very clear. He saw the almost warehouse looking shed with its large windows and multiple visionscreens just past the bedded tractor field markers and in the very center of that marker there was something silvery which cast a shadow of its own; a ship, a liner.

There was a tap on the control-room door. It was Bazil who had been jarred from his nap when the ship came out of overdrive.

"Anything happening?" he asked uneasily.

"I just sighted the ship we're going to take," said Vash.

Bazil looked unhappy to hear this news. He withdrew, leaving Vash to plot out the extremely roundabout course he must take to end up with the liner and the yacht traveling in the same direction and the same speed, so capture would be possible.

He put the yacht on the line required. He threw on full power. Actually, he headed partly away from his intended victim so as not to raise suspicion from the liner's crew.

The little yacht plunged forward. Nothing seemed to happen. Time passed and Vash had nothing to do but worry, so he worried.

Bazil tapped on the door again. *"Is it about time to get ready for a fight?"* he asked dolefully.

"Not yet," said Vash. *"I'm currently running away from our victim, now."*

Give it another half hour. The course changed. The yacht was now behind the landing grid just low enough to see the underbelly and its massive turbine operated propellers. The visionscreens of the sky port were the only thing standing between them and their prey. The course of the small ship curved now. It would pass almost close enough to clip the lowermost tips of Nemo Vesta's ground edge. There was nothing for Vash to do but think morbid thoughts, so he thought them.

The Lawlor drive began to burble and whirl. He cut it off. He sat gloomily in the control room, occasionally glancing at the nearby expanse of mottled surfaces and hulking geared propellers. Its attraction bent the path of the yacht. It was close enough that to look as if now the view appeared as a parabolic curve in the visionscreens.

Presently Vash found the liner. It rose steadily. The grid still thrust it upward with an even, continuous acceleration. It had to be not less than forty thousand feet out before it could take to overdrive, but at that distance it would have an outward velocity of its own which would take it the rest of the way out on its own power. At ten thousand feet, certainly, the tractor-fields could let go.

They did. Vash could tell because the liner had been pointed base down toward the grid when the tractor fields picked it up. Now it wobbled slightly with a steady sway. It was free. It was no longer held solidly. From now on it floated up on its own aether and momentum.

Vash bit at his fingernails, then quickly stopped when his memories reminded him of how his mother used to slap his hands when she caught him doing it. There was nothing to be done for thirty minutes more, and then twenty, ten, five, three, two—then the liner was barely twenty feet away when Vash fired his rockets. They made a colossal cloud of vapor as he repositioned.

The yacht stirred faintly, shifted deftly, lost just a suitable amount of velocity—which now was nearly straight up from the sky port—and moved with precision and directness toward the liner. Vash stirred his controls and swung the entire vessel. Here, obviously, he could not use the overdrive for its proper purpose. But a switch cut out certain elements of the Lawlor unit while cutting in others, which made the modified drive-unit into a ball lightning projector.

A flaming speck of pure incandescence sped from the yacht's bow through empty space between the small vessel and the liner. It would miss— No. Vash was able to arc it left and it struck the liner's port hull. It would momentarily paralyze every bit of electrical equipment in the liner. It would definitely not go unnoticed.

"Calling liner," said Vash painfully into the ship's archaic communicator. "Calling liner! We are the pirates known in these parts as the Equalizers," Using the name of his grandfather's notorious group, knowing that the name would immediately strike fear. "We are attacking your ship. You have ten seconds to get into your lifeboats or we will hull you!"

He settled back, again biting at his fingernails. He was acutely disturbed. At the end of ten seconds the distance between the two ships was perceptibly less. He flung a second ball lightning bolt across the diminished air space. He sent it whirling round and round the liner in a tight spiral. He ended by having it touch the liner's bow this time. Liquid light ran over the entire hull.

"Your ten seconds are up," he said worriedly. *"If you don't get out—"*

But then he relaxed. A boat-blister on the liner opened. The boat could not release by its self. It could not possibly take on its complement of passengers and crew in so short a time; the opening of the blister was merely a sign of surrender.

The two first ball lightning bolts were miniatures. Vash now projected a full-sized ball. It glittered viciously across the emptiness, the plasma and aether necessary for its existence furnishing a medium for radiation. It sped toward the liner and hung just off its side, menacingly. The yacht moved steadily closer; ten feet then nine…

"All out," said Vash regretfully. *"We can't wait any longer!"*

A boat darted away from the liner. A second, then a third and fourth and fifth; the last boat lingered desperately. The yacht was less than a few feet away when the last lifeboat broke free and plunged frantically toward the landing grid.

The other boats were already streaking downward, trails of rocket-fumes expanding behind them. The crew of the landing grid would pick them up for safe and gentle landing.

Vash sighed in relief. He played delicately upon the yacht's rocket-controls. He carefully maneuvered the very last of the novelties he had built into an originally simple Lawlor drive-unit. The two ships came together with a very distinct metal on metal clashing sound that seemed horribly loud to the seven voluntold crewmen.

Bazil jerked open the control room door with a face white as death.

"W-we hit something! Wh-when do we fight?"

Vash said ruefully: *"I am so sorry, I forgot to tell you. The fighting's over. But bring your stun-pistols anyway. No one would deliberately stay behind, but someone might have gotten left behind in the hurry."*

He rose from his seat, to take over the ship that he had just single-handedly captured, feeling a sense of despair that his grandfather wasn't there to witness the event.

Chapter 9

Normally, at a steady overdrive cruising speed, it would be a day and a half's journey from Nemo Vesta to Port Barogate, but Vash made it in just under a day. There was reason for his haste. He wanted to beat the news of his piracy to the port. He could endure suspicion, and he wouldn't mind doubt, but he did not want certainty of his nefarious behavior to interfere with the purposes of his call. Sky marshals at this point in the game would be a major defeat and would further give Vash reason to believe the fates had conspired against him. No, for this once, he woefully pleaded and begged that fate would not give him any more obstacles to contend with.

The sky yacht, sealed tightly, was left to float solitarily in the sea with bladders half full, just enough to ensure the nose cone be kept above sea level. Vash then loaded his crew and lofted the big ship to travel alone and land by way of the landing grid on Port Barogate. It glittered brightly as it descended. When it touched ground and the grid's tractor fields cut off, it looked very modern and very crisp and strictly businesslike. Actually, the capture of this particular liner was a bit of luck, for Vash. It was a medium ship of five thousand tons burden, specifically designed for service stops. It was brand-new and on the way from its builders to its owners when Vash interfered. Naturally, though, it carried cargo on its maiden voyage.

Vash spoke curtly to the control room of the grid. *"I'm non-sked,"* he explained. *"It's a new ship. I've got a last-minute charter party over on Nemo Vesta and I have to get rid of my cargo. How about shifting me to a delay space until I can talk over my load with some brokers?"*

The tractor fields came on again and the liner moved very delicately to a position at the side of the grid's central space. There it would be out of the way allowing other ships to be guided in. Vash made sure to dress himself carefully in garments that he had found in the skipper's cabin. He found Bazil wearing an apron and an embittered expression on his face. He ceased wielding his mop as Vash halted beside him.

"I'm going ashore," he said crisply. *"You're in charge until I get back."*

"In charge, in charge of what?" demanded Bazil bitterly. *"Of a bunch of male housemaids! I run a mop! And me a Toffpointian gentleman! I thought I was being a pirate! What do I do? I scrub floors! I wash paint! I stencil cases in cargo holds! I paint over names and put others in their places! Me, a Toffpointian gentleman, or at least I was at one point!"*

"No," said Vash. *"A pirate. If I don't get back, you and the others can't work this ship, and presently the police of Port Barogate will ask why. They'll recheck my careful forgeries, and you'll all be hung for piracy. So don't let anybody in. Don't talk to anybody. If you do—pfft!"*

He drew his finger across his throat, and nodded as he jaunted cheerfully out through the crew's landing-door at the base of the ship. He went across the tarmac and out between two of the gigantic control feed arches of the grid. He then hired a ground vehicle.

"Where to sir?" asked the driver.

"Hm-m-m, where to indeed?" said Vash. *"There's a firm of lawyers.... The name escapes me at the moment, however."*

"My apologies sir, but there's millions of 'em here," said the driver.

"No, this is a special one," explained Vash. *"It's so dignified they won't talk to you unless you're a great-grandson of a client. They're so ethical they won't touch a case of under a million credits. They've got about nineteen names in the firm title and—"*

"Oh!" said the ground-car driver. *"That'll be— Oh heck! I can't remember the name either. But I'll take you there. I know exactly who you are talkin' about."*

He drove out into traffic. Vash relaxed. Then he tensed again. He had not been in a city since he stopped briefly in this one on the way to Toffpoint. The traffic was abominable. And he, who'd been in various pitched battles on Toffpoint and had only lately captured a ship — Vash grew apprehensive as his ground-car charged into the thick of hooting, rushing, squealing vehicles. When the car came to a stop, he found himself quite relieved.

"It's there, just past the central guard tower," said the driver. *"You'll find the name soon enough on the directory wall."*

Vash paid the driver, then cut past the empty guard tower and went inside the gigantic building. He looked at the directory wall and shrugged. He went to the downstairs guard. He explained that he was looking for a firm of lawyers whose name was not on the directory list. They were extremely conservative and of the highest possible reputation. They didn't seek clients.

"Rooms forty-two and forty-three," said the guard, frowning. *"I ain't supposed to give it out, but—floors forty-two and-three."*

Vash thanked the guard and assured him that he didn’t hear the information from him and then went up the stairs. He was unknown to anyone at this firm mind you, so the receptionist looked at him with surprised aversion; *"I have a case of space piracy,"* said Vash politely. *"Could I speak with a member of the firm, please?"*

Ten minutes later he eased himself into one of the high-back leather easy chairs in the main lobby. A gray-haired man of infinite dignity soon showed and said: *"Well?"*

"I am," said Vash modestly, *"a pirate. I have a ship in the sky port with very convincing papers and a cargo of Regalia, furs, jewelry and more from the Nemo Vesta area, and a rather large quantity of rather fine bobbles and minerals from a few other places. I want to dispose of the entire cargo and invest a considerable part of the proceeds in conservative stocks on Port Barogate."*

The attorney frowned with somewhat of a shocked look about him. Then he said carefully:

"You have made two statements that bring a concern. One was that you are a pirate. Taken by itself, that is no concern of mine. The other, however, is that you wish to dispose of certain cargo and invest in reputable businesses on Port Barogate. I assume that there is no connection between the two observations."

He paused. Vash said nothing, so the elderly attorney went on, trying to speak with a higher level of education:

"Of course, our firm is a law firm and not in the business of brokering sales. However, we can represent you in your dealing with some of the local brokers if that is what you are looking for. And obviously we can advise you in the legal bits and matters."

"I wish to also purchase," Vash said with calm resolve, *"a complete shipload of agricultural machinery, a microfilm technical library on vision-tape, machine tools, vision-tape readers, generators, and such other things along those lines."*

"Hm-m-m," said the elderly attorney, now intrigued by Vash's requests. *"I will send one of our clerks to examine your cargo so he can deal properly with the brokers. You will tell him in detail what you wish to buy."*

Vash then quickly stood up, extending his hand in polite gesture. *"I'll take him to the ship right now if you wish."*

He was mildly surprised at the smoothness with which matters were proceeding, yet still had a worry of concern in the back of his mind to take care of the matter before sky marshals were dispatched. Vash took a young clerk to the ship. He showed him the ship's papers as edited by himself. He took him through the cargo holds. He discussed in some detail what he wished to buy.

Not long after the clerk left, Bazil came to complain again.

"Look here!" he said bitterly, *"we've scrubbed this ship from one end to the other! There's not a speck or a finger mark on it. And we're still scrubbing! We captured this ship! Is this what you call a pirate's revel?"*

Vash looked at him and simply said: *"There's money coming. I'll let you boys ashore with some cash in your pockets presently. Just wait a bit longer."*

An assortment of local brokers soon came, escorted by the clerk who had examined the cargo. They squabbled furiously with each other as to who would be the best one to do the transaction. There was no question as to the dignity of the firm that the clerk represented, so if it was said that this was a good deal, then the brokers would fight tooth and nail to have the opportunity to do business with the firm so as to gain more esteem in the eyes of the citizens of Port Barogate.

There was no suspicion—no overt suspicion anyhow—as to where the cargo had come or if it were legal or pirated. Soon the furs went. The clerk painstakingly informed Vash that he could only gain a specific price in the barter. More brokers from other firms soon came; the jewelry went. The lawyer's clerk jotted down figures and worked out gross from net. The bulk of everything else was taken over by a group of brokers joining forces due to the fact that none of whom could handle the loads alone.

Vash drew cash from the present earnings and sent his seven disgruntled Toffpointians ashore with a thousand credits apiece. With bright and shining faces and a change in their previous demeanor, they headed for the nearest pub.

"As soon as my ship's loaded," Vash told the clerk with a grin as he watched them leave the loading bay, *"I'll want to get them out of jail."*

The clerk nodded. He brought salesmen of agricultural machinery, representatives of microfilm libraries and vision-tape devices, manufacturers of generators, etc. Vash bought left and right. Delivery was promised for early morning.

"Now," said the clerk, "about the investments you wish to make with the balance?"

"I'll want a reasonable sum in cash," said Vash as he reflectively contemplated the amount still unused. *"But.... well ... I've been told that insurance is a fine, conservative business. As I understand it, most insurance organizations are divided into divisions, which are separately incorporated. There will be a life-insurance division, a casualty division, and so on. Is that right? And one may invest in any of them separately?"*

The clerk said impassively: *"I was given to understand, sir, that you are interested in risk-insurance; more specifically, risk-insurance covering piracy. I was given quotations on the risk-insurance divisions of all Port Barogate companies as well as some on other colonies. Of course, those are not very active stocks, but if there were a rumor of a pirate ship acting in this part of the galaxy, one might anticipate—"*

"I do," said Vash. *"Let's see. ... My cargo brought so much.... Him-m-m.... My purchases will come to so much. Hm-m-m.... My legal*

fees, of course.... I mentioned a sum in cash. Yes. This will be the balance, more or less, which you will put in the stocks you've named, but since I anticipate activity in them. I'll want to leave some special instructions to accompany payouts, dividends on increase, etc."

He gave a detailed, thoughtful account of what he anticipated might be found in news reports of later dates. The clerk noted it all down, passively so as to be typed up official at a later date. Vash added instructions with detail and direction.

"Yes, sir," said the clerk without hint of intonation when he was through. *"If you will come to the office in the morning, sir, the papers will be drawn up and matters can be concluded. Your new cargo can hardly be delivered before then, and if I may say so, sir, your crew won't be ready. From the personal observations I made as they left, I'd estimate two hours of festivity for each man tonight, followed by a good fourteen hours or so for recovery."*

"Thank you," said Vash. *"I shall see you in the morning. Thank you for your expediency in these matters."*

He sealed up the ship when the clerk had departed and soon after had an empty feeling of loneliness as he was made suddenly aware by the echoes in the hull that he was the only living thing in the ship. His footsteps echoed hollowly down the catwalk towards the sleeping quarters, so he began to whistle just to break up the monotony of the silence.

Vash went rather forlornly to the cabin once occupied by the liner's former skipper. His loneliness increased. Today's actions were the ones, which bothered his conscience and gave him pride all at the same time. He felt troubled by the piracy, happy that he was helping a greater cause, saddened by the many he had forced away from the liner and possibly forced their jobs from, yet pleased that he did something that his grandfather would have been overjoyed to see.

He reflected that his grandfather would not have been disturbed about such a matter or felt bad for committing piracy on those who could afford it and that the elderly pirates would have felt at ease with no compulsions to recompense for their actions. It was his conviction that piracy was an essential part of the working of the world's economic system. Vash, indeed, could remember him saying precisely:

"I tell you what, piracy's what keeps this whole world's business thriving! Everybody knows business suffers when retail trade slacks down. It backs up the movement of inventories. They get too big. That backs up orders to the factories. They lay off men. And when men are laid off, they don't have money to spend, so retail trade slacks off some more, and that backs up inventories some more, and that backs up orders to factories and makes unemployment and hurts retail trade again. It's a feedback y' see?" It was his grandfather's custom, at this point, to stare shrewdly at each of his listeners in turn and point a finger into their chest.

"But suppose somebody pirates a ship? The owners don't lose. It's insured. They order another ship built right away. Men get hired to build it and they're paid money to spend in retail trade and that moves inventories and industry picks up. More'n that, more people insure against piracy. Insurance companies hire more clerks and bookkeepers. They get more money for retail trade and to move inventories and keep factories going and get more people hired.... Y'see? Its piracy that keeps business on this entire planet spinning!"

Vash had his doubts about his grandfather's logic, but it could not be entirely wrong. He'd put a good part of the proceeds of his piracy in risk-insurance stocks, and he counted on them to make all his actions as benevolent to everybody concerned as his intentions had been, and were. But he feared that it might not be true enough. It might be less than ... well ... sufficiently true in a particular instance. And therefore—

Then he saw how things could be worked out and so that there could be no doubt about it, he began to work out the details step by step in his mind. He drifted off to sleep in the act of composing a letter in his head to his grandfather on the pirate colony of Gibbit Cove.

When morning came, large catawheel transports came with gigantic agricultural machines of a sort in tow that would normally never be shipped by sky freight in this quantity. Generators, both large and small turbines, tanks for water collection, vision-tape machines with boxes full of tape for them, followed these in single file. There were machine tools and cutting tips—these last deliveries were vast in quantity—many of which the emigrants of Ivoryhelm probably would not have been expecting, and might not even recognize. The cargo holds of the liner were filled from wall to wall.

Vash went to the office of his newly found attorneys where he read and signed all of the papers, in an atmosphere of great ethically persuasive purpose, knowing that what he was doing was to right a wrong on someone who did not disserve the wrong. The attorney's clerk accompanied him to the police office across the way, where seven dreary Toffpointians with much deserved hangovers tried dismally to cheer themselves by memories of how they found themselves in their current state.

Vash posted bond for them and transported their slow-moving carcasses to the ship, all the while being as boisterous and loud as possible for his own amusement. The clerk produced a rather small, but weighty box with an air of extreme solemnity as he looked in every direction to ensure that no one was watching from the shadows.

"The currency amount, which you asked for, sir."

"Thank you," said Vash. *"That, then concludes our business at this time?"*

"Yes, sir," said the clerk. He hesitated, and for the first time showed a trace of human curiosity. *"Could I ask a question, sir, about piracy?"*

"Of course; however, I may not have an appropriate answer for you." Vash retorted. *"Go ahead."*

"When you ... ah ... captured this ship, sir," said the clerk hopefully, *"did you ... ah ... shoot the men and keep the women?"*

Vash sighed. *"As much as I hate to spoil a very enlivening theory,"* he said regretfully, *"no. These are modern days. Efficiency has invaded even the pirate business. I used my crew for floor-scrubbing and cookery."*

He closed the ship port gently and went up to the control room to call the landing grid operators. In minutes the captured liner, loaded down again, lifted toward the upper stratosphere with the aid of the grid's massive control arms.

And the entire journey back to Toffpoint, with all of the excitement of the piracy waning, was as anticlimactic as a stroll through the park. There was no trouble finding the sky yacht that had been left in its remote, stationary orbit in the sea. Vash sent out an unlocking signal, and a keyed transmitter beacon on the yacht began to send a signal on which Vash was able to hone in on. When the liner nudged alongside it, Vash's last rigged contrivance kicked into operation and the yacht clung fast to the under-belly of the larger ship's outer hull and both ships, now tethered, jumped into a state of overdrive, or as much as a fully loaded dirigible towing a yacht could. There were a few pauses for repositioning, as Vash had still not come to terms with the position finding equipment and had to rely on old fashion astrogation. The stopover on Port Barogate had caused some delay and took longer than expected, but Vash arrived back at Toffpoint air space within a day of standard travel should he have come directly from Nemo Vesta. It took no time at all locating and getting into orbit alongside the junk yard space fleet of the emigrants. Shortly thereafter he called the leader's ship with only mild worries about possible disasters that might have happened while he was away.

"Calling the Ivoryhelm leader," he said crisply. *"Calling the leader's ship! This is Vash Rayburn, reporting back from Nemo Vesta with a ship and machinery contributed for your use!"*

The harsh voice of the bearded old leader of the emigrants seemed somehow broken when he replied. Whereas his previous conversations were harsh, he now called down blessings on Vash. Then there was the matter of getting emigrants on board the new ship. They didn't know how to use the boat-blister lifeboat tubes. Vash had to demonstrate. But shortly after there were fifty or so of the citizens from Ivoryhelm, feverishly searching the ship surprised and somewhat incredulous to the bounty, reporting what they found.

"It's impossible!" said the old man almost in tears. *"It's impossible!"*

"I wouldn't say that," said Vash. *"It's unlikely, but it's happened before. My only fear is it's not enough."*

"It is ... many times what we hoped," said the old man humbly.*" We are more grateful than we can begin to express in words."*

Vash took a deep breath. *"I'd like to take my crew back home now if you would allow,"* he explained. *"Then I will come back and ... well ... perhaps I can be useful explaining things. And I'd like to ask a great favor of you ... for my own work."*

"But naturally," said the old man. *"Of course. We will await your return. Naturally! And ... perhaps we can ... we can arrange something—"*

Vash was relieved. They were passionately excited over the agricultural machinery, but they seemed rather uncertain over the microfilm library and the vision tape devices.

The vision-tape instructors were the objects of polite comment only. Vash felt a vague discomfort. There seemed to be a sort of secret desperation in the atmosphere, which they would not admit or mention. But he was coming back of course, so he would explain everything in full when he arrived.

He brought the sky boat over to the new liner. He hooked onto a lifeboat blister and his seven crewmen crawled through the lifeboat tube. Vash then pulled away quickly before somebody thought to ask why there were no lifeboats in the places so plainly made for them.

He headed downward when the landmarks on Toffpoint's surface told him that Fairbeard's castle would shortly come around the next mountain line. The boat's rocket-tanks had been refilled, and he burned fuel recklessly for no other reason than to make a dramatic landing within a hundred yards of the battlements where Adeline had once thoughtfully had a coil of rope ready for him.

Heads peered at the lifeboat over those same battlements now, but the gate was closed. It stayed closed. There was somehow an atmosphere of suspicion amounting to enmity. Vash knew now that he was an unwelcome visitor.

"All right, boys," he said resignedly. *"Out with you and to the castle. Before you go, here is your loot from the voyage"*—he'd counted out actual cash for each of them, more than any of them had seen handed out by Lord Fairbeard—*"and I want you to take this box to Lord Fairbeard. It's a gift from me. And let him know*

that I wish to consult with him about co-operation between the two of us in some future plans I have. Ask if I may come and talk to him."

The seven former spearmen, now official pirates, tumbled out. They marched gleefully to the castle gate. Vash saw them tantalizingly displaying large sums in cash to the watchers above them. Bazil held up the box for Fairbeard. It was the small, but weighty box the clerk had turned over to him, with a tidy sum of cash in it. The sum was partly depleted, now with Vash paying off his involuntary crew as if they'd done the fighting they'd expected and he'd thought would be necessary. But there was still more in it than Fairbeard would have gotten from Nemo Vesta for selling him out.

The castle gate slowly opened, as if the retainers on the other side were still leery of those who were entering. The seven went in, carrying the box for Lord Fairbeard.

Some time passed while Vash, alone with his thoughts, went over every possible argument he meant to use against the good Lord Emory Demetrius Fairbeard. He needed to make up a very great sum, and it could be done thus-and-so, but thus-and-so required occasional piratical raids, which called for pirate crews, and if Fairbeard would not encourage his retainers then he could easily go to another chieftain, of course, but he knew what kind of scoundrel Fairbeard was and it’s better to do business with a scoundrel that you can read as opposed to one that you can’t. He'd have to find out about another man and frankly, he didn’t want to make the effort.

Nearly an hour elapsed before the castle gate opened again. Two files of spearmen marched out. There were eight men with a sergeant in command. Vash did not recognize any of them. They came to the lifeboat. The sergeant formally presented an official message. The Lord Fairbeard would admit Vash Rayburn to his presence, to hear what he had to say.

Vash felt excessively uncomfortable waiting, he'd thought about that secret despair in the emigrant fleet. He worried about it. He was concerned because Fairbeard had not welcomed him with cordiality, now that he'd brought back his retainers in good working order. In a sudden gloomy premonition, he checked his stun-pistols. They needed charging. He, fortunately, had managed it from the lifeboat unit before going to the castle. He sighed with a slight relief at this added modicum of security.

He walked slowly toward the castle with the eight spearmen surrounding him as cops had once done to him on Nemo Vesta. He did not like to be reminded of it. He frowned to himself as he went in the castle gate, and along a cold stone passage, and up stone stairs into the great hall of state. Lord Fairbeard, as once before, sat peevishly by the huge fireplace. This time he was almost inside it, with its hood and mantel actually over his head. The Lady Adeline sat there with him.

Lord Fairbeard seemed to put aside his peevishness only a little to greet Vash.

"My dear fellow," he said complainingly, *"I don't like to welcome you with reproaches, but do you know that when you absconded with that lifeboat, you made a mortal enemy for me? It's a fact! My neighbor, on whose land the boat descended, was deeply hurt. He considered it his property. He had summoned his retainers for a fight over it when I heard of his resentment and partly soothed him with apologies and presents. But he still considers that I should return it to him, whenever you appear here with it!"*

"Oh," said Vash. *"That's too bad."*

Things started to appear ominous. The Lady Adeline looked at him strangely. As if she tried to tell him something without speaking it. She looked as if she had been recently weeping.

"To be sure," said Fairbeard fretfully, *"you gave me a very pretty present just now. But my retainers tell me that you came back with a ship, a very fine ship. What became of it? The landing grid has been repaired at last and you could have landed it. What happened to it?"*

"In truth, sir, I gave it away," said Vash. He saw what Adeline was trying to tell him. One corridor ... no, two ... leading toward the great hall was filled with spearmen. His tone turned cynical, bordering on sardonic. *"I gave it to a poor old man."*

Fairbeard just shook his head.

"That's not right, Vash! That fleet overhead, now. If they are pirates and want some of my men for crews, they should come to me! I don't take kindly to the idea of your kidnapping my men and carrying them off on piratical excursions! They must be profitable! But if you can afford to give me presents like that, and be so lavish with my retainers ... why I don't see why—"

Vash grimaced. *"I came to arrange a deal on that order,"* he said with a level of distain.

"I must say that I have not heard it but I don't think I like it," said Lord Fairbeard somewhat irritated. *"I prefer to deal with people direct. I'll arrange for the situation with the landing grid and it's necessary repair, and I can arrange for a regular recruiting service, which I will conduct personally,"* Fairbeard added. *"But you ... you are irresponsible! I wish you well, but when you carry my men off for pirates, and make my neighbors into my enemies, and infect my daughter with strange notions and the government of a friendly neighboring colony asks me in so many words not to shelter you any longer ... why that is the end of it, Mr. Rayburn. So, with great regret—"*

"The regret is mine," said Vash methodically, and somewhat casually given the situation. Vash aimed a stun-pistol at a slowly opening door. He pulled the trigger. Yells followed its humming, because not everybody it hit was knocked out. Nor did it hit everybody in the corridor. Men came surging out of one door, and then two, to reluctantly acquire the attention of his weapons.

Then a spear went past Vash's face and missed him only by inches. It buried its point in the floor. A whirling knife spun past his nose at the very moment he glanced up. There were balconies all around the great hall, and men popped up from behind the railings and threw things at him. They popped down out of sight instantly. There was no rhythm involved, just random objects coming from all sides. He could not anticipate their rising, nor could he shoot them through the balcony front. More men infiltrated the hall, getting behind heavy chairs and tables in order to push toward him as makeshift shields and barricades from Vash's weapon. More spears and knives flew as if having minds of their own.

"Vash!" cried the Lady Adeline, in a stressed high-pitched scream.

Thinking that maybe she had an exit for him to make it into, he quickly sprang to his feet to dart past flying blades to her side.

"I ... I didn't want you to come," she wept. *"I had hoped that you would be done with us."*

Seeing that Vash was in position with the Lady Adeline, most of the men halted their barrage assault. Then one man popped up and hurled a knife. The clang of its fall was a very lonely one as it missed its target, but hit the floor just short of Adeline's foot. Fairbeard yelled at retainer.

"You idiot! Think of the Lady Adeline!"

The Lady Adeline suddenly smiled tremulously. *"Of course!"* she said with a sudden realization. *"They don't dare do anything while you are so close to me!"*

"Do you suppose," asked Vash, *"I could count on that?"*

"I'm certain of it!" said Adeline. *"And I think you'd better use it to your advantage if you hope to get out of here alive."*

"Then my lady, I must humbly beg your forgiveness," Vash said politely as he bowed a slight nod in her direction while keeping his eyes fixed on hers.

No sooner was the apology off of his lips, he swung the willing hostage up and over his shoulder. With a stun-pistol in his free hand he headed down the hall.

"Outside," she said almost cheerfully as if excited at the concept of being kidnapped by a pirate. *"Get out the side door and turn left, and nobody can jump down on your neck. Then left again to the gate."*

Vash, only able to make eye contact with her posterior, obeyed without hesitation. Now and again, he got in a pot shot or two with his pistol. Fairbeard had turned the castle into a very pretty trap.

The Lady Adeline said plaintively, *"This is a terribly undignified position for a lady to be in,"* only able to see where they have been. *"I can't see where we're going. Where are we now?"*

"We're almost at the gate," panted Vash feverishly. *"And now here we are,"* as he lunged out of the massive entrance to Fairbeard's stronghold. *"I can put you down now."*

"I wouldn't," said the Lady Adeline, secretly enjoying the idea of Vash carrying her off as a prize won in battle. *"In spite of the fact that we are out of the castle, there are still battlement posts who could reach you from here. I think it best that you make for your lifeboat exactly as we are."*

Again, Vash obeyed the lady Adeline without a word, racing across the open ground. Howls of fury followed him. It was evidently the opinion of the castle that the Lady Adeline was to be abducted in the place of the seven spearmen recently returned.

Vash, breathing hard, reached the lifeboat. At that point he put Adeline down and said anxiously: *"Are you alright my lady? I'm very much in your debt! I was in a spot there!"* Then he nodded toward the castle. *"They are upset, aren't they? They must think I mean to kidnap you from the sounds of it all."*

The Lady Adeline beamed as her face lit up at the prospect. *"It would be wonderful... I mean, absolutely terrible if you did,"* she said, trying to hide her hopefulness. *"I couldn't do a thing to stop you! And a successful public abduction's a legal marriage, on Toffpoint! Wouldn't it be just absolutely terrible?"*

Vash mopped the sweat from his brow and patted her reassuringly on the shoulder.

"Don't worry!" he said warmly. *"You just got me out of an awful fix! You're my friend! And anyhow I'm going to marry a girl on Nemo Vesta, named Jessica. Good-by, Adeline! Keep clear of the rockets and thanks again."*

He went into the boat port, turned to beam almost paternally back at her, and shut the port behind him. Seconds later the lifeboat took off. It left behind clouds of rocket smoke.

Though Vash hadn't the faintest idea of it, along with a fuming Lord Fairbeard, he had also left behind a very irate lady whose irritation could not be measured.

Chapter 10

It is the custom of all men, of all ages, in every corner of the world, to be utterly and absolutely obtuse where women are concerned. Vash was no different as he went skyward in the lifeboat with feelings of warm gratitude toward the Lady Adeline as if she were a younger sister. He hadn't the slightest clue that she, who had twice spoiled her father's skullduggery so far as it affected him, felt anything but the friendliest of feelings toward him. He remembered that he had kept her from the necessity of adjusting to matrimony with the Lord Seymour. It did not occur to him that most girls intend to adjust to marriage with somebody, nor did he even suspect that it is a feminine instinct to make a highly dramatic and romantic production of their marriage so they'll have something to be sentimental about in later years, such as being carried off by a strong sky pirate after fighting off hordes of her father's retainers; no, this was something that would not have entered Vash's mind at all.

As Vash drove forward, the sky became deep purple, and then black velvet set in as flecks of fiery stars began to decorate the vastness. He was relieved by the welcome he'd received earlier today from the emigrants, but he remained slightly puzzled by a very faint impression of desperation remaining. He felt very virtuous on the whole, however, and his plans for the future were specific. He'd already composed a letter to his grandfather, which he'd ask the emigrant fleet to deliver. He had another letter in his mind—a form letter, practically a public-relations circular—which he hoped to whip into shape before the emigrants got too anxious to be on their way. He considered that he needed to earn a little more of their gratitude before asking a favor.

For himself, he anticipated only the deep satisfaction of accomplishment. He'd wanted to do great things since he was a small boy, and even greater things in the fields of mechanics and electronics since his discovery of the manuals in his adolescence. When he'd found those textbooks in the libraries of looted ships, he knew that he would someday be an engineer. He'd gone to Nemo

Vesta in the hopes of great achievements. There, of course, he failed because in a fascist economy industrialists of the state consider that freedom is the privilege to be stupid without penalty. In other economies, of course, stupidity is held to be the duty of administrators. But Vash now believed himself in a situation of having knowledge and abilities, which were needed by people who knew their need and appreciated those who could help them, unlike certain individuals.

It wasn't until he'd made contact with the fleet, and was in the act of maneuvering the lifeboat to a side-blister on the liner hull that doubts again filled his mind. He had done a few things—accomplished a little. He'd devised a broadcast-power receptor, a microwave projection pistol and he'd turned a Lawlor drive into a ball lightning projector and worked out a few more minor things like that, but it turns out that the first had been invented before by somebody on one of the floating cities, and the second was a Teslian design that anyone could have made with some basic education on how Tesla's mind worked and the third was standard practice on Gibbit Cove. He began to lament for he still felt that he hadn't done anything of real significance.

When he made fast to the liner and crawled through the boat-tube to its hull, he was in a state of doubt, which passed very well for modesty to those greeting him as he entered.

The bearded old man received him in the skipper's quarters, which Vash himself had occupied for a few days. He looked very weary. He seemed to have aged quite quickly, in hours since Vash last saw him.

"We grow more astounded by the minute," he told Vash heavily, *"by what you have brought us. Ten shiploads like this and we would be better equipped than we believed ourselves in the beginning. It looks as if some thousands of us will now be able to survive our colonization of the New Ivoryhelm."*

Vash looked at him through dreary eyes. The old man put his hand on Vash's shoulder.

"We are truly grateful," he said with a drawn attempt at warmth. *"Please do not doubt that! It is only that ... that—we cannot help but wish that ... well, instead of unfamiliar tools for metal-working and machines with tapes.... we wish that, instead of these*

unfamiliar devices that we had more of the tools that we are most accustom too!"

Vash's jaw dropped in disbelief. The people of Ivoryhelm wanted more of the archaic machinery that they had been using and could not see any value at all in the newer, more productive pieces that he had acquired for them. Most of them could only look forward to starvation when the ship supplies were exhausted, because not enough ground could be broken and cultivated early enough to grow food enough in time for everyone in the fleet.

"Would it," asked the old man desperately, *"be possible to exchange these useless machines for others that will be more helpful to us?"*

"Let me speak with your mechanics, sir," snapped Vash unhappily. *"Maybe something can be done."*

He restrained himself from verbally tearing into the leader as he went to where the mechanics of the fleet looked over their treasure-trove. He'd come up to the fleet again to gloat and do great things for people who needed him and knew it. But instead, he faced the hopelessness of people to whom his utmost effort seemed mockery because it was so far from being enough.

He gathered together the men who'd tried to keep the fleet's ships in working order during their flight. They were competent men, of course. They were resolute in their commission to keep things going, but now they had given up hope. Vash began to lecture them. They needed machines. He hadn't brought the machines that they wanted, but he had brought the machines that could be used to make them with. Here were automatic shapers, turret lathes, dicers, etc. In another holding area there were cutting-points for machines; these machines could make machines the colony on the New Ivoryhelm would require and this way, could be modified to fit the environment. He'd brought these because they had the raw material, the ships themselves! Even some of the junk they carried in crates was good metal, merely worn out in its present form, but usable to make new mechanics for their use. They could make anything they needed with what he'd brought them. For example, he'd show them how to make lumber saws for making building materials for housing, or maybe a piping lathe to create irrigation pipes…The possibilities were endless with the right education on the supplies and materials that lay before them.

The mechanics watched somewhat baffled at the crates of supplies with no sign of hope. *"I've brought you everything you need for where you are going!"* Vash insisted. *"You've got a civilization, compact, on this ship! You've got life instead of starvation! Look at this,"* pulling out some basic mechanics and tubing, *"With these items here, I can make a water pump to irrigate your fields!"*

Before their eyes he turned out an irrigation pump on an automatic steam powered shaper. He showed them that the shaper went on, by itself, making other pumps without further instructions than the by-hand control of the tools that formed the first one.

The mechanics stirred uneasily. They had watched without comprehension. Now they listened without enthusiasm. Their eyes were like those of children who watch marvels without comprehending what they saw. Vash looked at the awe in their eyes and almost felt like a magician doing tricks on stage.

He made a sled for transporting large items, whose runners seemed to hover on air, with a good inch between themselves and whatever object would otherwise have touched them. It was practically frictionless. He made a machine that molded nails by the hundreds in varying sizes—with just a few inputs of calculations. He made a power hammer which hummed and pushed nails into any object that needed to be nailed. Vash stopped abruptly, and sat down with his head in his hands. The people of the fleet faced so overwhelming a catastrophe that they could not see past the day-to-day survival mode that they had all taken. They could only experience it as it was happening.

Vash raised his head. The mechanics looked dully at him. *"You men do maintenance, right? You repair things when they wear out on the ships? Have you run out of some materials you need for repairs?"*

After a long silence between the men, a tired-looking man said slowly: *"On the ship I come from, we're having trouble. Our hydroponic garden keeps the air fresh, of course, but the water-circulation pipes are so far gone that there are literally open springs running through the belly of the ship, which is causing the hull to rusted through. We haven't had any pipe to fix them with. We have to keep the water moving with buckets."*

Vash got up. He looked about him. He hadn't brought hydroponic-garden pipe supplies, but he showed them that there were raw materials. He took a pair of power snips and cut away a section of cargo space wall lining that had been stuffed into a cargo bin as part of the junk given them. He cut it into strips. He asked the diameter of the pipe. Before their eyes he made pipe—spirally wound around a mandril and line-welded to solidity.

"I need some of that on my ship too," said another man. The bearded man said heavily: *"We'll make some and send it to the ships that need it."*

"No," said Vash. *"You will do no such thing. We'll send the other ships the tools they need to make their own. We will make the tools here. There must be other kinds of repairs that can't be made. With the machines I've brought, we'll make the tools to make the repairs. These picture-tape devices connected to these vision screens have reels of instructions that show exactly how to do it."*

It was a totally new concept for them to take in. The mechanics had immediate problems that needed to be addressed besides the overall impending disaster of the fleet; pumps that did not work, motors overheating and varying types of flight mechanisms slowly giving way causing ships to not maintain proper flight. They could envision fixing and rigging the problems at hand, and they could envision the long-term goal of what to do once they had transported the fleet to the new planet, but they could not imagine anything in between. They couldn't see getting from their current state of point A to the final goal of point B, but now they were capable of learning how to make tools for repairs, so potentially envisioning the next step was now around the corner.

Vash was patient to teach them. By the end of the first day of training there were five ships in varying staged of being brought back to better operating condition than they had worked at in years. Two days. Three. Mechanics began to come to the liner from the other vessels to learn what Vash had to teach. Those who'd learned first pompously thought themselves to be the star pupils and passed on what they knew to the others. On the fourth day one of the mechanics actually began to use a vision-tape machine to get information on a finer point in welding without being guided to do so. On the fifth day there were lines of men waiting to use them as Vash could now see that his work was getting easier.

On the sixth day a mechanic on what had been a luxury passenger sky liner many scores ago asked to talk to Vash via the ship communicator due to the fact that he had been too busy with his newfound knowledge to leave his vessel to visit Vash face to face. He'd been working feverishly at the minor repairs he'd been unable to make for so long. To get material he pulled a crate off one of the junk machines supplied the fleet. He looked it over. He believed that if a specific piece was made new, and then replaced, using sound metal, that the machine might be completely operational again.

Vash insisted that he come to the liner, which was now the flagship of the fleet for all things mechanical. Discussion began as blueprints were sketched and resketched. Shaping such large pieces of metal, which could be taken from here or there—shaping such large pieces of metal.... Vash began to draw diagrams. They were not clear. He drew more. Abruptly, he stared at what he'd outlined. Electronics.... He saw something remarkable. If one applied a perfectly well-known bit of pure-science information that nobody bothered with— He finished the diagram and a vast, soothing satisfaction came over him. *"We've got to get out of here!"* he said. "Not enough room!"

Vash looked about him. Insensibly, as he talked to the first man on the fleet to show imagination, other men had gathered around. They were all now absorbed in the descriptions that were described. *"I think,"* said Vash, *"that we can make an electronic field that'll soften the bonding forms between the crystals of steel, without heating up anything else, similar to a device I made on Nemo Vesta, but much stronger. If it works, we can make die-forgings and die-stampings seamless! And then that useless junk you've got can be turned back into raw material which can then be quickly stamped into useable parts."*

They listened in astonished silence, occasionally nodding as he spoke. They did not quite understand everything, but they had now made it a habit to believe anything Vash told them. He commissioned specific pieces to be brought to the huge cargo spaces of the ship the leader had formerly used.

"Hm-m-m," said Vash. *"How about duplicating these machines and sending them over?"*

They looked hesitatingly at the tool-shop equipment. The mere pressing of a few buttons, twists of a few knobs and pulling of a lever could program the machine to self-replicate.

The new machine shop, in the ancient ark of retired flying vessels made another machine shop to be placed on another ship. In the other ship that tool shop would make another which would find its way to another ship, which in turn....

By then Vash had a cold-metal die-stamper in operation. It was very large. It drew on the big ship's drive unit for power. One put a rough mass of steel in place between the dies and with one swift turn of a switch, engaged the power. For no more than a second or two, the steel was soft as putty. Then it stiffened and was warm. But in that second or so, it had been shaped with absolute precision to fit the piece that it was made for.

It took two days to completely duplicate the jungle-plow in new sound metal. What amazed the mechanics, however, is that with a few dials and knobs and the throwing of a switch, the machine began to recreate new, identical jungle plows with little effort on their part.

There were other enterprises on hand, of course. A mechanic who stuttered horribly had an idea. He could not explain it or diagram it. So… he just simply made it. It was an electric motor very far ahead of most of the machines of Ivoryhelm's current collection. This motor could run the liner itself with half the reserve currently needed and the design was simple enough that it could easily be modified and fitted to all of the larger vessels, even the large bladdered dirigibles.

Vash, himself, even woke from a light cat nap with a diagram burning in his head, as he often did when he was back on Gibbit Cove. He drew it out; half-asleep, and later looked and found that his unconscious mind had designed a power-supply system which made the one he had created on Nemo Vesta look rather primitive. More importantly, it could be built into a larger version to replace the transport system the small scout ship had been using to transport back and forth to the new planet they had found. Though Vash was still skeptical about living on new planets and being able to transport there instantaneously, he did see the scout ship do it and the theory was sound.

During the first six days Vash did not sleep for any length of time to speak of, and after that he merely cat-napped off and on, but he finally agreed with the emigrants' leader—now no longer fierce, but fiercely triumphant—that he thought they could go on to work on a larger version of their transport system that would take the entire fleet to the new planet. It was now that Vash felt confident enough that he would ask a favor.

The next morning, he propped his eyelids open, jumped to his paper and quill and wrote the letter to his grandfather that he'd composed in his mind in the liner on Port Barogate. He managed to make one copy, un-addressed, of the public-relations letter that he'd worked out at the same time. He put it through an ansible facsimile transmission machine and managed to address and send fifty copies to their proposed locations. Then he yawned uncontrollably, feeling ready for a long hibernation.

Still yawning, he went to take leave of the leader of the people of Ivoryhelm. The leader looked up to him as a savior of his people and simultaneously down on him as a son.

"I think everything's all right," said Vash, still yawning from exhaustion. *"You've got a dozen machine shops that are fully functional as well as some enthusiastic mechanics, now, soaking in the vision-tape materials and finding out more than they guessed there was, and they're starting to think for themselves and create; I think you'll make out just fine now."*

The bearded man looked at Vash and said humbly: *"I was waiting until you said all was well to ask this of you, but now that we can see our future again, will you come with us?"*

"OH No-o-o," said Vash. He yawned again. *"I have my work here and there's an ... obligation I have to meet before I think about uprooting again."*

"It must be very admirable work," said the old man wistfully. *"I wish we had more young men like you among us."*

"You have," said Vash. *"I just trained them and they will be giving you trouble presently."*

The old man turned down his head and laughed for the first time in what seemed like years for the elderly leader. He then looked at Vash very affectionately and nodded his head in agreement before glancing down toward the letters Vash had handed him.

"We will deliver your letters," he said warmly. *"First to Port Barogate, and then to Nemo Vesta. Then we will go on and let down your letter and gift to your grandfather on Gibbit Cove as you asked. After that we will be on our way to New Ivoryhelm. Our mechanics will work at building machines while we are in overdrive."*

Vash nodded exhausted as he stretched his arms out trying to reinvigorate himself.

"So," said the old man contentedly, *"we hope that you will pardon us if we only let down your letters using drop balloons, and don't actually visit those planets? We have prejudices with two of them as you know."*

"Perfectly satisfactory," said Vash. *"I understand and am fine with it as long as they get to their final destinations."*

"The mechanics you have trained," said the old man proudly, *"have prepared a little gift for you in appreciation for all you have done. It is not much, but we did see how you enjoyed the space yacht, so we upgraded it and fit it with a small tool shop. You will also find that the operations deck has been outfitted with a small Ansiblary Resonance Modulation Unit with the coordinates preprogrammed into a specific dial combination that will bring you into the outer aether of New Ivoryhelm. I know that you have not actually used the device and may not trust it, but it is there for you none the less and will guide your vessel safely to us, if even for a visit.!"* The old man then scratched his chin and said, *"unfortunately, we still haven't worked out all of the kinks and the jump drains the power very quickly, so the current ship's abilities will allow enough for one jump before the entire ship's power reserve is drained, but I am sure that a man of your means might find a way to fix that."*

Vash would have been more touched by the generosity if they had just presented it to him instead of being told about it ahead of time, but one of the men entrusted with the job of modifying the vessel had harassed Vash constantly for advice in a manner that led to suspicion. He had a strong idea of what he was getting. The sky yacht, now equipped as a potential space yacht, was completely refurbished and fitted with everything the emigrants could provide down to new layers of paint.

He affected the appearance of great surprise and expressed unfeigned appreciation. Barely an hour had passed before Vash transferred to his new vessel with the absconded lifeboat locked in position in the boat port just under the dual aether bladders. He watched as the emigrant fleet headed out toward the emptiness of the sea in order to gain enough open space to open the jump hole and resume its valiant journey. Vash allowed his mind to wander on the facts that merely days prior, this was a journey of failure for them, but now, in fact, the colony on New Ivoryhelm was starting out better-equipped than most fully settled and pre-established colonies.

He allowed himself a moment of self-appreciation before he laid down and went to sleep. He'd nothing urgent to do, except allow a certain amount of time to pass before he did anything. He was exhausted. He slept almost a full day before waking up and then ate a bite, and went back to sleep again. On the whole, the spinning planet that he looked down on did not notice the difference. Stars flamed in emptiness, and planets rotated sedately on their axes. Comets flung out gossamer veils or retracted them, and sky liners went about upon their lawful occasions. Lovers swore by stars and moon along with many other various things which had absolutely nothing to do with Vash, so he slept in peace.

When he finally woke again, he was totally rested, and he reviewed all his actions and his situation. It appeared that matters promised fairly well on the emigrant fleet now gone forever, with only a dissipating vapor trail lofting in the aether where the fleet once took port. They would remember Vash with affection for a decade or so, and after that would be taught to the young as a legend who single handedly saved their entire civilization. He then felt a sense of reality and thought how settling a new world would be enthralling and important work and that no one would think of him at all, after a certain length of time. He then allowed his mind to snap back to an obligation he'd assumed on their account that needed to be addressed post haste.

He considered his own affairs. He had told Adeline that he was going to marry Jessica. The way things looked, that was no longer so probable. Of course, in a year or two, or a few years even, he might be out from under the obligations he now considered due. In time even the Nemo Vestaian government would realize that Tesla's death ray announcement would only be that of theory and do not actually exist, and a lawyer might be able to clear things for his return to Nemo Vesta. But—Jessica was a nice girl.

He frowned. That was it. She was a remarkably nice girl. But Vash suddenly doubted if she were a delightful one. He found himself questioning that she was exactly and perfectly what his long-cherished ambitions described. He tried to imagine spending his declining years with Jessica. He couldn't quite picture it as exciting as he once did. She did tend to be a little insipid—And her father, he couldn't forget about her father.

Presently, gloomy and a trifle dogged about it, he locked his new vessel in an orbit above Toffpoint where he then transferred to the lifeboat, now with updated equipment and rockets, to head down toward Toffpoint. Being fully rested, he had work to do, which could not be neglected any longer. To carry out that work, he needed a crew able and willing to pass for pirates for a pirate's pay. And there were innumerable castles on Toffpoint, with quite as many shifty noblemen, and certainly no fewer plunder-hungry Toffpointian gentlemen hanging around them. Lord Fairbeard's castle had one real advantage and one which existed only in Vash's mind.

Fairbeard's retainers all knew that Vash had led their companions to loot; Large loot. He'd have less trouble and more enthusiastic support from Fairbeard's retainers than any other.

The illusion that he had, being that he had the common sense of a man, was that the Lady Adeline was his firm personal friend with a no-nonsense attitude about her. Vash would soon come to realize that this was a very great mistake on his part.

He landed for the fourth time outside Fairbeard's castle. This time he had no booty-laden men to march to the castle and act as heralds of his presence. The lifeboat's visionscreens showed fairbeard's stronghold as immense, dark and menacing. Banners flew from its turrets, their colors bright in the ruddy light of the dimming sunset. The gate remained closed. For a long time, there was no sign that his landing had even been noted. Then there was movement on the battlements, and a figure began to descend outside the wall. It was lowered to the ground by a long rope.

It reached the ground and shook itself. It marched, toward the lifeboat through the red and nearly level rays of the dying sun. Vash watched with curiosity and a frown as he noticed that this wasn't a retainer of Lord Fairbeard. It assuredly wasn't Adeline. He couldn't even make out its gender until the figure was right next to the hull.

Then he looked astonished. It was his old friend Derk, who had arrived on Toffpoint a long while since in the vary lifeboat Vash had been using ever since. Derk had been his boon companion in the days when he expected to become rich by splendid exploits in mechanics and electronics. Derk was also the character who'd conscientiously told the authorities about Vash and his invention, when they found his power-receptor sneaked into a Mid-Continent station and a stray corpse coincidentally outside.

He opened the life boat's port and stood in the opening. Derk had been a guest—or at least an inhabitant—of Fairbeard's castle for a good long while now. Vash wondered if he considered his quarters cozy and if he had been locked in at night as Vash was.

"Evening, Derk," said Vash cordially. *"You're looking well!"*

"I do? Well, I don't feel it," said Derk dismally. *"I feel like a fool in the castle yonder and the police official I came here with has gotten quite grumpy and snaps when I try to speak to him."*

Vash said gravely: *"I'm sure the Lady Adeline—"*

"A tigress!" interrupted Derk bitterly. *"We don't get along at all."*

Looking at Derk, Vash found himself able to understand why. Derk was the sort of friend one might make on Nemo Vesta for lack of something better. He was well meaning and might be capable of splendid things—even heroism under the right conditions, but under the current conditions, he was appallingly too civilized for the culture of Toffpoint.

"Well! Well!" said Vash kindly. *"And what's on your mind, Derk? What brings you over the wall to make this visit?"*

"I came," Derk said with a scowl, *"to plead with you again, Vash. You must surrender! There's nothing else to do! People can't have death rays, Vash! Above all, you mustn't tell the pirates how to make them!"*

Vash was puzzled for a moment. Then he realized that Derk's information about the fleet came from the spearmen he'd brought back, loaded down with cash. Derk hadn't noticed the absence of the flashing lights at sunset—or hadn't realized that they meant the fleet had gone away.

"Hm-m-m?" pondered Vash out loud. *"And why is it that you don't think I've already done it?"*

"Because they'd have killed you," said Derk. *"Lord Fairbeard pointed that out. He doesn't believe you know how to make death rays. He says it's not a secret anybody would be willing for anybody else to know. But... you know the truth, Vash! You killed that poor man back on Nemo Vesta. You must sacrifice yourself for humanity! You'll be treated kindly!"*

Vash shook his head. It seemed somehow very startling for Derk to be harping on that same idea, after so many things had happened to Vash, but he didn't think Derk would actually expect him to yield to persuasion. There must be something else. Derk might even have nerved himself up to something quite desperate.

"Now, tell me why did you really come out here, Derk?"

"To beg you to—" Then, in one instant, Derk made a hysterical gesture toward his belt as Vash pulled the stun pistol that he had been holding inconspicuously the entire time and fired. A small object left Derk's hand as his muscles convulsed from the stun-pistol bolt. It did not fly quite true. It fell a foot or so to one side of the boat port instead of inside, which was its intended target.

It exploded luridly as Derk crumpled from the pistol bolt. There was thick, strangling smoke. Vash disappeared. When the thickest of the smoke drifted away there was nothing to be seen but Derk lying on the ground and thinner lofting of smoke slowly drifting out of the still-open boatport.

Nearly half an hour went by when, slowly, figures came very cautiously toward the lifeboat from the castle. Bazil was their leader. His expression was mournful and depressed. Other brawny retainers came uncertainly behind him. At a nod from Bazil, two of them picked up Derk and carted him off toward the castle.

"I guess he got it," said Bazil dismally. He peered in to the boatport and shook his head.

"Wounded from the blast, maybe, and just crawled off to die." He peered in again and shook his head once more. *"No sign of him."*

A spearman, now just behind Bazil said: *"Dirty trick Lord Fairbeard played! I was with him to Nemo Vesta, and he paid off good! A good man! Shoulda been a chieftain! Good man I tell ya!"*

Bazil entered the lifeboat. Gingerly. He wrinkled his nose at the faint smell of explosive still inside. Another man came in followed by another.

"Say!" said one of them in a conspiratorial voice. *"We got our share of that loot from Nemo Vesta but he had a share, too! What'd he do with it? He could've kept it in this boat here. We could take a quick look! What Lord Fairbeard don't know won't hurt him!"*

"I'm going to find Vash first," said Bazil, with dignity and remorse. *"We just won't carry him outside just yet so that Lord Fairbeard knows we're looking for loot, but I'm going to find him first."*

There were other men in the lifeboat now; a full dozen of them. Their spears were very much in the way.

Masked by the clanging around of the retainers' spears and daggers, the boat door closed quietly thanks to the new parts. The retainers stared at each other with surprise as the locking-dogs grumbled for half a second or so, sealing the door tightly. Fairbeard's retainers began to babble in protest, some suddenly remembering how their last encounter with piracy began.

There was a roaring outside. The lifeboat stirred. The roaring rose to thunder. The boat lurched. It flung the spearmen into a sprawling, swearing, terrified heap at the rear end of the boat's interior hull.

The boat went on to quickly reach the outer aether again. In the control room Vash said dourly to himself: *"I'm in a rut! I've got to figure out some way to ship a pirate crew without having to kidnapping them every time. This is starting to get rather monotonous!"*

Chapter 11

There was a disturbance in the air, which seemed to be shared by all the members of Vash's new crew, on the way back to Nemo Vesta. It was not exactly reluctance, because there was self-evident enthusiasm over the idea of making a pirate voyage under him. So far as past enterprises were concerned, it was obvious that Vash, as a leader, was the answer to a Toffpointian gentleman's prayer. The partial looting of Seymour's castle, alone, would have made him a desirable leader. But a crew of seven, returned from a voyage in the skies to display wealth which amounted to that only spoke of in fables of lands lost in the great flood. No one really knew if these places actually had existed, but they were now used as synonyms of uncountable riches. It was now a fact that when men went off with Vash, they came back rich.

But nevertheless, there was still an unshakable discomfort about the atmosphere in the renovated yacht. Now in the yacht, they were quite docile about it because none of them knew how to get back to ground. Vash left the lifeboat fixed with an onboard trigger/timing signal set to be engaged from a homing device in which he had placed underneath a decorative brocade on the lapel of his Vest, He drove his wonderful new yacht well out of Toffpointian visual range before setting coarse for Nemo Vesta.

Within hours he noted the disturbing feel of things. His followers were not happy. They moped. They sat in corners and submerged themselves in misery. Large, massive men with drooping scowls—ideal characters for the roles of pirates—tended to squeeze tears out of their eyes at odd moments. When the ship was a few hours into its journey, the atmosphere inside it was that of a funereal. The spearmen did not even gorge their stomachs on the food with which the yacht was now amply stocked. And when a Toffpointian gentleman lost his appetite, something had to be wrong.

He called Bazil into the control room. *"What's the matter with the gang?"* he demanded somewhat vexed. *"They look at me as if I'd broken all their hearts! Do they want to go back?"*

Bazil heaved a sigh, indicating depression beside which suicidal mania would be hilarity. He said pathetically: *"We cannot go back. We cannot ever return to Toffpoint. We are lost men, doomed to wander forever among strangers, or to float as corpses in the sea."*

"What happened?" demanded Vash. *"I'm taking you on a pirate cruise where the loot should be a lot better than last time!"*

Bazil wept. Vash was astonished as he regarded his whiskery countenance, contorted with grief and dampened with tears.

"It happened at the castle," said Bazil miserably. *"That man Derk, from Nemo Vesta, had thrown a bomb at you. You seemed to be dead. But Lord Fairbeard was not sure. He fretted, as he often does. He wished to send someone to make sure. The Lady Adeline said; 'I will make sure!' She called me to her and said, 'Bazil, will you fight for me?' And there was Lord Fairbeard suddenly nodding beside her. So, I said yes, my Lady Adeline. Then she said; 'Thank you. I am troubled by Vash Rayburn.' So what could I do? She said the same thing to each of us, and each of us had to say that he would fight for her. To each she said that you troubled her. Then the good Lord Fairbeard sent us out to look at your body. And now we are disgraced!"*

Vash's mouth opened and closed and opened again as he remembered this small item of Toffpointian etiquette. If a girl asked a man if he would fight for her, and he agreed, then within a day and a night he had to fight the man she sent him to fight, or else he was disgraced. And disgrace on Toffpoint meant that the shamed man could be plundered or killed by anybody who chose to do so, but indignant authority would hang him if he resisted. It was a great deal worse than outlawry. It included scorn and contempt and opprobrium. It meant dishonor and humiliation and admitted degradation in the annals of Toffpointian history. A disgraced man was despicable in his own eyes and Vash had now kidnapped these men who'd been forced to engage themselves to fight him, and if they killed him they would obviously die as none of them knew how to fly the vessel and it would surely crash into the sea, and if they didn't they'd be ashamed to stay alive. The moral tone on Toffpoint was probably not elevated, but etiquette seemed to be a force that went higher than good judgment.

Vash thought it over. He looked up suddenly. *"Some of them,"* he said wryly, *"probably figure there's nothing to do but go through with it, eh?"*

"Yes," said Bazil dismally. *"Then we will all die."*

"Hm-m-m," said Vash. *"The obligation is to fight. If you fail to kill me, then that isn't your fault, is it? Am I correct to assume that if you are conquered by me, you're in the clear?"*

Bazil said miserably: *"True. Too true! When a man is conquered... he is conquered. His conqueror may plunder him, when the matter is finished, or he can spare him, when he may never fight his conqueror again."*

"Then draw your knife," demanded Vash. *"And come at me."*

Bazil bewilderedly made the gesture. Vash leveled his stun-pistol to Bazil and said:

"Bzzz! You are now conquered. You came at me with your knife, and I shot you with my stun-pistol. It's all over. Right?"

Bazil blankly looked at him, not quite sure of the gesture that had just transpired and then he spontaneously beamed ear to ear. With his newfound expression, he expanded, he gloated, he frisked around like a schoolgirl. He practically wagged a nonexistent tail in his exuberance. He had been shown an out when he could see no out due to his mourning of the situation in front of him. Vash's grandfather would have used the opportunity to pint out one of his colloquial phrases, long since burned into Vash's brain; *"A man simply can't read the label from inside the bottle."*

"Send in the others one by one," said Vash. *" So that I can take care of them post haste, but Bazil—why did the Lady Adeline want me killed?"*

Bazil had no idea, but he did not care. Vash didn't care either, or at least didn't show it. He was bewildered and more inclined to be indignant. A noble friendship like theirs is obviously one filled with controversy and one should only take it at face value. A spearman came in and saluted. Vash went through a symbolic duel, which was plainly the way the thing would have happened in reality. Others came in and went through the same process. Two of them did not quite grasp what was going on as they were more known for their brawn than their brains and did not quite understand that it was a ritual, and he had to actually shoot them in the knife arm. After, he hunted in the ship's supplies for ointment to apply on the blisters that would appear from stun-pistol bolts at such short range. As he bandaged the places, he again tried to find out why the Lady Adeline had tried to get him carved up by the large-bladed knives all Toffpointian gentlemen wore. Nobody could seem to enlighten him. Still, he played that it did not really concern him even though it was obvious now that it did.

After the mock battles, the atmosphere on the ship improved remarkably. Since each theoretic fight had taken place in private, nobody was obliged to admit a compromise with etiquette and Vash's followers ceased to brood at that point. They developed huge appetites. Those who had been aground on Port Barogate told zestfully of the monstrous hangovers they'd acquired there. It appeared that Vash was revered for the size of the benders he enabled his followers to hang on.

But there remained, in Vash's mind, the fact that the Lady Adeline had tried to get him massacred. He puzzled over it. The little yacht sped through the outer atmosphere toward Nemo Vesta. He tried to think how he had so wrongfully offended Adeline. Being a man's man and not one of the natural understandings of women, he could think of nothing. He set to work on a new electronic setup, which would make yet another modification of the Lawlor Drive possible. He almost felt bad to have to crack into the control panel again and make another rigged switch after the mechanics of Ivoryhelm painstakingly redesigned it with custom fittings and switches just for him. This was going to be the trickiest rigging of all. It required the homemade vacuum tube he had created earlier to burn steadily when in use. But it was a very simple idea. Lawlor drives and landing grid force fields were formed by not so dissimilar generators, and ball lightning force fields were in the same general family of phenomena. Suppose one were to make a field generator that could work as a grid field, but had to be on a ship if it was to work, capable of creating all those allied, associated, similar force fields with the mere turn of a knob and flip of a switch? If a ship could make the different fields of landing grids, ball lightning, thrust ports, etc., it should be most useful to pirates.

Vash's present errand was neither pure nor simple piracy, but piracy it would be. The more he considered the obligation he'd taken on himself when he helped the emigrant-fleet, the more he doubted that he could lift it without long struggle. He was preparing to carry on that struggle for a long time. He had, more or less, resigned himself to the postponement of his personal desires. Jessica, for example. He wasn't quite sure— Perhaps, after all—

Time passed, and he finished his new electronic modification. He came out of overdrive and made his astrogation observations and corrected his course, all the while telling himself that when he had the time, he needed to learn how to use the onboard navigation controls. Finally, off in the starboard viewscreen, Nemo Vesta appeared. It writhed and spun in the vast silence of emptiness over the Earth as the under mechanics kept the stationary colony with its burbs in a harmonious orbit.

Vash drove to a point still above the five-diameter limit of Nemo Vesta as he had done before. He interestedly switched on the new control, which made his drive-unit manufacture landing-grid-type force fields. He groped for Nemo Vesta, and felt the peculiar rigidity of the ship when the field took hold somewhere underground. He made an adjustment, and felt the ship respond. So now, instead of pulling a ship to the ground, as the landing grid did to make the vessel stationary enough for the grappling arms to connect, the setup he had made now pulled the ground toward the ship. When he reversed the adjustment, instead of pushing the ship away to empty aether, the new field pushed against the floating city itself.

There was no practical difference, of course. The effect was simply that the sky yacht now carried its own, built-in landing grid. It could descend anywhere and ascend from anywhere without using rockets. Moreover, it could hover, drawing from the repelled force of the other body as opposed to using up its own power to stay lofted. It would also eliminate the constant back and forth to and from the lifeboat.

Vash was pleased with how well it worked. He took the yacht down to a bare four-mile altitude. He stopped it there. It was highly satisfactory for its maiden trial. He made quite certain that everything had worked, as it should before he made a call on the communicator.

"Calling ground," said Vash. *"Calling ground. Pirate ship calling ground!"*

He waited for an answer. Now he'd find out the result of very much effort and planning. He was apprehensive, of course. There was much responsibility on his shoulders. There was the liner he'd captured and looted and given to the emigrants. There were his followers on the yacht, now enthusiastically sharpening their two-foot knife blades in expectation of loot. He owed these people something. For an instant he thought of the Lady Adeline and wondered how he could make reparation to her for whatever had hurt her feelings that made her so cross that she would try to get his throat cut.

A whining, bitterly unhappy voice came to him. *"Pirate ship!"* said a mournfully melancholy voice, *"we received the fleet's warning. Please state where you intend to descend, and we will take measures to prevent disorder. Repeat, please state where you intend to descend and we will take measures to prevent disorder— "*

Vash drew a sharp breath of relief. He named a spot—a high-income residential suburb community some forty miles from the capital. He set his controls for a very gradual descent. He went out to where his followers made grisly grinding noises with occasional sparks as they honed their knives for potential battle.

"We'll be landing," said Vash sternly, *"in about twenty minutes of an hour. You will go ashore and loot in parties of not less than three! Bazil, you will be ship guard and receive the plunder and make sure that nobody from Nemo Vesta gets on board. You will not waste time committing atrocities on the population! Our time here is short, so stick to looting and nothing more."*

He then went back to the control room and turned the communicator to general-communication bands and listened to the broadcasts coming from down below.

"Special Emergency Bulletin!" boomed a voice. *"Pirates are landing in the community of Periwatch, a half mile from Nemo Vesta City. The population is instructed to evacuate immediately, leaving all action to the police. Repeat! The population will evacuate Periwatch, leaving all action to the police. Take nothing with you. Take nothing with you. Leave at once."*

Vash nodded approvingly. The voice boomed again: *"Special Emergency Bulletin! Pirates are landing ... evacuate ... take nothing with you.... For your own safety, leave at once...."*

He tuned in to another broadcast where an overly excited voice barked:

"... Seems to be only the one pirate ship, which has been located hovering in an unknown manner over Periwatch. We are rushing vision tape recording crews to the spot and will try to give on-the-spot, as-it-happens coverage of the landing of pirates on Nemo Vesta, their looting of the community of Periwatch, and the traffic jams inevitable in the departure of its citizens before the pirate ship touches ground. For background information on this, the most exciting event in the world history since the visitors and the flood, I take you to our editorial rooms." Another voice took over instantly. *"It will be remembered that it was merely a few days prior that there was a gigantic pirate fleet flying overhead, which sent down a communication to the Nemo Vestaian government, warning that single ships would appear to loot and giving notice that any resistance—"*

Vash felt a contented, heart-warming glow. The emigrant fleet had most faithfully carried out its leader's promise to let down a letter from the fleet while in full effect, covering the entire sky with its full fleet. The emigrants, of course, did not know the contents of the letter. They would not send anybody down to the surface; because of the fears they had toward those who had taken the hospitality of their forefathers and abused it, only to follow up with threats to them.

Blithely, and cheerfully, and dutifully, they would give the appearance of monstrous piratical strength that Nemo Vesta would be no match for. They would awe Nemo Vesta thoroughly with their enormity and then add fear as the entire fleet vanished as quickly as they came before a single sky marshal could be contacted. And then they'd go on, faithfully leaving similar letters and similar impressions on Port Barogate, and other well-to-do colonies until the stock of addressed missives had run out. They would perform this kindly act out of gratitude to Vash and then move out of the current orbit into that of their newfound planet, if in fact they had actually been able to find another planet.

With every colony they visited, the citizens of that colony would be left with the impression that the fleet overhead was that of bloodthirsty sky-marauders who would presently send single ships to collect loot—which must be yielded without resistance or else. Such looting expeditions were to be looked for regularly and must be submitted to under penalty of unthinkable retribution from the monster fleet of ghost pirates.

Now, as the yacht descended on Periwatch, it represented that mythical but impressive piratical empire of Vash's sole contrivance. He listened with genuine pleasure to the broadcasts as he flipped back and forth from station to station. When low enough, he even picked up the pictures of highways thronged with fugitives from the to-be-looted suburb community. He saw their police directing the traffic of both flying and ground transports. He saw other traffic heading toward the capital. Nemo Vesta was one of the most highly civilized colonies on the planet, at least out of all of the manufactured colonies currently aether stationed, and its citizens had had no worries at all except for the bouts of occasional boredom. When something genuinely exciting turned up, they wanted to be there to see it.

The yacht descended below the clouds. Vash turned on an emergency flare to make a landing by. Sitting in the control room he saw his own ship as the broadcast vision tape crews clustered about and picked it up, relaying it to thousands of viewscreens across the colony. He was impressed. It was a glaring eye of fierce light, descending deliberately with a dark and mysterious craft behind it. He heard the chattered on-the-spot news accounts of the happening. He saw the people who had not left Periwatch yet joined by avid visitors from other communities on the sky colony. He saw all of them held back by police, who frantically shepherded them away from the area in which the pirates should begin their horrid deeds.

Vash even watched pleasurably from his control room as the broadcasters daringly showed the actual touch-down of the ship, giving second by second account as if it were the final days of the colony as they knew it; the dramatic slow opening of its entrance port: the appearance of authentic pirates in the opening, armed to the teeth, bristling ferociously, glaring about them at the near-silent, near-deserted streets of the city left to their mercies; this voided space left for the pirate's plundering.

It was a splendid broadcast. Vash would have liked to stay and watch all of it. But he had work to do. He had to supervise the pirate raid from beginning to end.

It was, as it turned out, simple enough. Looting parties of three pirates each moved skulking about, seeking plunder. Quaking vision tape recording crews dared to ask them, in shaking voices, to pose for the vision tape recorders. It was a request no Toffpointian gentleman, even in an act of piracy, couldn't possibly refuse. They posed, making pictures of malignant ruffianisms with visions of skullduggery in their eyes; truly a visual spectacle to behold. Vash thought, *"I wonder what Lord Fairbeard would say to see his retainers in such a display...He would be peevish in his resolve that his actions did not afford him the opportunity to be a part of it."* He snickered to himself at the thought of, yet again, making Fairbeard disappointed.

Commentators, adding informed comment to delectably thrilling pictures, observed that the pirates wore Toffpointian costume, but observed crisply that this did not mean that Toffpoint as an entity had turned pirate, but only that some of her citizens had joined the pirate fleet.

The crews then asked apologetically if the pirates would permit themselves to be broadcast in the act of looting. Growling and grunting savagely to give their public what they wanted, and occasionally throwing in a fiendish *"Ha!"* they obliged. The crews actually began to help the looters pick out good places to plunder that would make for the best lighted pictures. The pirates cooperated in fine dramatic style, giving Vash a sense of honor to be in the working presence of such thespians. Thousands watching vision sets all over the flying colony, shivered in dramatically delicious horror as the pirates went about their nefarious enterprise of gain.

Presently the police could not hold the press of onlookers back. They surrounded the pirates. Some, greatly daring, asked for autographs. Girls watched them with round, frightened, fascinated eyes. Younger men found it vastly thrilling to carry burdens of loot back to the pirate ship for them. Bazil complained hoarsely that the ship was getting overloaded. Vash ordered greater discrimination, but his pirates by this time were in the position of directors rather than looters themselves. Romantic Nemo Vestaian admirers smashed windows and brought them treasure, for the reward of a scowling acceptance.

Vash eventually had to call off the pirates in training, both his crew and the citizens that were now helping because the ship's cargo hold *"was loaded from tip to gill,"* as Vash's grandfather used to say. He called back his men, however, one party of three did not return. He took two others and fought his way through the mob. He found the trio backed against a wall while hysterically adoring girls struggled to seize scraps of their garments for mementos of real, live pirates looting a Toffpoitian town! Vash, in all of his years on Gibbit Cove, had never heard a tale of pirate groupies. This would definitely be one to tell his grandfather one day.

Breaking away the would-be celebrities from their newfound adoring fans, Vash got them back to the ship. Somewhat blushful as they entered the ship, their clothes were in shreds. Vash, being the last to enter the ship, had to fight his way out of the mob in order to get in. Cheers rose from the onlookers as he got the landing port shut only by the help of police who kept pirate fans from having their fingers cut off in its closing deck port.

Then the piratical space yacht rose swiftly toward the stars leaving their adoring fans to clean up the mess and return to the doldrums of Nemo Vestaian life.

Roughly an hour later there was barely a sign of decline in the excitement inside the ship. Vash's followers still picked, floated, and danced over the plunder that had been tucked everywhere. It was so full that it began to crowd the living quarters as the men sorted and picked. It threatened to interfere with the astrogation of the ship. Vash came out of the control room annoyed at the spectacle.

"Break it up!" he snapped. *"Pack that stuff away somewhere! What do you think this is? It's a pirate ship...My pirate ship, not your house."*

Bazil gazed at him abstractedly, not quite able to tear his mind and thoughts from this completely unimaginable mass of plunder. Then intelligence came into his eyes—as much as could appear there. He grinned suddenly. He slapped his thigh.

"Boys!" he gurgled out as if drunk. *"He didn't see what we got for him, did he?"*

The others stopped their inventory check and beamed as they looked at Bazil and then to Vash. They got to their feet, weighed down and dripping with jewelry. Bazil went ponderously to one of the two staterooms the yacht contained. At the door he turned, expansively in a grandiose gesture.

"She came to the port," he said exuberantly, *"and said we looked like we were men from Toffpoint and asked if we did indeed come from there, so I said we did. Then she asked, did we know somebody named Vash Rayburn and I said we did and if she'd step inside the ship, she'd meet you. And here she is!"*

He unfastened the stateroom door, which he had barred from without. As he opened the door, Vash hesitated and then looked in. Bazil said, *"Come on now,"* then grabbed, and pulled at something in the dark. Vash went ill with apprehension as to who this might be. He groaned as the something inside the stateroom sobbed and yielded to Bazil's tugs.

It was Jessica that Bazil pulled out into the catwalk of the yacht. Her nose and eyes were red from terrified weeping. She gazed about her in purest despair and horror. She did not see Vash at first and feared the worst for a moment. Her eyes were filled with the brawny, piratical figures who grinned at her in what she took for evil gloating at their conquest.

She wailed even louder now, fearing the worst that would befall her at the hands of these barbarians.

Vash swallowed, with much difficulty, and said sickly: *"It's all right, Jessica. It was a mistake. Nothing will happen to you. You're quite safe with me! Don't worry about these scabs, they are now much too famous now to worry with harming a single young lady"* he gives a halfcocked glance with a smirk in the direction of the crew. *"...I mean with the pick from all of their young Nemo Vestaian groupies and all."* The three, still in their torn and tattered clothes looked down with embarrassment.

Chapter 12

Now with everything squared away on the ship and Jessica calmed, Vash stopped off at Port Barogate properly by landing grid, to consult his lawyers. He felt a certain amount of hope for good results from his recent raid on Nemo Vesta, though he still felt desperation about Jessica. Once she was confident of her safety under his protection, she basically took over the operation of the spaceship. She displayed an overwhelming ingratiating, saccharinely delightful manner that was appalling to the members of the crew. She was sweetness and light among criminals who respectfully did not harm her, and she gave a womanly charm to the atmosphere of the vessel until Vash's followers were close to mutiny.

"It ain't that I mind her being a nice girl an all," one of his mustachioed crewmen explained almost tearfully to Vash, *"but she is wanting, I fear, to make a nice girl out of me!"*

Vash, himself, cringed from her social etiquettes. He could gladly have put her ashore on Port Barogate at this point with ample funds to return to Nemo Vesta, but she was most reproachfully helpless. If he did put her ashore, she would confide to all who would listen of her kidnapping and the lovely behavior of the pirates until nobody would believe in them any more as rough vandals—which would be fatal to his plan.

He went to his lawyers, brooding. The news astounded him. The emigrant fleet had appeared over Port Barogate on the way to Nemo Vesta. Before it appeared, Vash's affairs had been prosperous enough. Right after his previous visit, news had come of the daring piratical raid, which captured a ship off Nemo Vesta. This was the liner Vash brought in to Port Barogate. All merchants and ship owners immediately insured all vessels and goods in transit at much higher valuations. The risk-insurance stocks bought on Vash's account had multiplied in value. Obeying his instructions, his lawyers had sold them out and held a pleasing fortune in trust for Vash.

Then came the fleet over Port Barogate, with its letter threatening colony-wide destruction if resistance was offered to single ships, which would land, and loot later on. It seemed that all commerce was at the mercy of the marauders from the sky. Risk-insurance companies had undertaken to indemnify the owners of ships and freight in emptiness. Now that an unprecedented pirate fleet ranged and doubtless ravaged the skyways, the insurance companies ought to go bankrupt. Owners of stock in them dumped it at any price to get rid of it. In accordance with Vash's instructions, though, his lawyers had faithfully if distastefully bought it in. To use up the funds available, they had to buy, not only all the stock of all the risk-insurance companies of Port Barogate, but all stock in all off-colony companies owned by investors on from there.

Then time passed, and ships arrived unmolested in port. Cargoes were delivered intact. Insurers observed that the risk-insurance companies had not collapsed and could still pay off if necessary. They continued their insurance. Risk companies appeared financially sound once again. They had more business than ever, and no more claims than usual. Suddenly their stocks went up—or rather, what people were willing to pay for them went up, because Vash had forbidden the sale of any stock after the pirate fleet appeared.

Now he asked hopefully if he could reimburse the owners of the ship he'd captured off Nemo Vesta, by which they informed him that he could. Could he pay them even the profit they'd have made between the loss of their ship and the arrival of a replacement? He could. Vash wanted to completely compensate all who were negatively affected by his theft of the liner. The attorneys had to be creative with how they went about with this reimbursement, but it was done. After which, Vash's attorney told him of the net amount he still laid claim to in his account.

Vash found himself shocked and somewhat appalled and brooded over his position. He wasn't a businessman, nor did he wish to be. He hadn't expected to make out so well. He had thoughts of laboring for years; then, perhaps, to make good the injury he'd done the ship owners and merchants in order to help the emigrants from Ivoryhelm, but it was all done, and here he was sitting on a fortune and the framework of a burgeoning financial empire. This was a shock to his system and placed an almost irritable snag in his plans. It is safe to say that he didn't like it one bit.

Gloomily, he explained matters to his attorneys. They pointed out that he had a duty, an obligation, from the nature of his unexpected success. If he let things go, now, the currently thriving business of risk insurance would return to its former unimportance. His companies had taken on extra help. More bookkeepers and accountants worked for him this week than last. More mail clerks, secretaries, janitors and scrubwomen. Even more vice presidents! *"Mr. Rayburn, you would administer a serious blow to the economy of Port Barogate if you caused a slackening of employment by letting these companies go down,"* the older gentleman said. *"A slackening of employment would cause a drop in retail trade, an increase in inventories, a depression in industry...."*

Vash thought of his grandfather. He had written to the old gentleman and the emigrant fleet would have delivered the letter. He couldn't disappoint his grandfather!

He morbidly accepted his attorneys' advice, and they arranged immediately to take over the entire first, second and third floors of the building their offices were in. Commerce would march on.

Vash then headed for Toffpoint. He had to return his crew, and there was something else, actually several something else's that needed to be handled. He arrived in the upper orbit listening for the call-signal the lifeboat would give for him to hone in on. He had left the lifeboat stationed in orbit should there be a situation of emergency and he lost his yacht, so now he found it, just outside the gravity field of Toffpoint and yielded the yacht by its side to pick it up. As he maneuvered alongside the lifeboat, however, there was blinding light everywhere. Alarms rang. Lights went out. Instruments registered impossibilities of electrical magnitudes, the rockets fired and spat as they shut down and refired, and the whole ship reeled. Then a voice roared out of the communicator:

"Stand and deliver! Surrender and be allowed to ground. But should you hesitate I'll hull you and heave ye out to the aether without so much as a balloon to break your fall!"

Vash winced as he recognized the voice over the communicator. Stray sparks had flown about everywhere inside the vessel, leaving everyone stunned. A ball lightning bolt, even of only warning size, makes things uncomfortable when it strikes. Vash's fingers tingled as if they'd been asleep and the nerves were just now getting feeling back. He threw on the transmitter switch and said annoyed, yet somewhat jovial:

"Hello, grandfather. This is Vash. How long have you been out here waiting for me?"

He heard his grandfather laugh with sarcastic delight. *"Not long dear boy, just long enough to get irritated that you weren't here to greet me proper."* Not long after, a badly battered, blackened and scuffed old craft, telling a story of years of piracy, came rolling up on rocket-impulse and stopped with a billowing of rocket fumes. Vash threw a switch and used the landing grid field he had created for use on Nemo Vesta in yet another fashion. The ships came together with fine precision, lifeboat-tube to lifeboat-tube. He heard his grandfather utter in amazement as to how timed and perfect the butting of the two were.

"That's a little trick I worked out, grandfather," said Vash into the transmitter. *"Come aboard. I'll pass it on."*

His grandfather presently appeared, scowling and suspicious. His eyes shrewdly examined everything, including the loot tucked in every available space. He snorted.

"All honestly come by I suppose," said Vash morbidly. *"It would seem that a scheme of mine paid off better than I had planned for and now I've got a license to steal. I'm not sure what to do with it though."*

His grandfather stared at a placard on the wall. It said archly: *"Remember! A Lady is Present!"* Jessica had put it up as a reminder to the crew about their manners.

"Hm-m-m!" said his grandfather. *"What's a woman doing on a pirate ship? That wasn't mentioned in your letter, ol' boy!"*

"They get on," said Vash, wincing, looking around to make sure Jessica wasn't in earshot. *"Like mice; surely, you've had mice on a ship, haven't you? Just when you think you have gotten rid of them, another crawls on board to find shelter. Come in the control room and I'll explain everything."*

And explain, he did, up to the point where his arrangements to pay back for a ship and cargo he'd given away turned into a runaway success, and now he was responsible for the employment of innumerable bookkeepers and clerks and such in the insurance companies he had now come to own. There was also the fact that as the emigrant fleet went on, some fifty more colonies scattered along air, sea and land, would require the attention of pirate ships from time to time, or there would be disillusionment and injury to the economic system.

"Organization," said his grandfather, *"does wonders for a tender conscience like you've got. What else?"*

Vash then explained the matter of his crew. Fairbeard might affect to consider them disgraced because they hadn't cut his throat. Vash had to take care of the matter. And then there was Jessica.... Adeline came into the story somehow, too. Vash's grandfather grunted and scratched his head as to how his grandson, the dreamer who didn't want to be a pirate in the first place was now leading pirate raids that kept an entire industry alive.

"We'll go down and talk to this Lord Fairbeard character," he said pugnaciously. *"I've dealt with his kind before. While we're down there, your Cousin Ernest can take a look at this new grid-field job you've worked up. We'll put it on my ship."* He looked through one of the visionscreens, *" Hm-m-m—about what time is it on the ground? You never land long after daybreak. Early in the morning, people just ain't at their best. Makes for sharp conversation and ill will."*

"It's not too late, sir," Vash said. *"Will you follow me down?"*

His grandfather nodded briskly, took another comprehensive look at the loot from Nemo Vesta, and crawled back through the tube to his own ship.

So it was not too long after dawn, in that time-zone, when a sentry on the battlements of Fairbeard's castle felt a shadow over his head. He jumped a foot and stared upward. Then his hair stood on end. He stared, unable to move a muscle.

There was a ship above him. It was not a large ship, but he could not judge of such matters since the only vessels that he had seen of recent days were that of the lifeboat. Rockets did not support this ship as it maneuvered, nor were the propellers engaged. It should have been falling horribly under its weight, but instead, it floated on with very fine precision, like a ship being landed by grid, and settled delicately to the ground some fifty yards from the base of the castle wall.

Immediately thereafter there was a muttering roar. It grew to a howl—a bellow; it became like thunder. It increased from that to a noise so stupendous then it ceased altogether to be heard, and was only felt as a deep-toned battering at one's chest. When it ended there was a second ship resting in the middle of a very large scorched place close by the first.

Neither of these ships were lifeboats. The silently landed vessel, which was the smaller of the two, was several times the sizes of the only craft ever seen on Toffpoint outside the skyport. Its design was somehow suggestive of a yacht. The other, larger, ship was blunt and soiled and battle worn, with patches on its plating here and there.

A landing ramp dropped down from the battered craft. It neatly spanned the scorched and still-smoking patch of soil. A port opened. Men came out, following a jaunty small figure with belligerent gray whiskers. They dragged an enigmatic object behind them.

Vash then came out of the yacht. His grandfather said waspishly: *"This the castle?"*

He waved at the massive pile of cut gray stone, with walls twenty feet thick and sixty high.

"Yes, sir," said Vash, noticing a look of apathy at the structure as if his grandfather wasn't impressed.

"Hm-m-m," snorted his grandfather. *"Looks kinda flimsy to me!"* He waved his hand again at a couple of gents on the old ship. *"You remember your cousins Randall and Jasper?"*

Vash gave a familiar, matter-of-fact nod to them even though he hadn't seen any of them for years, but they were his kin and to not acknowledge knowing them would have been an insult. They wore commonplace, workaday garments, and carried weapons slung negligently over their shoulders as they drug a cryptic object behind them without particular formation or apparent discipline, but they looked the part of pirate.

Vash and his grandfather strolled up to the castle gate, their companions a little to their rear. They came to the gate and nothing happened. Nobody challenged them or even addressed their arrival, almost as if there was a peevish refusal to associate with anyone who now landed in ships on the front lawn.

"Shall we hail them?" asked Vash.

"Nah!" snorted his grandfather. *"I know his kind! Make him bring the first advances."* He waved to his descendants. *"Open it up."* Pointing to the cryptic thing that they were lugging.

Cousin Jasper casually pulled back a cover and reached in and began to throw switches.

"Found a Power Broadcast Unit." grunted Vash's grandfather, *"It was on a ship we took some months ago. Hooked it to the ship's overdrive. When you can't use the overdrive outside of the ship, you still got power. Your Cousin Ernest whipped this thing up for us to use."*

The enigmatic object made a rather spiteful noise. The castle gate shuddered and fell halfway from its hinges. The thing made a second noise. Stones splintered and began to collapse. Vash admired the immense power that this device had. Three more unpleasing but not violently loud sounds came from the machine as the cousins took turns playing with the dials. Half the wall on either side of the gate was turned to rubble, collapsing inside the castle's proper boundary.

Figures began to wave hysterically from the battlements. Vash's grandfather yawned slightly, as if this was common everyday routine for him.

"I always like to talk to people," he observed, *"when they're worryin' about what I'm likely to do to them, instead of what maybe they can do to me."*

Figures appeared on the ground level. They'd come out of a sally port to one side. They were even extravagantly cordial when Vash's grandfather referenced that it might be more convenient and prudent on their part to talk over his business inside the castle, where there would be an easy-chair to sit in.

With haste, the gentlemen invited him and all of Vash;s grandfather's companions in to meet with the, now, fearful and complying Lord Fairbeard. Once well within the walls, two members of the crew from the old warhorse pirate ship stood station on either side of the now dismembered portcullis should there be need for exterior support to assist in a hasty escape.

Presently they sat beside the fireplace in the great hall. The good Lord Emory Demetrius Fairbeard, now quite visibly jittery, shivered next to Vash's grandfather. The Lady Adeline appeared; icy-cold and defiant. She walked with frigid dignity to a place beside her father. Vash's grandfather regarded her with a wicked, estimating gaze.

"Not bad!" he said brightly. *"Not bad at all!"* Then he turned to Vash. *"Those retainers coming?"*

"On the way as we speak," said Vash. He was not happy and grumbled to himself as he noticed the Lady Adeline, in looking over the men, had passed her eyes over him as if he hadn't even been there.

There was a murmurous noise. The dozen spearmen came marching into the great hall. They carried loot. It dripped on the floor and they blandly ignored such things as stray golden coins rolling away from them. The stay-at-home inhabitants of the castle gazed at them in joyous wonderment.

Jessica came following behind. The Lady Adeline made a very slight, almost imperceptible movement back as Vash said desperately:

"Adeline, I know you hate me, though I can't guess why. But here's a thing that ... has to be taken care of! We made a raid on Nemo Vesta ... that's where the loot came from ... and my men kidnapped this girl ... her name is Jessica by the way ... and they brought her on the ship as a present to me ... because she'd admitted that she had known me! Jessica's in an awful fix, Adeline! She's alone and friendless, and ... somebody has to take care of her! Her father will come for her eventually, no doubt about that, but until then, someone has to look out for her in the meantime, and I can't do it!" Vash felt hysterical at the bare idea. *"I just can't!"*

The Lady Adeline looked at Jessica who wore the brave look of a girl so determinedly sweet that nobody could possibly bear it.

"I'm ... very sorry to be an imposition," said Jessica to her new hosts, *" I've been the cause of poor Vash becoming a pirate and getting into such dreadful trouble. I cry over it every night before I go to sleep. He treated me as if I were his sister, and the other men were so gentle and respectful that I ... I think it will break my heart if they are punished. When I think of them being executed with all that dreadful, hopeless formality—"*

"On the colony of Toffpoint," said the Lady Adeline rather practically, *"we're not very formal about such things. Just cutting somebody's throat is usually enough. But he treated you like a sister, did he? Bazil?"*

Bazil swallowed hard, internally bemoaning the fact that he was now drawn into this conversation. He'd been beaming a moment before, with his arms full of silver plate, jewelry, laces, and other bits of booty from the Nemo Vestaian suburb, but now he was not so sure of himself and said desperately:

"Yes, Lady Adeline. But not the way I would have treated my sister if she had been onboard. My sister bit me when she was little, slapped me when she was bigger, and scorned me when I grew up. Don't get me wrong, I am fond of my sister, but if she ever lectured me because I wasn't refined, or shook a finger at me because I wasn't gentlemanly— Lady Adeline, I would have strangled her most enjoyably!"

There was a certain gleam in the Lady Adeline's eye as she said warmly to Vash:

"Of course, I'll take care of the poor thing! I'll let her sleep with my maids and I'm sure one of them can spare clothes for her to wear, and I'll take care of her until a space liner comes along and she can be shipped back to her family. And you can come to see her whenever you please, to make sure she's all right!"

Vash's eyes tended to grow wild. His grandfather cleared his throat loudly. Sensing his grandfather's verbal nudge to get on to other topics, Vash then said somewhat doggedly:

"My good Lady Adeline, you asked each of the men if they'd fight for you. They said yes. You sent them to cut my throat. They didn't.

But they're not disgraced! I want that to be clear here and now! They're good men! I ask that you nor your father see them as disgraced for failing to assassinate me! I beat them single handedly as they fought long and hard to follow your order."

"Of course, they aren't disgraced," conceded the Lady Adeline with a sarcastic sweetness to her voice as she looked over the men. *"Whoever heard of such a thing?"*

Vash wiped his forehead with his sleeve realizing a sense of relief that the men wouldn't be harmed. Fairbeard then opened his mouth fretfully. Vash's grandfather, however, forestalled his words and spoke up first.

"Now I take it that you've gotten word about that big pirate fleet that's been floating around these parts? Eh? It belongs to my grandson, Vash. I run a squadron of it for him. He's a wonderful boy, my grandson! Bloodthirsty crews on those ships, but they love that boy!"

"Very interesting to hear," said Lord Fairbeard with a definite nervous stutter to his voice.

"My grandson likes your men," confided Vash's grandfather. *"He used them multiple times now and says they make nice, well-behaved pirates. He's going to give them stun-pistols and a sonic cannon like the one that smashed your gate. They are the only men on Toffpoint with guns like that! Seize the skyport over yonder and put in a sophisticated power broadcast system like those on the sky colonies, and make sure nobody else gets stun-weapons. They would run, not only this colony, but all of the surrounding land mass villages and ports. Your men'll love it. They will follow Vash anywhere on the planet and bring home loot that you couldn't imagine."*

Lord Fairbeard, coming to a sudden turn of situation as he came to harsh memory of how he treated Vash previously, began to quiver with anxiety. The idea of his men all following Vash and taking over quickly hit him as quite horribly plausible. He'd had the scheme of the only stun-weapon-armed force on Toffpoint, himself. He knew his men tended to revere Vash because of the plunder his followers seemed always to acquire. Fairbeard found himself in a very, very uncomfortable situation to say the least. Bored men from the battered vessel now slowly and methodically started making their way in and stood about his great hall, slowly causing his feeling of uneasiness to grow into full on intimidation. They were unimpressed as they looked around. He knew from their looks, that they were stacking up the odds should they try to take over the castle and were sure that they could bring his castle down about his ears in minutes if that is what they chose to do.

"But ... if my men—" Fairbeard's voice quavered. *"What of me?"*

"Minor problem," said Vash's grandfather blandly as he gave a slight wink in Vash's direction. *"The usual thing would be pffft! Cut your throat."* Running his spindly index finger across his throat as he rose from his seat. *"Reckon we can decide on that later, no doubt. What say you Vash?"*

"I've brought back my men," growled Vash as he glared down Fairbeard, *"and Jessica's taken care of. We're finished here."*

He turned headed abruptly for the great hall's farthest door. His grandfather followed him briskly, and the now crowd of unsavory characters that had mingled in from the old vessel, who were in actuality, mostly Vash's first and second cousins, came after them as they walked outside the castle.

Vash said spitefully: *"Why did you tell such a preposterous story, grandfather?"*

"It wasn't preposterous," said his grandfather. *"Sounds like fun, to me! You're tired now, Vash, with all of those newly developed responsibilities and such, and you probably need to take a rest. You and your Cousin Ernest can get together and fix those new gadgets on my ship. I'll take the other boys for a run over to that port village that we saw on the way in, surely by now they've heard news of the pirates. The boys have been itchin' for a run ashore, and there might be some good loot. Your grandmother's quite fond of seascape art from them places. I'll try to pick some up for her every chance that I get."*

Vash just shrugged. His grandfather was a law unto himself. Vash then looked over and saw his cousins bringing horses from the castle stables, and a very casual group went riding away as if on a pleasure excursion. As a matter of fact, it must have been, because it was Bazil who guided them.

For the rest of that morning and part of the afternoon Vash and his Cousin Ernest worked on the old, battered ship's Lawlor Drive. Vash was pleased with his cousin's amazement and respect for his device. He, too, gave an honest, unfeigned admiration toward the cannon that Ernest had designed. Presently they reminisced about their childhood. It was pleasant to renew family ties like this.

The riders came back about sunset that evening. There were extra horses, with loads. There were cheerful shouts and merriment. His grandfather came into Vash's ship.

"Brought back some company," he said. *"Sky liner landed while we were there. He said he was a friend of yours. A quite congenial fellow and he seems to thinks quite highly of you!"*

A large figure followed his grandfather in. A large figure with snow-white hair who walked in very amiable and relaxed; it was the Intercolonial Ambassador to Nemo Vesta.

"Hard-gaited horses, Vash," he said wryly. *"I need a chair, a soft chair, and a drink. I traveled a good many miles to see you, and it wasn't necessary after all. I've been talking to your grandfather."*

"Glad to see you, sir," said Vash slightly reserved as he brought him a chair.

His Cousin Ernest brought glasses, and the Ambassador buried his nose in his and did not come up for air until the glass had been emptied, then he said in satisfaction:

"A-a-ah! That's good! Very capable man, your grandfather; I watched him loot that town so quick and easy. It was a beautifully impressive and professional job that he made of it! He got some homespun sheets for your grandmother. But about you..."

Vash sat down across from him as his grandfather just leaned against the port door and puffed silently on his mechanical tobacco vaporizer. His other cousins, who had been escorting the ambassador, left post haste as the ambassador waved a hand indicating he no longer needed their services.

"The reason I started here," he observed as he started nursing another drink, *"because it appeared to me as if you were running wild. That move you did with the fleet, now ... I know something of your ability. I thought you'd contrived some way to fake it. I knew*

there couldn't be such a fleet. Not really! That was a sound job you did with the emigrants, by the way. Most praiseworthy! And the point was that if you ran hogwild with a faked fleet, sooner or later the sky marshals would have to cut you down to size. And you were doing much too good work to be stopped!"

Vash just blinked expressionless as the ambassador continued.

"Satisfaction my dear fellow," said the ambassador as he leaned back to have his glass filled for a third time, *"is well enough. But satiety is death. Nemo Vesta was dying on its feet. Nobody could imagine a greater satisfaction than curling up with a good tranquilizer in front of a visionscreen full of nonsense! You've ended all of that! I left Nemo Vesta the day after your raid and already, the young men were trying to grow mustaches, the textile mills were now dying brightly colored felts for garments. Jewelers were turning out stun-gun shaped pins for ornaments and Toffpointian style knives as brooches and hair pins, while the song writers had eight new tunes on the air about pirate lovers, pirate queens, and dark ships that roam in the blackness of night. Three new vision-play series were to start that same night with space-piracy as their theme, and one of them claimed to be based on your life believe it or not."* The ambassador's beard scuffed across his glass as he took a momentary pause in his speech to take another drink.

"I would make them pay for that, Vash!" His grandfather interjected. The ambassador continued, *"In short, Nemo Vesta had rediscovered the pleasure of fear and the excitement of not knowing what would happen next or to whom. People who watched that raid on visionscreens had thrills they'd never swap for tranquilizers in a million years and the ones who actually mixed in with the pirate raiders— They, vicariously, became pirates for a day thanks to you, Vash!"*

Vash said, *"Hm-m-m,"* as he felt that a comment was in order, but there was nothing else to be said.

"Now, your grandfather and I have canvassed the situation thoroughly! This good work must be continued. Diplomatic Service has been worried all along the line. Now we've something to work up. Your grandfather will expand his facilities and snatch ships, land and loot, and keep piracy flying. Your job is to carry on the

insurance business. The ships that will be snatched will be your ships, of course. No interference with legitimate commerce. The intercolonial piracy-risk insurance companies, well you, will pay for the landing-raids. In time you'll probably have to get writers to do scripts for your men and maybe even some acting classes, but not right away. You'll continue to get rich, but there's no harm in that so long as you re-introduce romance and adventure to a world headed for decline. Savages will not invent themselves if there are plenty of heroic characters—of your making! —To slap them down! I have already been in communications with the sky marshals and they will be working on a special sky force with the sole obligation to fight the dreaded pirates. Of course... they will be hand selected and not pose a threat, just enough to create the vision of a good guy in the eyes of the populous."

Vash said rather ruefully: *"But I like working on mechanical and electronic gadgets. My cousin Ernest and I have some things we want to work on together. I ended up on Nemo Vesta because I wanted to get away from piracy."*

His grandfather snorted defiantly at his comment. About that time one of the cousins came in from outside the yacht. Bazil followed him, glowing. He'd reported the looting of the sky port village, and Lord Fairbeard had gone into a tantrum of despair because nobody seemed able to make headway against these strangers. Now he'd turned about and issued a belated invitation to Vash and his grandfather and their guest the ambassador—of whom he'd learned about from Bazil—to dinner at the castle. They could bring their own guards.

Vash would have refused, but the ambassador and his grandfather were insistent. Unwillingly he found himself seated drearily at a long table in a stone-walled room lighted by very smoky torches. Lord Fairbeard, still jittering, displayed a sort of professional conversational charm. He was making an urgent effort to overcome the bad effect of past actions against Vash by fawning all over him with conversational brilliance and false pieties. The Lady Adeline sat quietly with jewels at her throat. She looked most often at her plate. The talk of the old trio became profound and monotonous. They talked administration, practical politics and economics.

The Lady Adeline looked very bored as the talk went on long after the meal was over. Fairbeard said brightly, to her:

"My dear this conversation must sound tedious to you! Young Vash looks uninterested, as well. Why don't you two walk on the battlements and talk about such things as persons your age would find interesting?"

Vash rose, gloomily. The Lady Adeline, with a sigh of polite resignation, rose to accompany him. The ambassador said suddenly:

"Oh, Vash! I forgot to tell you! They found out what killed that man outside the power station!" For a second, Vash showed no comprehension, so the ambassador explained, *"The man your friend Derk thought was killed by death rays. It happens that he' had gotten a terrific load on that night and was quite intoxicated, you know—and climbed a tree to escape the pink, purple, and green bison he thought were chasing him to gore him... well, I am not entirely for sure about that part, but none the less, he climbed too high, a branch broke, and he fell across a generator line and was electrocuted, which led to the burn marks and death that your device was accused of. I'll take it up with the court when I get back to Nemo Vesta. No reason to lock you up any more, you know, well not for murder anyway...maybe piracy."* He said with a grin. *"You might even try selling the Power Board on using your receptor, again!"*

"Thanks," said Vash politely. He then added, *"Lord Fairbeard actually has that Derk and an official from Nemo Vesta here now. If you would, you can tell them the story and that they may go home."*

He accompanied the Lady Adeline to the battlements. The stars were very bright. They strolled along the edge as Adeline stopped and looked at him. *"What was that the Ambassador told you?"* she asked.

He explained the whole ordeal with vigor and excitement. Once finished, however, he lowered his tone and added morbidly that it didn't matter. He could go back to Nemo Vesta now, and if the ambassador was right, he could even accomplish things with his mechanics and electronics. But he wasn't interested in his goals anymore. It was odd that he'd once thought such things would make him happy.

"I must confess that I thought," said the Lady Adeline, in her gentle melancholy demeanor, *"that I would have been happier with you dead because you had made me so angry, but I found I was so wrong."*

Vash fumbled around in his mind for the meaning behind what she said, still being the dense man that he was, but he did sense some sort of cryptic meaning to it all. It wasn't quite an apology for trying to get him killed, but at least it was a disclaimer to future intentions that brought his mind some comfort. Still, however, he couldn't put his finger on why she wanted him dead in the first place nor what she was implying now.

"And speaking of happiness," she added in a slightly different tone, "this young lady Jessica...." He shuddered, and she said: *"I spoke with her in detail and she is so sickeningly sweet and thought that since she was like a sister to you, that you wouldn't mind if I played matchmaker."*

"What did you do?" Vash asked nervously. "*I arranged a meeting between her and Lord Seymour." She said wryly "We're on perfectly good terms again, you know; since he found that my father and I had wanted you dead and he wanted vengeance for the violent molestation of his pride, apologies were given and an alliance was made. I introduced him to Jessica and She of nature, was sweet as vanilla ice cream with maple syrup on a hot summer day. He absolutely loved it! She gazed at him with pretty sadness and told him how terribly romantic it was that he risked life and limb to carry off the woman of his dreams and couldn't see any man doing that for her. He humbly admitted that one look in her eyes had him strongly thinking about it and she swooned instantly! They go together like strawberries and cream! I had to leave, or become unladylike by losing my meal in front of them. I think I made a match that will wear through the fabric of time."*

Then she said tranquilly: *"But seriously, you ought to be perfectly happy. You now have everything you ever said you wanted... Well,"* Adeline looked off toward the two vessels parked on the front lawn of the castle, *"except a delightful girl to marry."*

Vash squirmed in his boots as Adeline continued. *"With all that we've been through, I think that we're good friends by now and you did me a great favor once so I'll return it. I'll round up some really delightful girls for you to look over."*

"I think I heard my grandfather call," said Vash somewhat alarmed at the direction this conversation was going.

"The only thing is— I don't know what type of girl you like. You said delightful and it is clearly obvious that Jessica isn't it."

Vash shuddered, thinking that he had once wanted such a sugary mess.

"What is your definition of delightful, anyway?" asked Adeline. *"What type of girl would you say I was?"*

Finally hitting him like a Lawlor Drive lightening ball to the forehead, realizing what Adeline had been subtly skirting around for some time; Vash said somewhat questioningly, *"Delightful?"*

The Lady Adeline stopped and looked up at him. She said approvingly with a smirk: "*I was wondering if that was ever going to occur to—"*

Before she could even finish her sentence, Vash wrapped his arm around her waist and pulled her up in a tight embrace where he quickly placed a firm kiss on her lips that stifled the rest of her words. He kissed her at first as if amazed at himself for even trying it, and then quickly became more enthusiastic upon noticing she was kissing him back.

While still in their embrace, there was a large sonic sound from the direction of the front lawn. A distortion in the air directly in front of Vash's ship began to form and then an opening about the size of the ship began to grow.

Vash and Adeline ran down the cold gray steps of the battlement, through the, now rumbled and messed front gate toward the ships as a vortex of wind began to create a gale matching that of a strong sea storm.

As they came upon the vessel, Bazil with one of Vash's cousins, came running out of the back port bay of the sky yacht.

Vash yelled to Bazil and grabbed his arm as he attempted to run by. *"What happened? What did you do?"*

"It wasn't me Lord Rayburn, it was your cousin!" Yelled back Bazil, trying to be heard over the loud torrent of wind and debris spiraling toward the front of the ship. *"He didn't understand what the device was that the emigrants had installed on the deck, so he began adjusting and I guess that his curiosity led in a direction he didn't mean for it to. We must leave before the storm devours us!"* With that, he pulled his arm away and ran toward the castle.

As Vash turned, Lord Fairbeard, the ambassador and Vash's grandfather were all out inspecting the situation.

Vash yelled for them to take the Lady Adeline to a safer location. Before leaving her side though, he pulled her in for one more kiss, this one longer than the last. "My dear, you need to go to safety. I just found you and my dreams won't be complete should something happen to you. Go! I will try to shut this thing off and shall return shortly!"

As soon as the words left his mouth, he pulled himself away from her grip and ran toward the open rear port of the yacht. His cousin Ernest was still inside trying to disconnect the wiring from the power source.

"It seems to be self-feeding; I can't get it to disengage!" Exclaimed Ernest as he continued to pull wires.

Vash then said with solemn conviction toward the idea that he was presenting, *"I will go out and try to block the focal array on the front of the ship. That should disrupt the beam long enough for you to shut it down!"* No sooner did he say this, he was out of the ship making his way through the flying sod and other debris toward the array with a transmission disc he pulled from the rear radio receiver system that he was intent to place in direct line between the array and the vortex.

The opening of the vortex began to get larger, by this time, it was large enough to drive the ship through. He held up the disc and placed it in front of the beam as it appeared work and the vortex began to shut down as the wind began to die and the opening began to get smaller.

He looked into the drive window of the vessel at his cousin, who was now nervously watching along with everyone at the castle who had gathered along the battlements to see what was going on from a safe distance.

The victory over the machine was not long won, however, as the beam soon bore a hole through the disc. The sonic vibrations of the beam suddenly regaining focal strength pushed Vash back, sending him through the smaller, yet stabilized vortex.

As Vash fell in, the opening soon closed as the power cell completely drained, Adeline screamed with panic as her father pulled her to his chest to divert her eyes from the quickly closing vortex that swallowed Vash.

Sometime…and somewhere later, Vash wakes to find himself on a secluded, white sand beach…

Ahhh! But that's another story.

Other Books by Phantom Script Publishing

Kinetic Kopy

Jesus Was a Prepper

Would Jesus be a Blogger?

If you enjoyed this story, keep an eye out for works by this author

Airship Memoires: A Pirate's Past

Hunt for the White Vaewolf

A Rip in the Wall

The Faustian Ring

Uncaging the Devil

www.ingramcontent.com/pod-product-compliance
Lightning Source LLC
LaVergne TN
LVHW012049160826
845678LV00014B/2753

9798758380789